Nina's Vermeer

Nina's Vermeer

NINA'S ISLAND

Gabriel H. L. Jacobs

ISBN: 0692398538
ISBN 13: 9780692398531
Library of Congress Control Number: 2015903586
Gabriel H. L. Jacobs, Shaw Island, WA

Front Cover: Jeune femme se peignant by Salomon de Bray. Courtesy the Louvre.
Back Cover: Unloading lobsters in Stonington, ME

*To Deborah who has made this and so many
other things possible with her love and caring*

Author's Notes and Acknowledgements

WHAT IMPELLED ME TO WRITE this book? I wanted to explore my interests in mind reading, what a healthy and positive approach toward sexuality could be like, how to create an ideal learning environment, Dutch 17th century painters, and quality watercolor painting. I am fascinated by life on small islands compared to small town living on the mainland and that is the setting.

When I look back at my professional career in education, the years I spent teaching glow with greater luster than the years I spent as a principal. I have long been intrigued by the learning process and have pursued practices that focus on the learner. I have tried to share the process and its pleasure in this book. I am in the most ideal teaching situation on my small island. I am teaching French to a group that is anxious to learn and happy to help me improve how I work with them. They are teaching me a great deal about learning, for which I am grateful.

My book, *When Children Think* (about keeping journals of new ideas) reflects my striving to find better ways to stimulate thinking. The results my students produced in their journals of new ideas motivated me to search for even better ways to have them think more profoundly. That search is described in my thesis, *The Creative Act and The Creative Process*. My search continued in this book.

I owe much to my wife Deborah's inspiration. She was the ideal person to talk through ideas with, and she suggested many things I have incorporated into the book. I don't think this book would have come to be without her. I own its shortcomings. I won't share those.

I am indebted to Karen Story and Lucy Elenbaas who have patiently edited the manuscript and guided me, Lorrie Harrison from whom I have learned a great deal about writing, my writing group who has been supportive and made many suggestions, and Jed Lengyel who has helped me with some technical aspects of physics. Eileen Lorenz and Nicole Didier corrected the French in the manuscript but I did not always heed their advice. Thus the mistakes in French are mine.

I wish you pleasure in reading this book. It was a labor of love and very satisfying to create. During my many times of rereading, there were parts when I found myself in tears of joy and sadness.

Table of Contents

Description of Characters

———

A<small>LAN</small> B<small>LACK</small> – S<small>ANFORD</small> B<small>LACK</small>'<small>S</small> identical twin brother.

Amanda Fessenden – Red (Nathan's) sister.

Anita Hall – Runs general store and post office.

Brian Hackworth – on sailboat Sloop du Jour anchored in Megantic Harbor.

Bonnie Hackworth – on sailboat Sloop du Jour anchored in Megantic Harbor.

Carrie – Seth's wife

Bradley Bartlett – aide to Sanford Black and hatchet man for him.

Cal – Christine's boyfriend.

Captain Joe – Captain of the ferry.

Christine – student of Nina's.

Citronelli – car company in France owned by Nicole's family pre WWII.

David Chenoweth – painter who was taught by Ogie to do old Dutch masters. Native of Megantic.

Eliot Corvissiano – peripherally involved in shooting over lobster territory.

Henry Olds – school board chairman and owner of the airstrip.

Jason – charged in lobster territory shooting.

Jenny T. – Russ Fessenden Sr's lobster fishing boat.

Jonathan – town clerk of Megantic.

Jonathan Logan – school board member.

Judah Worthington- owner of Island Art Gallery on Megantic.

Karl Funderburk – medically murdered Ogie's and Nina's father and made it appear as a heart problem. Married Ogie's mother and kept her drugged and a prisoner in his psychiatric clinic.

Korzybski – Good friend of Ogie's and partner in the art gallery that represents him. Loaned his house on Megantic to Ogie.

Le Brun – Art dealer and co-owner with Korzybski of art gallery.

Marianne – successful well known sculptor and mother of Melanie

Melanie – Marianne's daughter who was driven to find her father.

Nicole – Nina and Ogie's mother. Was French and raised Nina and Ogie in French.

Nina – Ogie's brilliant 16 year old sister who graduated from high school at 13. Worked as sternman on lobster boat and substitute taught in Megantic High School.

Ogie McMaster – Nina's older brother. Has increasing mind reading ability. Used to create new/old Dutch Masters and now does highly coveted watercolors that are sold by le Brun.

Oliver McMaster – Ogie and Nina's father. Nicole's first husband.

Owen Cartwright – Ogie's incognito name.

Renee Liegeois – French Canadian origin and Principal of Megantic School.

Robert Hatfield – NY Times columnist held prisoner by Karl Funderburk.

Roger Burgess – Sheriff on Megantic.

Russ Fessenden Sr. – Red's grandfather and owner of the Jenny T. Lobsterman and on the school board.

Russ Fessenden Jr. – Red's father and son of Russ Sr.

Pearl Fessenden – Russ Jr's wife & mother of Red (Nathan). Nina's aide.

Red (Nathan Fessenden) grandson of Russ Fessenden Sr. Works as sternman for his grandfather and falls in love with Nina.

Sanford Black – Assistant Secretary of Defense and twin of Alan Black.

Description of Characters

Sashi – Natasha Aleksandra Lebedeva – Ogie's off again on again girlfriend. Government employee in intelligence. Is fluent in Russian, English, French and god knows what other languages. Her avocation is working in le Brun's art gallery.

Seth – Nicole's brother and Ogie's and Nina's uncle. He and Carrie raised Nina after she turned eight.

Mrs. Tyler – French teacher Nina is substituting for.

Glossary

——

STERNMAN – SOMEONE WHO WORKS on a lobster boat but not in charge of it.

Lobstering – Not officially a verb but it is used as a verb in this book.

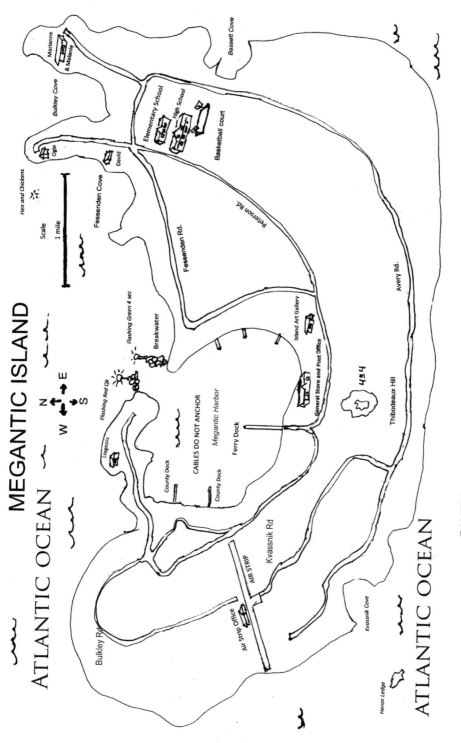

MEGANTIC ISLAND

ATLANTIC OCEAN

ATLANTIC OCEAN

CAUTION DO NOT USE FOR NAVIGATIONAL PURPOSES

N
W E
S

Scale
1 mile

Hen and Chickens

Marianne & Melanie

Bulkley Cove

Bassett Cove

Ogle

David

Fessenden Cove

Elementary School

High School

Basketball court

Peterson Rd.

Fessenden Rd.

Avery Rd.

Flashing Green 4 sec

Breakwater

Island Art Gallery

Flashing Red Qk

Liegeois

County Dock

County Dock

CABLES DO NOT ANCHOR

Megantic Harbor

Ferry Dock

General Store and Post Office

454

Thibodeaux Hill

Bulkley Rd

Air Strip Office

AIR STRIP

Kvassnik Rd

Kvassnik Cove

Heron Ledge

MEGANTIC ISLAND

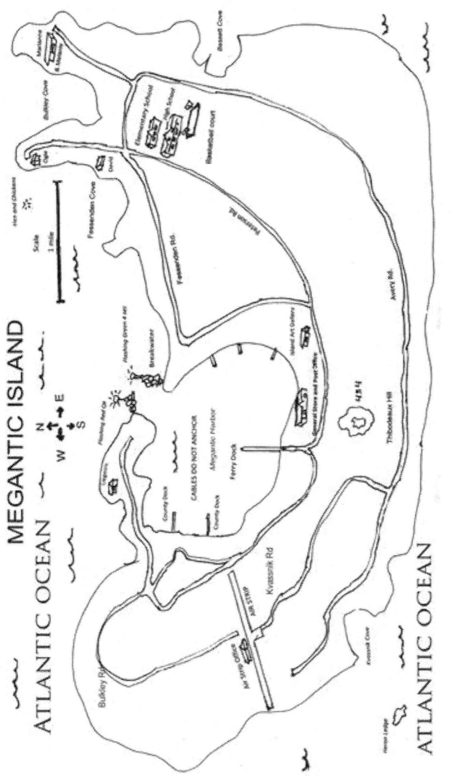

ATLANTIC OCEAN

ATLANTIC OCEAN

CAUTION DO NOT USE FOR NAVIGATIONAL PURPOSES

CHAPTER 1

Ogie

———

Ogie didn't understand why the people around him couldn't hear the banging in his chest. Even when he'd escaped from the courthouse eight years ago, the sound hadn't been this loud. He was panicked, because he read in Anita Hall's mind that there were federal agents on the incoming ferry.

Usually if he breathed in deeply and held it a few seconds, his panicky heart went back to normal. After what felt like an eternity of controlled breathing, the pressure and sound of his heart finally eased.

Living with the constant threat of going to prison for life was incarceration in a different form.

He could no longer laugh at himself. His years on the run had frozen his sense of humor. He had become a stranger to himself. He missed the company of his freer self. The tension of always evading the law had twisted his insides, and he wondered if it was permanent.

He smiled wryly, which he didn't mistake for his lost sense of humor. He didn't know whether he would ever again laugh without restraint. That he was conscious of this was good. That he saw no solution was dismal.

He had long ago given up his anger about the injustice of his case and his stepfather's role in it. He knew his anger was like taking poison and hoping Karl, his stepfather, would die. It would be nice if Karl did, but Ogie knew that hoping for it was killing him, not Karl.

Anita Hall ran the store at the ferry dock and always had the Marine VHF radio on. She'd learned from the ferry captain about the two federal agents on board.

Searching Anita's mind, Ogie couldn't find anything about the agents' purpose. She probably didn't know anything more. His internal debate was agonizing. Should he stay at the ferry landing, attempt to read the minds of the Feds, and risk re-arrest? Or should he go to plan B before it was too late?

Plan B meant leaving Megantic Island. Megantic provided more security for him than any other place. If he left, there would be a mountain of problems finding another home. Money was not an obstacle, but finding somewhere he would not arouse suspicions presented difficulties. He didn't want to use his Social Security number or his driver's license. His computer-savvy friends had created these for him, and they had worked so far. They had inserted what was necessary into the Social Security system and he had a new work history and a new number. They had done similar things with a birth certificate and the DMV. Good as his friends were at doing these things, Ogie didn't like using fake documents because why take unnecessary risks? Banking, using credit cards, car buying, house rental, and purchasing online were things made complex or impossible by changing identities and locations. Large cash purchases were awkward and he had been refused when trying to do it. The ten thousand dollar reporting trigger on transactions meant that there were many things he could not buy.

Getting to live on Megantic was a stroke of good fortune. His agent, Korzybski, had a summer place he rarely used, and he let Ogie stay there. At first he had wanted to leap at Korzybski's offer but was reluctant to take advantage of him. Korzybski overcame his reluctance, saying, "How many choices do you have? *Noli equi dentes inspicere donati*—Don't look a gift horse in the mouth." Ogie knew this was his polite way of saying, "don't be the other end either." Ogie quickly realized there was no future in counting the horse's teeth. He needed to climb on and go.

His mind-reading skills had progressed considerably since he first became aware of them. For a long time, he'd been doubtful of their reality. Now he easily read most people's thoughts within a hundred feet, and sometimes beyond. Reading current thoughts was easy. But reading people's previous thoughts was limited, and only worked with people he knew well.

Sometimes he could plant thoughts in people. This allowed him to guide those who were suspicious of him to think about him differently. While he was shaky at this, it often worked. It had kept him safe on Megantic. Being in a small community and rarely dealing with people who didn't live on the Island, he didn't have to constantly steer people away from wondering about him. Once he'd guided a Megantican away from their suspicions, he didn't have to do it again.

He had been arrested eight years ago for attempting to free his mother from imprisonment by his stepfather, Karl. Karl kept her drugged and isolated at his psychiatric hospital. Ogie's attempt to free her resulted in his being convicted of kidnapping. Being a mind reader enabled Ogie to escape during his sentencing hearing. He knew that if he were caught, it would mean life in prison.

Roger Burgess, the Island's Deputy Sheriff, entered the store. Ogie scanned his mind. Roger was there to meet the ferry. When someone asked Roger what he was doing, Ogie read his thinking: *"Must make up a reason because the Feds want it kept quiet."* Roger hesitated and said some federal agents were coming to coordinate security matters. Ogie kept probing but got no further.

With his beard and different hair color, Ogie assumed that if the Feds were looking for him, they wouldn't spot him right away. And then he realized his faulty reasoning. If they were after him, they would know he was here, and even with his changed appearance he would be caught.

He decided to stay in the store while the ferry tied up. He spotted the Feds by their thinking and then, when they emerged from the cabin, by their dark suits. *"What kind of a cock-and-bull cover story is 'coordinating security' anyway?"* one of them was thinking. *"These days, everything is accepted if national security is given as a reason. How stupid is it for us to come here to pick up a package at an art gallery? There must be more to it."*

Ogie's knees shook with relief. They weren't here for him! After he calmed down, he wondered why the Feds would have any interest in the art gallery on Megantic. Ogie supposed the story would come out sooner or later. With a population of 725, it didn't take long for people to put pieces together.

When he read that they were picking up a Vermeer at the Island Gallery and then going to see David Chenoweth, Ogie became nervous again. Creating legitimate reproductions of Vermeers and other Dutch masters was David's business. It had been Ogie's. Ogie had trained David.

Then Ogie heard a familiar female voice in his mind: *"I wonder how I will find him?"* It sounded like his sister, Nina. He couldn't believe someone else would have Nina's voice, whether spoken or in their thoughts. This voice was lower than he remembered. After the Feds had climbed into Roger's car and driven away, Ogie walked toward the ferry to get a look at whom he was hearing.

He didn't recognize her at first. He hadn't seen her in eight years. Her nervous smile betrayed her insecurity, her wide grin begging kindness from the strangers surrounding her. Again he heard her voice in his mind: *"I must not ask for directions. It's too dangerous for Ogie and I don't even know what name he's using. I hope he won't be angry at my coming here."*

The sensations in his chest and throat were manifestations of the love and warmth he felt seeing Nina. The Feds and Nina's unexpected arrival took all his emotional reserves. Nina paused when he approached her because his appearance had also changed.

When he went to hug her, her tallness startled him. She was almost as tall as he was. Her cheekbones were high and pronounced. She had become extraordinarily beautiful. She had obviously given thought to making her appearance low key. But her natural beauty made it impossible. Her well-worn jeans and denim shirt weren't chic but revealed a lovely figure. Her hair was just long enough for a pony-tail. There was hardly any sign of the child she had been. What with the symmetry of her features, her unblemished complexion, and an assured walk, she had turned male heads on her short trip from the ferry.

The first thing she said to him was, "I know I shouldn't have come because it puts you in danger. But it was so long since…I've desperately needed and missed you. Seth has been a gem, but he's not you."

He was anxious to get her in his car before too much of the Island was witness to their reunion. He knew questions and speculation would come regardless. He needed to think of what he would say to explain her presence, and what their relationship was.

At the house, Ogie encircled her with his arms and pulled her into him, hugging her with a desperation born of being starved for family for so many years. His tears dropped onto her hair and his arms felt weak. He could feel Nina shaking.

He had been living with the knowledge that he didn't know when, if ever, he would see her again. He had anesthetized his feelings about her to prevent them from running rampant. It felt unreal that she was here and part of his life again. The sensations in his chest and throat eased. He felt weak, but he knew he had to indoctrinate Nina to how she should conceal his identity.

"Does Seth know where you are?" Ogie asked. He read in her, *"If I don't tell him the truth, he will know it anyway. He always has."*

"He knows how anxious I am to be with you. I didn't tell him where I was going, but I know he knows. Ogie, I want to live here with you, I need to. I've lived with this emptiness for so many years, and I can't face leaving you again."

"Nina, you have to remember that my name here is Owen Cartwright. You must use it and you know why. Practice it and use it, even when we're together. Staying here is another matter."

"What can be so complicated? You've been safe here for eight years."

"People wonder about me. Anyone new stirs up curiosity. On this Island, people know each other better than in small towns on the mainland because they encounter each other in more places. There are a multitude of places to meet—in the store, the school, on the ferry, on the few roads, in the limited ways to earn a living, and in recreation. They know or knew each other's parents and grandparents. Newcomers are fascinating because they're not the same old, same old. It's not so much a hunger for gossip as it is wanting to know more of what someone is like and how they fit in. I have avoided almost everything social. I rarely go off the property. It's painful because I enjoy being with people. On rare occasions when I do, I'm tense because I have to be careful of what I say. You too will have to be careful of what you tell people about our lives. For instance, you shouldn't say anything about where your mother is and why she is there because someone could put together those facts with what has been published about me as a wanted felon."

"But..."

"Nina, with very little information, people draw incredibly accurate and inaccurate conclusions. There are things I would like to do on this Island, but I have to be careful about what I do and how I do it. It's heartbreaking to withhold myself. I know how good-hearted you are, and you would have a hard time holding back."

"Isn't there anyone you are close to?"

"David Chenoweth is the one person I am somewhat close to. He apprenticed with me and now does the same kind of painting I used to do. While I haven't told him about my so-called checkered past, I am certain he has figured out that I have compelling reasons to say little and be asocial. But even with David, you will need to be discreet about our history."

"Let me have a trial period to see if I can do it?"

Ogie read in her thoughts that she was determined to protect him, which reassured him.

"One mistake could lead to revelations that would be a disaster for me. Let's leave it for now and discuss it later. There is much to catch up on. I am starved for news about you and Seth. Korzybski is limited in what he knows about the family and can't take too many chances communicating with me in order not to reveal where I am. I want to know everything that has happened to you in all these years, and hear about Seth and the family."

Interrupting their conversation, a mangy black cat went straight to Nina, sniffed her, and jumped up on her lap. Nina sat still while the cat sniffed some more, did a few circles in preparation for settling, and then curled itself down on her lap. "Who's this?" she asked.

"It's the first time he—I assume it's a he—has come all the way into the house. He's feral. He started hanging around a few weeks ago and I've fed him on the porch. He hasn't come close enough for me to touch him. I forgot you always had magic with animals. You haven't lost it."

Nina slowly moved her hand to the cat's back and lightly rested it there before stroking and scratching his fur. The cat responded with a purr loud enough for Ogie to hear at the other end of the couch. With its head, the cat pushed Nina's hand to continue the stroking.

"Have you named it?"

"No, but I can see that it has just abbreviated in two minutes the whole complex legal process of adopting you. You will have to do the naming."

After turning the cat on its back as if it were a baby—Ogie was astounded the cat put up with it—Nina determined that he was indeed a male. "Fra Angelico he will be. What better name for a cat living in a painter's house? His nickname for family and other intimates will be

Frangelo." Looking at both of them, Ogie thought it was a marriage made in heaven. The look in Nina's eyes was the ecstasy of a parent-less child finding love, and the cat's feelings reciprocated Nina's.

Ogie knew there was no way Nina was going to leave. She was hungering to be with him, and now with Frangelo. Frangelo had cemented his future with his seduction of Nina. Ogie knew he had to ensure that her being on the Island wouldn't reveal his identity. She might have to use a different name. He needed to think about it.

CHAPTER 2

Ogie

———

OGIE COULD SEE IN NINA'S mind that something fierce was happening. He didn't want to spook her by looking in more thoroughly, but her distress was such that he had to know what was going on. She was in turmoil. Her emotions were mixed. She was disturbed by his sensing things about her she hadn't told him and angry because he hadn't explained his disappearance from her life. But she was comforted by being with him. She knew he must have had extraordinarily good reasons to have placed her with Seth, but that didn't make her feel better. She could feel him in her mind but thought it was her imagination. He was failing in trying not to give away that he was intruding on her psyche.

She broke down with convulsions of upset when he asked her what was wrong. She could hardly get the words out her body was so racked with waves of emotional pain. He turned himself inside out to send soothing and calming feelings to her. "Abandoned, not loved, a living nightmare, no one there for me, no idea what to do for myself, and only eight," were some of the words coming out in a raging torrent. When she was calmer, she said, "How could you have left me when our mother was already taken from me?" and then after a silence, "I'm sorry I let go like that. I know you have done your best for me to be well cared for. Seth and Carrie couldn't have been better. But it felt horrible. And the worst was not knowing if I would ever see you or Mom again. If I had known there was a possibility of being with you, I wouldn't have despaired."

"Nina, I'm amazed you have come out of that trauma as well you have. Yes, it hurts like mad, but you have transcended that awfulness and become a beautiful, whole human being. It must have taken extraordinary effort to not let yourself go before this. I don't know where to begin to explain what happened. It is an untouchably long and ugly chapter. It will take time to explain it and understand it."

"Ogie, oops, I mean Owen, please begin. There is nothing worse than not knowing the whys of you deserting me and losing Mom. Even though I knew that you had to hide and protect me from Karl, I felt abandoned and unloved."

"Nina, this may help you understand what was going on. When I visited Mom and Karl, I was shocked at Mom's condition. Karl had her heavily drugged. You were miserable there. You begged me to take you away, which is why you ended up at Seth's. I tried to see Mom every day and find out what was going on with her. At first, Karl went through the motions of being gracious and invited me into their house. I was overwhelmed by the luxury of it. It had to have been at least 14,000 square feet. There were two swimming pools and a lap pool. There was an airstrip with a jet on it that had the logo of the hospital and Karl's name. When I first knew Karl, there was no sign of his being a wealthy man. I didn't think running a private psychiatric spa would be that kind of a moneymaker.

"Mom could barely recognize me. I never understood Karl's explanation about why he was keeping her sedated. His ostensible reason was that she was still recovering from the death of our father. After I started questioning him about Mom, he avoided me.

"During my visits, I saw a number of other people in the same sedated state. In talking with other 'patients' and their families, I found there were political motives on the part of the people who had them committed. Karl's psychiatric hospital is a fraud. I begged Karl to release Mom to me. He refused, saying that it wouldn't be in her best interest.

"I read, I mean I sensed in Karl that even if I could take her, I wouldn't get anyplace because he'd accuse me of kidnapping, and he had the local and state officials in his pocket. Mom was in no condition to evade the guards and get out, even with my help. The only thing left was to keep coming back to see if I could get Karl to change his mind about me seeing her. I had no luck.

"While trying to visit Mom, I came to know other patients. One was Robert Hatfield, who had been a major writer for the New York Times. He was being held prisoner-patient there and believed it was because he had investigated 9/11 and the frauds connected with our going to war in Iraq and Afghanistan. From him, I learned that Karl had important people put in his so-called care by the administration. With that kind of backing, there was little hope for me to get Mom out. Karl was supported financially and legally by the administration, using their powers under the Patriot Act.

"I had odd feelings about Karl before they were married. He was in an unseemly hurry. When I suggested that they wait a little longer after dad's death, Karl told Mom it was just a Freudian thing on my part."

After a long and thoughtful pause, Nina asked, "When did Karl build his sanitarium?"

"What are you getting at?"

"Where did he get the money to build it?"

Ogie read in her mind that she was wondering if there was a connection between Karl's wealth and his marriage to their mother. He didn't think it likely, because his mother wasn't well off. But he could see Nina sensed a connection.

She was searching back to a conversation Karl and her mother had when she was six. It had to do with France, and Karl's anxiousness to go there. Karl had been asking her mother questions about the family's car factory, which was sold before WWII. Nina asked Ogie, "Does the word Citronelli mean anything?"

"Yes. It was a car with an air-cooled engine made before the war. The factory that made them belonged to Mom's family. Why do you ask?"

"I heard Mom and Karl talking about it before they moved to the west coast. I don't know if it's important, but Karl couldn't let go of knowing more about Citronelli. Do you think that could have anything to do with his having the money to build that fancy hospital?"

"Nina, I'm amazed at what you remember and what you could put together at that age. I think it's important. In what way, I don't know. It could be an explanation for why Karl is treating Mom like he does."

"Ogie, I mean Owen, you haven't told me how you escaped."

"Nina, that's a long story of its own. Let's save it for another time."

CHAPTER 3

Nina

——

NINA WAS WATCHING THE LOBSTERMEN get ready to leave. She was determined to go out with them. She chose a boat called the Jenny T, because its captain didn't jockey his craft around in cowboy roundup style like most of the others did. She introduced herself to Russ Fessenden and his grandson, Red, and screwed up the courage to ask if she could come along to watch. Russ growled a bit and told her she was going to get dirty, but she could come if she wanted to. He handed her some rubber boots and pants with suspenders and said, "You might as well give us a hand if you can. I hope you're as strong as you are purty."

Red looked as if he was fifteen or sixteen and carried himself in a serious way. Nina was used to her male age-mates being just a step less crazy than young children and saw them as foreign animals. She wondered whether Red had gone through that stage or whether he had skipped it entirely. Everyone else called him Red, but Russ used his given name, "Nathan." He treated him respectfully. It was fascinating to see the pleasure that grandson and grandfather had in their interaction with each other. It was subtle and you had to look carefully to see it because of Russ's gruff exterior.

As Nina climbed aboard the Jenny T, Red gave her an intense look. It was not the usual sexual looking over that so many boys and men did. Was it because she was, as native Mainers called it, "from away?" In any case, it was rare when anyone that young looked at her with such intensity. She decided to sort it out later.

She tried to stay out of the way. Every place she moved worked briefly until she found herself in the way again. Red was embarrassed about each encounter with her. She knew, because he overdid the "excuse me's." She thought it was shyness on his part. He must be feeling awkward around her.

As soon as they cast off, Red started filling bags with bits of fish. Nina looked a question at him and he said they were bait bags and he wanted to stay ahead of things. She motioned to him that she would like to do it. The sound of the engine made it difficult to converse, but he showed her how.

As they picked up their traps, Nina noticed that the colors of their lobster pot buoys matched the colors of the sideboards of the Jenny T. The way Russ and Red retrieved the traps looked as if it was done in one motion, but it was many steps. First Russ hooked the line, then pulled it in and put it on a hauler. The hauler's wheel and pulley system made it easier to pull in the heavy traps. There were two traps for each buoy. Red landed the first one on the gunwale, and Russ grabbed the second one. They opened the traps and with unbelievable speed sorted out lobsters, starfish, crabs, and sea urchins, throwing back all but a few lobsters. They put bait bags in the empty traps and pushed them overboard with the accumulated line and the buoy.

The process moved so fast that Nina couldn't see how she could help. By the time she thought of something she could do, Red had done it. The best she was able to do was try to anticipate where the next action would be and move out of the way.

Nina had many questions about how things worked but decided the men were too busy to answer. Finally when they were on their way back to the harbor, she asked Red, "How do you decide which lobsters to throw back?"

"If they're larger than five inches or smaller than three and a quarter inches, or if they're notched or berried, they have to go back."

"Why do the larger ones have to be returned?"

"Because they're the ones that will reproduce."

"What does 'buried' mean?"

"It's spelled b-e-r-r-i-e-d, not buried. It means a female lobster that has eggs attached to her. If we catch them and the flipper is notched, we know they are breeders. If they are berried but not notched, we have to notch the flippers. That tells anyone who catches that lobster they must return it."

"Does everyone do it?"

"Just about. If they don't, and if the Marine Patrol doesn't catch them, their neighbors will know when they see the catch. They probably won't turn them in, but word will get around and the others will make life miserable for the person who does it.

"We all depend on the lobster business. If they don't reproduce, it hurts all of us. So far the amount of traps being set every year has increased and yet the catch hasn't decreased. The laws seem to be working to help keep the business going and expanding."

"I see many of the lobstermen driving expensive pickups. Do they earn enough money for new ones?"

"You wouldn't believe how much some of them make. It can run as high as $300,000 per year."

"Doesn't your grandfather earn enough for a new truck?"

"He does, but he's too smart to spend his money that way."

"What do you mean?"

"He wants me and his other grandchildren to go to college. As long as we're serious, he'll pay for it. He's setting up a trust fund for college for all of us. He knows college will be very dear and that we'll have to live on the mainland. He says we should all know how to lobster and do everything connected with it, including boat repair, engine work, and carpentry, because if the lobster business should fail, we'd have a trade. But he also wants us to know more than that and have a choice about what kind of work we do."

"Do you want to go to college?" Nina asked.

"I do, but it scares me."

"Why?"

"Well, I've done OK in school, but we're more limited here, and I don't know if I could make it with students who've had a better education. And except for the summer people, I haven't had much contact with mainland people. All I know is here."

"What do you want to do?"

"I don't know enough about the mainland to know what I want to do. I've thought about teaching, but I don't know if I know enough to do that.

"What about you," Red asked. "How long are you going to be here? Do you go to college?"

"No, I don't go to college yet. I don't know how long I will be here."

"What do you do while you're here?"

"I help my brother and David Chenoweth."

"What do they do? And what do you do to help them?"

"They're both painters. It's hard to describe how I help them. David's field is one I'm interested in and know a good bit about. I help him with ideas, research, and when he needs a model, I do that."

"What do you mean 'his field'?"

"He paints pictures in the style of the old masters."

"You mean he makes forgeries?"

"No. It would be logical to think that, but that isn't what he does. Sometimes he copies the originals, which are sold as reproductions, and sometimes he creates new paintings in that style."

"And he can make a living doing that?"

"Yes. I don't know if he makes as much as you do lobstering, but I think he does well."

"Who does he paint like?"

"Well, Vermeer is one and Gabriël Metsu is another."

"I've heard of Vermeer. We saw a film in school about his work. He didn't paint many paintings. I would love to see David's new Vermeers. He must know a lot about Vermeer to be able to do that. What is Gabriël Metsu's work like and when did he live?"

"About the same time Vermeer did. His work looks similar, but it has a different feel to it."

"How about your brother? I've seen him painting. I haven't had a good look at what he does. Does his work sell well? I haven't seen his paintings for sale at the Island Gallery. How do you help him?"

"He has a gallery in Washington, D.C. His work sells for much more than paintings do here. I've only been here a month, and except for doing his housekeeping, mostly cooking, I can't help him. His painting doesn't involve the research that David's does."

Nina asked, "Both Owen and David are devoted to their work and tend to be private, but if I can get their permission, would you like to visit their studios?"

"Yes, but won't I be in the way?"

"You'd be in the way less than I've been in your way today."

When they returned to the dock, Nina helped them unload. When they were finished, Russ asked her how it had gone. "It was fascinating and I would appreciate it if I could come again."

"Do you think you could do Nathan's job?"

"Maybe...but not nearly as fast. He does so many things so quickly, and I don't know how yet."

"Watching you today, you're a quick study. Tomorrow when you go with us, get Nathan to show you what he does. I'll be off-Island next week and Nathan needs a sternman. It would be too slow if he had to do it all by himself. I'll pay you the beginning wage. Would you be able to do it all next week?"

"I'll check with Owen, but I don't see any problem." She saw a relieved smile on Red's face. She suspected he wanted her company even more than he wanted her help, which pleased her. It surprised her that she was pleased.

Seth, her uncle, had given her the gift of finding clarity for herself. As much of a pain in the ass as Seth had been when he made her clarify her thinking in the middle of her upsets, she now knew that it made her life richer. He taught her how to stop in the middle of things and ask herself: "What am I feeling and why am I feeling this way? What does it remind me of?" She knew she was going to analyze her feelings about Red further. She was elated at being both needed and wanted.

At home with Ogie, she recounted the day's adventures. He asked her about Russ's upcoming absence. "Obviously, you fit in well to be taken as a sternman. Russ appears to be a curmudgeon, but it's only his exterior. He's highly regarded as a sage. People go to him for help with their personal problems. His kids have all done a fabulous job raising their kids. The gossip is he set a tone for all of them that stuck. I haven't had a chance to get to know Red, although from afar he seems like a well put-together kid. What was he like?"

"It's hard to describe him. He was quiet at first and seemed as if he was afraid of me. When I asked him questions about lobstering, he was clear and concise. He and Russ have a special relationship. It didn't show in any obvious way, but there was a strong feeling of companionability. They work well together with almost no exchange of words. It was like watching a ballet. But I could see the pride and love in Russ's eyes when he was doing things with Red. And there was no resentment when Russ asked him to do things. It was all done in a low key way."

"Did Russ say anything about why he wasn't going to be here?"

"All he said was that he would be off-Island next week. I didn't ask him why."

"How do you feel about working as a sternman?"

"I'm nervous. I don't really know how to do it. But I have a feeling Red will be patient with me. I think that's his nature."

"How do you think it will go to be alone with him all day?"

"Ogie, what are you asking me? Are you asking if I'm afraid he'll make a pass, or are you asking if I'm scared of having to work a long day?"

"Both, I guess. But I'm more worried about Red than about you. That whole family is a very moral one and they take religious

18

injunctions seriously. I wouldn't like to see Red in a position where he would be tortured by his moral upbringing."

"And you think I would torture him?"

"No, I don't think you would do it consciously, but remember, you are a very attractive young woman."

"Ogie, I don't know how I feel about Red. Much to my surprise, I find him very nice and attractive. I never thought I'd find a boy my age a possible boyfriend. They're usually childish and only interested in sex. For all I know, he has a steady girlfriend. I don't know why you're assuming the worst about me."

"It's not the worst. If it's a caring relationship, it's the best. But I do want you to know the potential problems. I know you wouldn't do anything sexual with him unless you cared, but remember that caring includes his feelings. While you can assume he has a strong sex drive, you should also assume he will care about his family culture and what it would mean to violate it. He might think it would force a separation between him and everyone he knows and loves."

"Enough, Ogie. I haven't even figured out how I feel about him and you're assuming I'm going to be an evil seductress." Nina smiled at her brother, half amused by his teasing, and half annoyed because he seemed able to anticipate her thoughts before she had identified them herself.

"Not quite an evil seductress, but I just want you to know what you might be getting into. I think you'll find it an interesting day and I look forward to hearing about it."

CHAPTER 4

Nina

———

NINA AND OGIE WERE EATING dinner when David Chenoweth called out and walked in without knocking. He was upset. Ogie saw in David's mind that it had to do with the Feds. He read David's reluctance to discuss it because of Nina's presence.

Ogie was closer to David than to anyone else on the Island. David had been the caretaker of Korzybski's house, and when Ogie moved in, he was anxious to continue that work. It wasn't a heavy workload and Ogie could have taken care of the house himself. David was desperate to keep that small income because there was very little work available for him on the Island. He was a misfit. No one wanted to take him on as a sternman on a lobster boat and his reading and writing skills were limited. It wasn't that he wasn't bright. He was, but that and his long silences made people uncomfortable, which was misattributed to his lack of intelligence. He was obsessed with drawing and painting, which the Meganticans thought harmless enough, but it wasn't a way to earn a living. He was largely self-taught and his work was more sophisticated than Grandma Moses' primitive style. Ironically, his paintings in the Island Art Gallery sold better than anyone else's, but being 60 miles off the coast, Megantic didn't have that many tourists who bought paintings.

Years before, when Ogie arrived on Megantic and David saw Ogie's paintings of Island scenes, he was both awestruck and jealous. He recognized that Ogie's painting skills transcended any of the semi-pro/amateur work in the gallery. The next time David came to check the house, he asked diffidently if he could show him his work. It was a sketchbook and a watercolor. As Ogie studied the work, David held his breath and watched Ogie's face intently. David was sixteen then and Ogie couldn't believe he could have done such sophisticated work being self-taught. For David, the minutes Ogie was studying his work were an eon of his insides trembling.

Ogie had been at a loss for words he was so taken with David's ability. The pause exacerbated David's tension. He assumed Ogie was searching for a way to be polite about his criticism. He was poised to run off and leave his sketchbook and watercolor. Ogie saw this and put his hand on his shoulder and said, "Your work is unbelievably good." He was about to continue with specific comments when he realized David was so nervous he couldn't register the praise. Ogie said, "Please sit down. There is much to talk about your excellent work." David was just beginning to understand that what was to come wasn't going to be negative. Ogie went to get some tea and served it to him. He asked David questions about how he worked and became so accomplished.

Because art was David's passion, he could transcend his shyness and asked Ogie what it was he thought was so good. And Ogie told him it was his composition, color coordination, extraordinarily accurate rendering, his incorporating texture in all parts of his work, and his overall good taste. He asked David, "What do you hope to do with your ability?"

"I want to earn a living doing it. I know that art in our gallery doesn't sell well. I have made a small amount of money from my paintings, but not enough to live on. I've heard that there are many good artists on the mainland who cannot make money with their art. Do you earn money with your paintings? They are so good they must sell."

"I do. I have just begun to send my paintings of Megantic to my gallery. Because it is a new style for me, it hasn't caught on yet, but my agent assures me it will."

"What is your gallery like? Are my paintings good enough for it? Could you get me into it?"

"The clientele of my gallery are very sophisticated and the man running it wants a wide variety of styles of paintings. Your paintings would be too much the same type as mine, and that's why he wouldn't take you on. But you have given me an idea. I used to create and copy 17th century Dutch masters. I made a good living at it. My gallery would like me to make more of them, but for reasons I can't go into, I won't. I could teach you how to do it and I think you could fill the void for them. Would you like to try it?"

"I don't know. I don't even know what they look like. I might be able to copy a painting, but I don't know what you mean by creating one."

Now it was eight years later and David's high quality work with Vermeer, Metsu, de Bray and others was paying him handsomely. It required much concentration, time, and few interruptions. David was intense about his work, which was demanding, and it enabled him to be even more asocial than he was able to be normally. His income enabled him to move away from home and set up a studio within the house he was in the process of buying. Ogie was in awe of what David had learned to do with light, gradations of color, and exactness of detail. He was outdoing Ogie in the *métier* Ogie had taught him. His monastic life meant there was less chance he would inadvertently give Ogie away. While he hadn't learned of Ogie's checkered past, he knew there were things Ogie didn't want people to know, and he was wise and discreet enough not to discuss his observations about him with anyone.

Before he was arrested, Ogie had been an elementary school teacher. He'd supplemented his living by copying and creating Dutch 17th century art. He had painted mostly Vermeers but occasionally other artists, such as Gabriël Metsu. The paintings were sold under his own name and were of high quality. He had a hard time keeping up with the orders. He had been considering doing it full time until his difficulties with Karl.

David's appearance of youth belied his years of experience. Nina could see intelligence in his astonishingly large eyes. His face emanated goodness and something more she couldn't put her finger on. He had the mien of a fine, sensitive person, which usually doesn't show until one is older. Perhaps it was the lines around his eyes, or something about his mouth. His smile conveyed his comfort of living within his own skin, which was unusual for someone so young. He appeared to her to be somewhere between 25 and 35. She was certain that few of her contemporaries would find him attractive, but that was no surprise. She had always been different from her contemporaries.

Nina graduated from high school at thirteen. She could easily have done it sooner but decided, with her uncle Seth, that it wouldn't be a good idea. All her high school classwork was Advanced Placement. Much of her work had been with home-schooling equivalents, such as assisting in research labs, apprenticing with artists, and helping in foreign language immersion classrooms. Nina and Ogie were both native French speakers because of their mother. Nina's early fluency in a second language enabled her to readily pick up other languages.

In the few classes she took in high school, her relations with her classmates had been awkward. She surpassed them in everything but athletics because her age and size prevented her from keeping up with them. She overcompensated by becoming a trick basketball player. She used her shortness to astonishing tactical advantage, leaving her opponents in the dust, wondering what had happened.

In almost all subjects, she knew more than most of her teachers. Even though she tried to keep it under wraps, her inner genius wore through the thin patina of ordinariness she stitched together. Even when she said nothing in class, she couldn't hide the wisdom on her face from her teachers. Their body language showed the respect they had for her. This, and her being years younger, exacerbated the annoyance of her fellow students.

Her high school administrators decided she would be better off not continuing in that atmosphere and arranged for her to take her

SATs, the high school equivalency exams, and the New York State Regents exams. The very few questions she missed on those exams were because the exam writers were less knowledgeable than she was. She hadn't yet gotten to the point where she could relate to the more limited outlook of the people preparing the exam and thus be able to give them the answers they wanted.

Nina had always been fascinated by sex and had done considerable reading about it. But she never had the feelings for boys that the girls in school endlessly talked about. Sixty seconds in David's presence brought her that understanding. Ogie read her thoughts and was astounded at how quickly she changed. His serious sister all of a sudden had the body language of a sexpot. He looked at David to see his reaction. What he saw was a physical response to her beauty and her body, and the artist's ability to picture her in the nude, followed by a quick clampdown of his feelings and related thoughts. He hadn't even been introduced to her yet. For all he knew, she was Ogie's girlfriend, and that would put her off limits.

"David, this is my sister, Nina. She knows a good deal about the Dutch masters."

Just as Nina had immediately seen in David a look of intelligence, he saw the same in her. He felt a wisdom and composure emanating from her rarely seen in someone as young as she looked. That, her physical beauty, and her sensuousness made his breathing difficult, and he was momentarily inarticulate. The very solitary life he led contributed to his uneasiness. He was out of practice dealing with people and had almost no contact with attractive, eligible women. Because his fellow Islanders saw him as odd, girls had avoided him. He had learned to live with that. Nina was the first girl who looked at him with interest.

Ogie saw the pictures in David's mind. He saw David's confusion and conflict. He read in him, *"Maybe she is available after all."*

In Nina's response to David, she had become a new and different person.

Mind reading the intense emotions of both of them simultaneously was straining Ogie's circuits. Living a solitary life on the Island hadn't given his social-emotional muscles much exercise. He felt as if he was off-Island because the stimuli there were so many that a day on the mainland left him exhausted.

He knew David would treat Nina with respect if they became lovers. But it would be a grave danger to them should it happen because of Nina's age. David could be subject to prosecution as a sex offender, and Ogie would have his identity exposed. It was obviously premature to ask them to consider those consequences, but if he didn't, it would be too late to prevent it.

He could read in Nina's mind there was little chance he could talk her out of anything important to her. Her brilliance included a great deal of self-knowledge. She had read much psychology and was a follower of Jung. She was no longer tolerant of all the rules she'd had to live by as a child. The arrogance of the know-it-all adolescent was compounded and augmented by her intellect. That intellect helped put the brakes on her impulses because she did have the insight to see where her untrammeled impetuosity could lead. But although she knew enough not to do and say things that were hurtful, she wasn't about to be limited by the arbitrariness of convention or law.

David said to her, "Tell me about your art interests."

"I used to watch Ogie creating Vermeers and Metsus. I got caught up in it and have done a lot of reading about the Dutch 17th century art world. The more I read, the more intrigued I was. I don't think there's been much improvement in technical painting since then. The Wyeths and Ogie, oops Owen, are probably the only exceptions."

"Has your brother told you that I do the same thing he used to do?"

"Sketchily."

What Ogie read in her mind was, *"Why hasn't Ogie told me more about David, knowing we are interested in the same things in art? I* know *he is uncomfortable having contact with other Islanders, but David is different. I can sense he wouldn't be a threat to O."*

"What exactly do you do?"

"I paint in the style of Vermeer, Metsu, and Rembrandt. I've even dabbled with Salomon de Bray."

"de Bray? That's arcane. Are you earning a living doing it?"

"Well, let's say I get along. I spend a great deal of time study-ing their work. Sometimes I create new ones and sometimes I do reproductions."

"I know Ogie used to do that but he sold his paintings under his own name. Are you doing that or forgery? Isn't that what Han van Meegeren ended up doing?"

"I sell them under my own name."

"And people buy those paintings? Knowing they are not originals?"

"They buy enough to sustain me."

Ogie said, "He's modest. He earns a very good living."

"Which are more popular, your copies or your so-called originals? And if you're so good, why aren't you doing your own paintings?" Nina's intensity seemed like a challenge, but it was her enthusiastic interest. David felt it as a challenge and he hadn't been challenged in a long time. His business was ideal because he had very little contact with his agent, and less with buyers. He didn't need to do much read-ing and writing. He worked hard and long. He could work when he wanted to. No one told him what to do. "Why don't you come and see my work and tell me what you think? Maybe you will see why I don't do a different type of painting."

Ogie knew this was the beginning of what he hoped was not the end of all of them. He was reading David's feelings and his body and knew he was aroused. He saw no way he could prevent Nina from making the visit. The best he could do would be to go with them.

David had become so absorbed with Nina that he had forgot-ten his panic about the Secret Service wanting him to identify who painted a fake Vermeer.

At David's, Nina was awestruck and quiet for the first few minutes. "You've outdone van Meegeren and it looks as if you are well on your way to out-Vermeering Vermeer. How did you get that canvas? It can't be 17th century. And the azurite. My god, it's not possible for anyone to accomplish this, and certainly in someone not yet 25."

David chuckled at her patronizing tone. "Tell me more. Why are you certain of the quality of my work? And speaking of age, how can you know so much at your age, whatever it is?"

Ogie's moment had arrived. "She's sixteen, and you have just begun to see how impressive she is."

"Why have you never said anything about her?" It was rare that David asked Ogie a personal question. In all their time together, Ogie and David hadn't shared much personal information. Ogie didn't want to talk about his past and David was uncomfortable discussing the way Meganticans viewed him. Ogie had assumed that David's reluctance to talk about himself was because they had so many other things in common, such as their interests in painting, life on the Island, the effects of living alone, and politics. He read David's effort to close off his sexual interest in Nina, which was a relief.

Nina went to look at an unfinished painting in the back of the room, and asked David why the style and the subject matter were so different from the others. He told her he had an apprentice who was working on creating a Gabriël Metsu. Her ability to see the difference in painting style surprised him, and he asked her how she knew. Nina said it was a gut feeling, but additionally there was a difference in the direction of the brush strokes and other things she couldn't put her finger on.

Ogie asked her if she remembered Melanie Wright, Marianne's daughter. Nina remembered playing with Melanie when they were both six. He told her that Marianne was living on Megantic with Melanie, and that Melanie was David's apprentice. Nina said, "She is very good for sixteen. I remember how well she drew. She's obviously learned a lot from you, David."

"I would like to watch you work. May I?" David hesitated, and Nina went on. "You must need a model."

Ogie cringed, knowing she was thinking of nude modeling. "David, there are problems with that. You could be charged with child pornography."

"Who would tell?" Nina asked.

Nina might be an ideal model physically, but David sensed that she would be demanding. Nina obviously knew a great deal not only about the history of Vermeer, but also about techniques in painting. She would ask many questions and would break his concentration.

However, he needed a model. On this small Island, it was an understatement that nude modeling wasn't acceptable. Whoever would do it would be an object of curiosity at the least. Even clothed models were hard to find and he didn't want people to know what kind of painting he did.

David's selective mutism, or something close to it, had not only made Meganticans uncomfortable with him, it made him uncomfortable with them. He had been bullied when young and his reaction was to withdraw within himself. Now Meganticans saw how successful he was in his ability to buy a house and acquire things that made for a comfortable life. Some of his erstwhile tormenters were now trying to cozy up to him and he wanted nothing to do with them. The thought of letting them get close and learn what he was doing was repulsive. His time with Ogie was almost the only social time he had and he valued it highly. He owed Ogie everything that had made his life change from marginal to good. Desperate as he was for an intimate relationship with a woman, he had no intention of risking what he had with Ogie by becoming involved with Nina. He could tell she was attracted to him and he couldn't imagine a more perfect woman to be close to. He was sorely tempted by his need for a model, by her enthusiasm and knowledge about what he was passionate about in art, and of course by her attractiveness.

Nina sensed David's indecision. She knew Ogie would respect her enough to let her make her own decisions about modeling and, if it came down to it, about having sex with David. She knew she wanted to experience sex with a partner and hadn't been tempted before this. She was perceptive and wise in ways beyond her years. Finding a male her age who would be careful, considerate, and deliberate about sex with her seemed impossible. She was certain that what most boys lacked was an interest in knowing what she would want rather than just going through the motions of pleasing her in order to please themselves. Her reading of women's autobiographical erotica had been extensive. From that, she already knew how to please herself, so she saw little point in sex with a man unless it could transcend what she already knew.

She didn't know why she was so certain that David would be just right for her. Maybe it was that he had to be so careful and disciplined in his painting. Maybe it was the wisdom he emanated, or the lack of panting on his part. It was probably a combination, and being attracted to him was the icing on the cake. It felt as if it could be a blending of more than their bodies.

She didn't think she could convince him to be intimate with her. Nude modeling seemed to be a good way to start the process. Nina knew the child pornography issue Ogie raised was a straw man. Difficulties could be prevented by keeping what they were doing secret. However, if their relationship became known, she would probably be assigned a foster parent or put in a sheltered group home. It would be the end of her good life, just when it was beginning.

And of course there was the danger of Ogie's identity being revealed. Ogie had the most to lose. That would be intolerable for her. He was a loving brother who had gone to extraordinary lengths to protect her from Karl, her stepfather.

Ogie asked David about his upset when they were leaving. Having met Nina and feeling comfortable with her and with Ogie's invitation to talk, he said the Feds had come to see him and had sworn him to secrecy. Ogie read David's mind and saw a garbled image of a painting that Ogie had done years ago. He thought he caught something about Melanie and Marianne, as well as the Secret Service asking about him. David's fear was stimulating Ogie's. When Ogie calmed down, he realized that if the Feds were here about copied Vermeers, then there was more to it than capturing him on an outstanding warrant. But it could still be a disaster for him.

CHAPTER 5
Nina

———

OGIE HAD RECONCILED HIMSELF TO Nina posing with and working for David. David's paintings wouldn't be shown on Megantic and if they didn't have sex, neither of them would give off the gestures or clues that they were intimate. He wasn't comfortable with the risk, but it was important to Nina. He hoped she would find other things to put her intelligence to work on.

David began a new painting based on Nina. She had suggested it and wanted to pose for it. He had done extensive planning with her. It would be in Vermeer's style. He talked with Ogie to be certain he wasn't reluctant for Nina to do it. Anxious as David was to be to be intimate with Nina, he knew it could be a disaster. He could lose Ogie, who was his only friend and a major source of artistic and social stimulation. He owed his success and well being to Ogie. Oddly, he sensed that Ogie wouldn't be upset with such a relationship if there weren't the constraints of Ogie's need to avoid being known. That was something he had never understood and Ogie hadn't explained. He didn't know how Ogie could be unknown and at the same time be successful selling his paintings. He sensed Ogie wouldn't answer him if he asked about it but he didn't want to risk his relationship with him by pushing it. Nina made it clear she was hoping that by posing for David he would initiate sex with her. She hadn't said it in words, but David knew it. That she felt that way was going to make it harder to work with her. Her enthusiasm for creating a new Vermeer was overwhelming and she had done a full court press using her charm, which made it even harder to say no to her. David had managed to isolate his sexual feelings about her and felt he would be able to keep his emotional distance.

Ogie was reconciled to the arrangement. If he went too far trying to stop her, it could backfire. If Nina was frustrated by David keeping her at arms' length, it would be unlikely that either of them would give off clues they had been intimate. He also had the advantage of reading the minds of Meganticans, and if he thought someone were suspicious of what went on between David and Nina, he could insert thoughts that would distract them from that.

One of the problems of trying to be Vermeerish and do a nude was that there were no known nude Vermeers. Nina paraphrased a quote from "The Scotsman" to the effect that if Vermeer had painted nudes, he would have done it with soft side lighting, as he did most of his work. It was impressive how much she knew about David's field. In fact, he had yet to find her wrong about anything in any field. Her depth of knowledge was hard to believe. Sometimes her interpretation was not to his taste, but that was different.

Nina came up with a way to make Vermeer's transition to a nude less abrupt. She suggested to David to show the nude partially in a reflection in the glass of a painting or a mirror, and to show the rest of the figure as a shadow. Because so many of Vermeer's paintings had light coming in from the side, the shadow could incorporate a graduated chiaroscuro effect. He could already see much of the painting in his mind. If it sold, he'd feel morally obligated to give some of the proceeds to Nina. While she wasn't going to be doing the actual painting, she was helping structure it with her suggestions, and if she modeled, she was entitled to remuneration. She was so enthusiastic about using her knowledge that he didn't think the thought of money occurred to her.

When Nina returned to Ogie's after her first modeling session with David, she bubbled over with excitement. "He adopted my idea for structuring the painting! He wanted to know everything about the research I had done on Vermeer. He even made a mockup of the window, the wall, and the black and white tiles in so many of Vermeer's paintings. And he made the wall in the mockup an uneven plastered surface, just as Vermeer's original wall had to have been. He photographed my naked shadow and then put the photograph on the mockup wall. I don't know yet how he is going to handle my reflection in the mirror."

Nina was excited and also disappointed. Ogie read that she was unhappy that nothing but professional activities had occurred. He said to her, "Wonderful that you are being so useful to him. Are you bothered by something?" He knew what was going on in her mind but wanted to give her the opportunity to tell him. He read her thoughts, *"I know I don't need to be afraid to tell him what I want from David, but it isn't easy to do. I also know that he and David are close, and what if he were to discuss it with him?"*

Ogie was startled by feeling physically what was happening in her body. There was a tightness in her chest and yet it wasn't constricting. He could feel that her wanting to have sex with David was more than choosing someone she could trust who would be good to her. She had loving feelings for him. His ability to read feelings wasn't developed enough to identify all that was happening to her, but he did know she was fully taken with David.

"Nina, did David say or do anything to upset you?"

"No, it was what he didn't do."

"And?"

"Ogie, I've decided it's time for me to have sex. There hasn't been anyone I've trusted or been interested in until I met David. He's perfect because he's thoughtful, sensitive, and respectful. On top of that, he is luscious. But I never had the feeling of his looking at me in a sexual way. What's wrong with me that he hasn't given off the slightest hint that he's interested in me in that way? He's seen me naked and I know that my body is appealing."

"Nina, do you assume that every man wants to have sex with any woman who is available?"

"It seems like that."

"Yes, there is no question that many men are like that. But has it occurred to you that maybe you don't notice the ones who aren't?"

"But you told me that men have sexual thoughts much more frequently than women do."

"Dear Nina, of course. But there are some of us who are able to conceal it and not act on it. I'm assuming David is one of them."

"But still, I have the feeling that David likes me, and I assume he wouldn't want to use me as a model if he didn't think I was attractive."

"Nina, you're impressively bright. There is hardly anything you don't know or can't find out. But there are some things that come from more than reading and schooling and are not easily taught. They're social and emotional things that take years of living to become part of you. You haven't had much chance to deal with the delicate areas of intimacy and sexuality. It's not as simple as the in and out of intercourse. There's much more to sex than that."

"What can I do?"

"Nina, this is not about any inadequacies of yours. Can you think outside of yourself and come up with other reasons why it isn't happening?"

"Jesus, O, you're my brother, not my therapist. Tell me what you think."

"Yes, I could give you a long list of reasons and some of them might be right. However, if you analyze it for yourself, you'll be in a better position to act on your insights than you would if I told you what to do."

"You're doing just what Seth did to me. OK. But please tell me more about him from your perspective. It could help me."

"David is a very private person. He rarely asks personal questions. He hasn't told me much about his life and family and he hasn't asked me about mine, until you appeared. We talk very little about our previous lives. Yet we became comfortable with each other in a short time. You know why I guard my privacy, but I don't know why David guards his. It may be the degree of concentration he needs to do such precise work, it may be traumatic things he doesn't want to revisit, or that he is naturally solitary, or other things. I gather he was somewhat of a social outcast growing up on the Island. I was surprised he took to you so readily. I know recently there have been other women on the Island who've tried to get to know him, and in his kind way he has made it clear he's not interested."

Ogie continued: "He's superb at what he does. I'm in awe of what he can do and have come to see that his inventing Vermeers is more than slavishly copying a style. He's taking known ideas to new places. I find he has surpassed me with his incredible work with light and shading."

"There must be more you can tell me. The day I arrived I noticed he met two men who looked like FBI agents. What was that about?"

"I've no idea. Ask him. If he wanted me to know he would have told me. That I haven't pried is probably why we get along well."

"Who buys his paintings?"

"He has the same agent I have, who has well-off clients who like 17th century Dutch paintings, but either can't afford the originals or they are never for sale. David has more orders for paintings than he can produce, which is why his paintings sell for a great deal of money. It's rare for an artist as young as David to be able to earn as much as he does."

"Speaking of that, how do you manage to live in what looks like a comfortable lifestyle? How can your paintings sell when you're using a false name?"

"I don't date my paintings and so no one knows when they were done or where. By giving minimum information, my paintings are harder to track. I send them to a third party who turns them over to my agent. I've been blessed with a few collectors who are anxious to have them. The money is funneled to someone who can get it to me surreptitiously or can get me things I need."

"Is it Korzybski?"

"Nina, it's best you don't know. That way, if I'm arrested, you can't tell what you don't know."

"If you're incognito and the gallery doesn't tell their clients much about you, how have you become known and popular?"

"My agent turned my secretiveness into something that gives allure and makes my paintings coveted."

"O, you asked me how David posed me to do the shadow before I mentioned that he did a sketch of my shadow. You also said he used charcoal for the preliminary sketch. You weren't there and I didn't mention those things. You know he normally uses a pencil for preliminary work. How did you know he used charcoal?"

Ogie wasn't prepared for this conversation. If he told her about his mind reading, she might not believe him. If she did believe him, she would become uncomfortable around him, knowing he was reading her mind. If he denied his mind reading, she would be assiduous in observing him and making mental notes about his behavior. Living with Nina, he would always have to be conscious of the need to conceal his mind reading. Ogie didn't want anyone to know about his mind reading skills. Nina would be the least dangerous but could give him away inadvertently. Should he tell her about it before she figured it out for herself? If he didn't tell her now when she was suspicious, then when it came out later she would realize he had lied to her by omission. How should he tell her to minimize her upset?

"Nina, I don't know how to answer you. You have sensed something going on with me that I debated whether I should tell you. You're on the right track. Try to explain your puzzlement about what you noticed."

"Well, it's happened before. You seem to know what I'm going to say or do before I do it. When I arrived, you didn't seem as surprised as I thought you would be. I thought you gave in too quickly when

I said I wanted to pose and work with David. I knew you were worried about the legal aspects and the threat of your being exposed if David and I had sex. I felt you knew my determination and knew you wouldn't be able to stop me. I can't explain it other than to say you intuit incredibly well, but somehow it seems to go beyond that. I'm reminded of the feelings I had about you when I was a child. Then I couldn't articulate it the way I can now. So tell me what's going on with you."

"Nina, don't say anything until I finish because you need to hear the whole story before we can talk about it.

"When I was teaching, I was able to sense in my students when they were troubled and what it was that was troubling them. Somehow I knew what it was they didn't understand and was able to make it clear to them. If it was an emotional problem, I could do the same thing and alleviate their anxiety. I didn't understand what I was doing and didn't think it was abnormal. The parents' positive reactions to what was happening with their children became extreme. Not only did their children do astonishingly better in their schoolwork, but they became much better behaved at home.

"I learned from my principal how overwhelmed he was by parents wanting their children transferred to my class and he asked me what I was doing that caused it. It started me thinking. I began to log what was happening and saw a pattern to the sequence of when I identified the child's problem and what I did to help the child. In those days, my most intense interaction was with children. But then I noticed I was seeing—that's the best way I can put it—what was going on with adults. Sometimes I spooked adults by anticipating what it was they wanted or were going to say. I couldn't believe the reality of what I was able to do. Looking at my notes after a few months of making them, I saw that my ability to see into my students' minds and sometimes those of adults was getting better. I devised tests to substantiate what I was becoming. That forced me to believe I had this uncanny ability. There's more to my development, but we don't have to go into that now. I want to hear your reaction to what I've told you."

"Ogie, are you telling me you're reading minds?"

"Yes. It's just that I wouldn't describe it like that. I would say that I developed a way to recognize what is going on with people. Mind reading suggests something more complete and absolute. Some of the time, I see words and phrases, but much of the time it's amorphous."

"What am I thinking about now?"

"I can't tell you the specifics, but I see that you're upset and frightened by me. You think it was a mistake to come here. Having confirmed what you suspected, you're panicky."

"Of course I feel that way. Why didn't you tell me about this sooner?"

Ogie replied, "Would you have believed it if you hadn't experienced it?"

"I guess not."

"Are you willing to discuss it before you decide to leave?"

"What's there to discuss? I don't think I could stand living with you knowing that I'm never alone with my thoughts, that you know my feelings before I've sorted them out, that there is nothing I can do or think you aren't aware of."

"Nina, when you're absorbed in a book, how much do you hear of what's going on around you?"

"What's that got to do with this? You've seen that I don't even hear you when you call me when I'm reading. Sometimes you have to touch me to get my attention."

Ogie said, "Most of the time when I'm painting, cooking, doing other things, I also wash out what's going on around me."

"Ogie, what are you getting at?"

"Nina, I don't want to be peeking in at your thoughts and feelings. I have come to relish my enforced isolation. My painting absorbs me and I have had great pleasure in gaining new insights into it. It takes an incredible amount of concentration to make the breakthroughs I've made. I'm anxious to continue doing it. If I spend time trying to see what's going on in your head, I will be missing my satisfactions and losing out on my progress. Your arrival threw me. I had to adjust to learning who the sixteen-year-old you is, and of course I was and am scared of you doing something that would reveal my identity. Your actions and thoughts have relieved me of that worry. Now I don't have to pay close attention to what you're doing—particularly as you have begun to be immersed in Island life. I'm guessing that this is just the beginning for you. Getting to know Russ and have him approve of you will open many doors. Does this make sense? Can you believe that I really don't want to spend my time away from my own inner life? Do you understand that? While I've enjoyed living the reclusive life, I would be delighted to have you here, but not in a way that would deprive me of what I value."

"Ogie, that sounds great and like it could work, but I'm still scared of you sitting on my brain. How can I be certain that you won't pop in there at unexpected times when I'm unaware of it?"

"Nina, I can't promise you that won't happen. All I can say is that I will do my best not to. I don't want to lose you. We're the only family we have as long as Karl keeps Mom a prisoner. And it doesn't look as if he is going to let her go. Now that you understand that, would you be willing to try again? I will go back to giving my work my full attention. The result will be my usual intense concentration to the extent that I often don't even hear the phone ring."

Nina said, "I'm dubious, but I'll try."

CHAPTER 6
Red

———

IN DAVID'S STUDIO, RED SAID that the difference between seeing a reproduction of a painting and an original was the difference of night and day. He knew he was seeing copies. He asked David how he was able to get the right colors in his copies if he didn't have the original to work from. Nina and David were taken aback by his insights. It was not because Red was an unsophisticated Island boy. They would not have expected that observation from any non-painter. David asked him, "How did you know it would be a problem?"

Red paused and he struggled to trace his thinking. "That's tough to say. When I see tourists painting from photographs they take, I realize the colors can't be the same as the real landscape. They also don't get the color of the water right in their paintings. In the time it takes them to paint the landscape and houses, the light has changed, and then they paint the water with the light of that moment and not the light from when they painted the other parts. They don't remember what color the water was when they started."

"Do you think the tourists can be forgiven for that?" David asked. "That's a subtle difference."

"I suppose it is, but the color of the water is really important to us. It gives us information about all kinds of things, including where we are. It tells us the depth, the state of the tide, the strength of the current, and where the lobsters are, because they migrate depending on the season and water temperature."

"That's right," Nina interjected. "How did you know where we were in the fog? You said we were at Heron Ledge and you didn't even look at the GPS."

"I don't know how to explain it. I just knew. For me, it's the same as if I were on one of the roads here and you asked me where I was. I guess the answer is, I grew up here. Nina, you told me you grew up on your uncle's farm and that you knew each individual sheep. That's not something I could know unless I lived with them."

Nina, David, and Red then went to Ogie's house, and Nina showed Red Ogie's paintings. This was another revelation for Red. He turned to Ogie and said, "What a difference between what you paint and what I see in the Island Gallery. I've always admired the work of our local artists, and even some of the tourists. But this is different."

"How would you describe the differences?" Ogie asked.

"Another tough one!" Red wrinkled his brow. "It would be easy to say the quality is different, but that doesn't describe it. For one thing, the way you paint the water is more accurate than the way other painters do it."

"Red, you're a careful observer and have come up with good insights about these paintings. There are no right or wrong observations. It's not an arithmetic problem where the right answer is evident. It's a matter of how you see things and how you feel about them."

"Well, your paintings feel deeper," Red said. "There's a feeling that I could walk into them and move around. They have more texture, and now that I think about it, the colors are more interrupted."

"What do you mean by more interrupted?"

"It's the small things. The colors of things in your paintings aren't the same all over. There are variations, just like in real life. Water isn't one color all over. There are slight changes in the water from place to place depending on the depth, the way the wind is hitting the water, the angle of the sun, and when there are clouds. Other people's paintings have some of that, but not as much as yours do."

"I know now why Russ trusts you to run his boat and do his lob-stering. You're incredibly bright, and from what Nina tells me of your behavior on the boat, incredibly competent." He could see Red strug-gling not to show how pleased he was. He was raised not to show satisfaction with a compliment, but these people were making it hard for him to stick to his cultural norms.

"I thought of another thing about your paintings," Red went on. "They move more than other paintings."

"Do you mean vibrate?"

"Yes...that's the right word for it, although you wouldn't think of a still painting as vibrating. Mr. Cartwright, may I ask you a question?"

"Not if you're going to call me Mr. Cartwright."

"OK, Owen, although I don't understand why Nina calls you Ogie."

"That's a long story for another time. What was your question?"

"You have so much detail in every surface. Does it take you more time to do a painting than it takes other people? How long does it take?"

"It varies considerably, and I can't always predict. Sometimes a painting will take two hours, and there are other paintings that can take five or six hours or more."

"How do you handle the light changing during that time?"

"Well, that's a problem I wrestle with. The shadows are a major problem—they're always moving, and it's important for me to record them. To capture the light and shadows I do several things. First, I take pictures with my digital camera. They're not perfect, but they help.

"Sometimes I paint a little bit of the color of an object on a sepa-rate piece of paper before the colors have changed. Then when I get to that part of the painting I have a reference I can use.

"The third thing, but it's not as reliable, is to use my memory of the color."

"Which name do you prefer I use, Owen or Ogie?"

42

"I'm used to my family and those close to me calling me Ogie. Nina has made you a part of us. You're welcome to call me Ogie."

"OK, Ogie, may I ask you a personal question?"

"Ask away. I don't promise I will answer."

"Nina told me your paintings sell for a good deal more than paintings sell for in the galleries here. How much do your paintings sell for?"

"I suppose I invited that when I said you were becoming a part of us. Well, it depends on the painting. Size and how much work I have put into it are factors in pricing a painting. On average, they sell for $40,000."

"Wow! Do you sell many?"

"A man by the name of le Brun handles my paintings in his gallery. He takes half of the sales price. I probably sell half of the paintings I make. The average is eighteen a year."

Without a pause, Red said, "That's $360,000 a year. What do you do with it? It doesn't look as if you spend that much? Oops, I think I'm being too personal. I'm sorry I asked."

"Red, I will answer your question about what I do with my money. My needs are relatively modest. There is little I want that I don't already have. I work hard at my painting because it gives me great satisfaction. I save the money I don't spend because Nina will need it for college and I'm hoping to assist with some difficult family problems."

"Your dealer taking half doesn't seem fair."

"Think about what it takes to run a gallery in a fancy location in a big city. The rent is astronomical. Either he, or someone he pays, is in the gallery for ten hours a day. It costs him to advertise, have paintings prepared for shipping, pay the electric bill, taxes, etc."

"How many paintings do you do a year?"

"It depends. If I had to pick a figure, I would say about 30."

"What do you do with the ones you don't sell?"

"There are paintings I won't sell because they are too important to me. There are paintings I give away."

"I know I've been prying, but this is a completely new world for me. What makes a painting too important for you to sell?"

"The most likely reason is that I made a breakthrough with a painting. I learned something new. It could also be sentiment, because something in the painting has particular meaning for me. For instance, I've done some paintings in France, which is my mother's country, but I haven't had much time to paint there. Those paintings are important to me. There are paintings I painted for my satisfaction, knowing full well they would be unlikely to sell.

"OK, Red, enough about painting. I can answer more of your questions later. How about we have the dinner Nina invited you for?"

During dinner, the question of how long Red's grandfather would be gone, and what he was doing, came up. At first Red was reluctant to talk about it. Then he realized that Ogie, Nina, and David had taken him in as one of them, odd as that might have seemed to him before. They might be "from away," but it no longer felt like that. He wondered why. With many of the temporary people on the Island you had the feeling they saw the Islanders as not quite as bright as they were. It was subtle, and often showed itself in the form of their bending over backwards to be nice. There was none of that with Ogie, Nina, or David.

"As you know, we had that shooting over lobster territory a few months ago. Grandpa has been called to testify about it. They can't tell him in advance exactly which days he needs to be there, but he has to stand by. So we don't know how long he will be gone."

"Red," Ogie asked, "What can you tell us about the trial?"

"I know that Grandpa doesn't like having to testify. He has often said it's rare when justice comes out of a court. Even though he saw much of what happened, he doesn't think the right person is on trial. It really bothers him because he thinks Eliot Corvissiano is responsible. Eliot is his first cousin, and he likes him. Jason, who is charged with attempted murder, isn't liked by many, including Grandpa, but Grandpa doesn't think Jason should be on trial."

"What do you think?" Ogie asked Red.

"I really don't know. At first I thought it was clear cut, but after listening to Grandpa, I can see it isn't simple."

"I was never clear about what the disagreement was," Ogie said. "Could you explain it?"

"You may already know that the unwritten laws here are that lobster territories belong to the people who inherit them. It's a law that's more powerful than the written laws, such as no speeding. If you don't want to be hassled on this Island, you had better not poach on someone else's territory. If you do, the nicest thing that could happen to you is that no one will speak to you. You might not even be able to buy anything in the store—Anita doesn't want to face the wrath of the rest of the community. There's a good possibility that other things will be done. Sabotaging your traps, cutting your trap lines, and slashing your tires are some of the less violent ones. There is even some resentment against people who have only had their territory for two generations."

Nina said, "Is that why Joseph works as a sternman when he has his own lobster boat? I heard he built it when he was thirteen."

"Yes, he did, but he knows better than to try to run his boat here. He doesn't have a right to a territory."

"How did he manage to build his own boat?" Nina asked.

"His father builds boats on the mainland. He let Joseph use his molds for it. Joseph has helped out at his father's yard enough to know how to set up the mold and pull the hull and deck and do the carpentry. He cannibalized abandoned motors to put together a good one and did similar things with some of the other parts, including the GPS and the marine radio."

"If he has all of those skills, he ought to be able to get a good job."

"Well, he's only nineteen. I think he has the idea of going into business for himself, and working as a sternman enables him to save money to do that. His captain lets him sleep on the boat so he can save most of his money."

Ogie asked what happened when someone died and no one in the family wanted to use the territory. Could it be saved for the next generation or could the person inheriting the territory let someone else use it and then reclaim it later?

"There are several possibilities. You can rent it out or sell your territory."

"How do you that when the territories aren't legal entities?"

"It's the same as owning a territory in the first place. Everyone recognizes the change and the enforcement is the same. If you're really interested in the details, grandpa has some books that have the unwritten rules about lobstering and usufructuary." Red laughed. "I just realized that books with unwritten rules are a contradiction."

"That's one of the best oxymorons I've ever heard," Ogie laughed.

Red asked Ogie to define oxymoron, and then said, "You, Nina, and David use many words I don't know. How do you get to know so many?"

"Some of it comes from being older than sixteen, and some from what you spend your time doing. I don't have a clue what usufructuary means. Obviously, it has something to do with lobster territory."

"I picked it up from reading the written unwritten rules." Red smiled. "It means someone who has the right to use property he doesn't own."

Frangelo, who had been sniffing at Red's legs, startled Red by landing in his lap. Red, who only had experience with outdoor feral cats, was momentarily frozen. His mother, Pearl, was allergic to cats and so there had never been a cat in his house. Red didn't know what to do. He had no idea whether cats were allowed at the table and no idea what would happen if he lifted Frangelo off his lap. He was torn, not wanting to offend Nina, who had talked to him of her love of Frangelo, or Ogie, his host, or even Frangelo, for that matter. No one seemed to have noticed what happened and Frangelo had immediately settled down on Red and thus had a low profile. Red took the coward's way out and said nothing until it was time to get up from the table. When the others were standing, Frangelo's position became apparent and Red asked, "What should I do?"

Ogie said, "You'll have to stay there until he decides to get up. It may mean spending the night here. The only other person he honors like that is Nina."

Red had come to feel comfortable enough to know that Ogie wasn't serious, and he put his hands under Frangelo to lift him off. At that, Frangelo hissed until Red withdrew his hands. Ogie's words about staying the night came back to him and he thought of how he would explain to his mother why he couldn't come home.

Nina saw the panicked look on his face and took pity on him by picking up Frangelo, who went agreeably. It was a revelation to Nina to see Red, who was so self-assured, at a loss. She reassured Red by telling him she was impressed that Frangelo had chosen him.

At the door, Red said, "Ogie and David, I want to thank you for showing me, and explaining, your art work. Obviously, what you do is something very different from what I'm used to. Thank you for a great evening and for dinner. Nina, I'll see you at five tomorrow morning. It will be a longer day than usual because we're going to pull a string of Arthur Lyons' traps as well. He also has to be at court tomorrow and his traps need to be tended to."

"Yes," Nina replied, "I think I'd better go to bed now if we have to get up so early. Won't it bother some of the others if you pull someone else's traps?"

"They'll figure it out and will have heard where Arthur is. We often do that kind of thing for each other. They know me well enough to know I wouldn't do it without permission."

"Again, thank you and good night."

After Red and David had left, Ogie told Nina how gone Red was on her.

"I didn't see it. How do you know?"

"Well, do you want the short version or the long version?"

"Start with the short version."

"Whenever you weren't looking at him, he was looking at you with intensity, as if it would be the last time he would ever see you and he'd better memorize all the details before it was too late. As you moved around, he followed every step you made with his eyes, but he tried to keep me from seeing that. No question in my mind, he is your prisoner. Red is a fascinating person."

"Ogie, you must have seen more than you're telling. What else?"

"Well, there came a point when you and he reached for the same thing at the same time, and he touched your arm. He reacted as if he'd been burned. My sense is that he's so scared you might think he'll take advantage of you that he dare not reveal how he feels."

"What did you read in his mind?"

"That would be an abuse of my power. If I did it, it would undermine your trust in me, and you might inadvertently reveal to Red what I told you. In addition, it interferes in your life in ways that aren't helpful."

"How?"

"It deprives you of the opportunity to figure things out for yourself. It isn't as if you aren't capable."

"I'm not convinced. It's not as if I'm going to ask you all the time. It will only be when it's really important."

"That's when it's most important for you to struggle to figure things out for yourself. If I help you and short-circuit the process, I will be stunting your growth in acquiring insights."

"OK, but you're being a tease. Answer this question. Isn't there another important aspect to this? If you're reading my thoughts, aren't *you* likely to inadvertently act on them and stunt my growth?"

"Nina, I promised that I would do my best not to read your mind. I can't promise you I won't make mistakes, and if you think I'm making a mistake, tell me."

"You already made a mistake when you warned me about how highly moral Red's family is. Did you read me as having lecherous thoughts about Red? If you did, you need to read again. When I told you about him, I was thinking how nice he is. I had no thoughts about intimacy with him. I had seen him, and I still see him, as a cut above other boys my age. He's very nice and easy to talk with. He doesn't tease, like so many boys do, and he doesn't come on to me in a sexual way. I never have the feeling that he is looking to 'get some,' as it's often so crudely put among boys. He really is what he appears, which is a very decent, clean-cut person."

"Nina, I suggest you take another look at your feelings about Red."

"What do you mean?"

"I'm violating what I said I wouldn't do, which is tell you what I see in your mind. If you want to experiment with concealing your thoughts, I will help you. With some people I seem to be able to look around in their minds and read their history and experiences easily, and with others I have to work at it."

"What is it like with me?"

"It's hard to say. I work at not looking in your mind, but I have, inadvertently. I can't always tell whether I've read your thoughts, or whether I know your thoughts because I know you so well."

The next day on the Jenny T, Nina and Red were alone. Russ was on the mainland. She felt something different from Red. She had a hard time putting her finger on it. He seemed more respectful, but there was a different quality to it. Could it be that he was bending over backwards to make sure she didn't feel trapped with him? Maybe he felt differently about her after he had spent time with her in her element and had seen how knowledgeable she was in so many things. Maybe it had to do with having seen the nude drawings David had done of her. Red had been very quiet when he was looking at them, and avoided looking at her. He commented about many other paintings, but said nothing about the drawings.

As they worked together hauling traps, she saw what Ogie had mentioned last night. Red was afraid of touching her. Ogie had said that it was because Red was so attracted to her. Now she believed it.

On the way back to the mooring, Red asked her to take the wheel while he repaired traps. He gave her a compass course to steer. It was confusing at first because of the compass moving in the opposite direction from the wheel. After she mastered it, she asked Red if she could do some maneuvers with the boat. He told her to slow the boat down to ten knots. After a few sharp turns, she decided to try maneuvers she had seen Red and Russ do when they docked. She spotted a floating branch and turned the boat so it was both going forward and sliding sideways. Then she put it in reverse to stop. The first time she ended up short of it, but the next time she was right alongside, with the boat motionless. Red asked her to do it again, which she promptly did, with the same result. He asked her about her experience with boats.

"I've done some kayaking."

"Well, I suppose that could give you a feel for it. But I've never seen anyone inexperienced with motor boats be able to do what you did on your second try. Would you like to try docking her when we unload?"

"I don't have enough confidence to do that. Maybe with more practice."

When they docked, Nina followed with her mind and body exactly how Red was doing it. She knew she'd be able to handle it the next time.

After they were moored, Red said, "You said you would go to college. When will it be?"

"I haven't figured it out. I don't know what I want to study."

"Have you finished high school?"

"Yes...three years ago."

"You don't look old enough. How old are you?"

"I just turned sixteen."

"How did you do it? Are you some kind of genius?" As soon as that came out, he was embarrassed and realized he was being intrusive. He started to apologize.

Nina said, "Don't worry about it. Yes, I was able to finish high school in a very short time. Mostly they wanted to get rid of me."

"Why would they want to do that? Did you misbehave?"

"Well, I suppose you could call it that. I think they couldn't stand to see me bored and decided I knew everything already."

"Nina, you're pulling my chain. What really happened?"

"Red, what I'm going to say will sound conceited. I like to think it's not conceit but a description of who I am. They said I was a genius. The teachers knew I knew everything they did and more. Some of the teachers had difficulties with that and others were fine and even asked me to fill in gaps in their knowledge. Occasionally, they asked me to teach things.

"If it was only the teachers who had difficulties with me, it would have been OK. But my fellow students were uncomfortable and weren't as tolerant as the teachers. Of course there were those I could get along with, but some seemed to be threatened by me. And being threatened by the runt I was then made them feel undignified. When I started high school, I was ten and not big for my age. My voice was a child's voice and my vocabulary was that of an educated adult, which didn't help. The solution was to graduate me early. It was a great relief to me and everyone else."

"It's obvious that David and Ogie have a great deal of respect for you," Red said. "From what David said, you know more about some painters he's working on than he does. He told me you showed him some painting techniques of the old masters. It seems like there's nothing you don't know or can't do. I've never seen an apprentice sternman learn boat handling as fast as you. How can you find it interesting to stay here and why do you want to be a sternman?"

"Red, I don't know how to explain this, but I'll try. I'm a flesh and blood person. When I cut myself, I bleed. Yes, I can do many things well, but that doesn't make me a better person or a better human being. I know that real success in life has more to do with how you feel about yourself. When I was younger, I felt superior to people around me. I came to see that feeling that way didn't make me feel good. While I tried to hide it, my classmates sensed my attitude, and that's one reason they disliked me. I'm trying to learn to be a better person."

"My grandpa has said things very much like you said, about being a good person," Red replied. "He ties it in with religion, but I think he sees being a good human being as more important than being religious."

"I agree," Nina said. "I think true goodness and humility are more important than religious piety.

"Red, please tell me more about your life."

"What do you want to know?"

"What is high school like for you? How do you get along with your teachers? Are there cliques? Do you have a girlfriend?" and when he shook his head, Nina was surprised to find she was relieved. She didn't want to acknowledge it, but maybe Ogie was right after all.

"What do you mean, cliques?"

"People who stick together and won't have anything to do with others. They try to exclude them."

"In a way, that happens, but it's not as clear-cut as you described. Because it's a small school on a small island, we all know each other from when we were toddlers. Sure, there are people who aren't particularly friendly, but there are many things we have to do together outside of school, and being exclusive wouldn't work here."

"How about your teachers? Do you like them? Do you do well? Do you enjoy school?"

"It's kind of the same with the teachers. They've known us since we were small. They're part of everyday life outside of school. They're at community meetings, in the store, at dances, and at projects the whole community works on. From what I've seen on television, there's more distance between students and teachers on the mainland. Here, there isn't much choice about getting along with them. We have to, and they have to do the same. If we didn't, our lives and their lives would be miserable."

"What subjects make you the most curious?"

"Physics, but not what we are taught. Mr. Liegeois, our principal, has me do research in physics that goes beyond classical mechanics. He says I already know the classical, and what I don't know is easy enough to find out. He intrigued me when he told us that Newton was outdated and Aristotle even more so. At first it was hard to grasp that an object in motion tends to stay in motion. It's very hard to picture. But even harder to picture is what could be beyond Newton. It's like fantasy to think about, but it's intriguing."

"How?"

"Because there is a different set of rules when things get smaller. Did you know that when we look at particles, we change their behavior? It even happens with bigger objects. It ties in with what I've experienced, which is that when falling objects are unobserved, they don't go where you'd think they would. But for me, the really mind-blowing thing is that in quantum mechanics, particles can be in two places at once. They call it superposition."

Nina worked on not sounding condescending when she said, "Mr. Liegeois sounds like a great teacher. I'm impressed you have someone who can do what he does for you. Tell me more about two particles and their relationship."

"This gets even crazier. Apparently, they get mixed up with each other and coordinate aspects of each other. It doesn't matter how far apart they are in space and time. Trying to picture quantum mechanics is like overloading your circuits. You have to hold too many ideas in your mind at once."

Nina realized that Red was more than just bright. She already knew about quantum mechanics, but that it fascinated Red, and that the school recognized his intelligence, made her think about him in a different light. Up till now, she had seen him as capable, reasonably bright, and quintessentially very nice. It was uncanny that Ogie had known what she was feeling before she did. She was attracted to Red, but she hadn't given herself license to go there. She was just enjoying him for who he appeared to be. That, and his beautiful relationship with Russ.

But now that he had breached her snob level by revealing how bright he was, she felt a stirring she hadn't felt before. She wondered why she could only let an intellectual get close to her. Why couldn't she have just accepted him for the decent person he was? Well, she had, but not in the intimate emotional sense.

She thought about David, and what an intimate relationship would be like with him. But there were problems. He wasn't willing, although she sensed that he was tempted. And the more she came to know him, the more she saw how extremely introverted he was. She didn't think there was any way she could warm up to that.

She was giving second thoughts to the requirement that her first lover be older and more experienced. What if Red, who was at heart a gentle, caring person, would be willing to learn with her? That could be interesting, even though it was not what she planned. It also obviated the whole question of her being under the age of consent, which had the potential of making everyone's life a living hell.

Red interrupted her thoughts, "You look as if you already know about quantum mechanics."

"I do."

"Then you were testing me. Did I pass your test?"

"Yes, in a way I was testing you. But I was curious what your school was like, and how much you could learn there. Life on Megantic is so different from what I know that I want to know everything about it."

Nina could see that she'd made Red uncomfortable, and in his eyes she might have put herself in the position of the summer people looking down on the Islanders. She desperately wanted to change his feeling about that.

"Everything here is different from what I'm used to, Red. Living with Ogie and working with David, I'm in a culture I know. But I want to know more about the culture here, and that's why I asked if I could go out with you and Russ. If you had been visiting me on the mainland, wouldn't you be curious about how things worked there?"

"I hadn't thought of it like that," Red replied, "To me, our culture is the norm. What goes on on the mainland seems strange. I suppose it explains why the summer people and the visitors are the way they are. This place is very different for them."

"So what other things interest you, in school or out?" Nina asked.

"Why are you asking about me?"

"I think you're interesting. I'd like to get to know you better."

"I don't think of myself as interesting."

"I think Russ finds you interesting," Nina said. "He would like you to go to college. Has he said what he'd like you to study?"

"He thinks I should study liberal arts. I don't really understand what that means, but he says it will make me a richer person, and he's not talking about money."

"What do you think he means?"

"He talked about it being studies in many different things. It would give me a broader outlook, and it might also help me decide what I want to do."

"He's right. A good liberal arts education will do that."

"How do you know? You haven't done it yet."

"No, but I've been around enough people who have that I have a feeling for it. I've also visited college classes. I was thinking I might enroll but then decided it would be better if I postponed it."

Nina asked him, "What subjects don't you like?"

"French," Red answered, "because it's so boring. We have to memorize rules and vocabulary and we almost never talk about anything. If we learned it so we could use it, I might like it."

"Why is French part of the curriculum?"

"There are a lot of people of French Canadian descent on the Island, and they want to see the language continued. The principal is also originally French Canadian."

"*Je suis française*—I'm French," Nina said. "*Ma mere est française, et avec elle il faut que nous parlons français*—My mother is French, and we have to speak French with her."

"Nina, is there anything you don't know?"

"For true wisdom, I will quote Joseph Addison: 'The utmost extent of man's knowledge, is to know that he knows nothing.' I haven't gotten there yet. You're closer than I am."

"Why do you say that?"

"Because you know a great deal, but you're more humble than I am. I tend to be a know-it-all, try as I might to be more modest. Being a know-it-all slows down my learning. My hope for myself is that I remain conscious of what Addison said. I've read that scientists add two thousand pages of new knowledge every day."

"See, you've done it again. You even know about what we don't know." Red sighed.

"Well, let me compound my sin of knowing too much by telling you about John Locke. He talked about how the mind is shaped by experience, which creates sensations we reflect on. He says that is the source of all our ideas. The immediate object of knowledge is an idea, and because of that, man only has indirect knowledge. Locke says that knowledge is relational, consisting of the perception 'of the agreement or disagreement among ideas.' Thus it is impossible for man to have both the complex idea in mind and the real object, because every object is an idea."

"But how can that be?" Red asked. "After all, an object is an object. I can feel it, touch it, and taste it. Isn't that more than an idea? It has substance, so how can it be an idea?"

"But what happens when you stop touching it?" Nina asked.

"I have the picture of it in my mind," Red replied. He paused for a second before continuing. "Wow, I never thought about what happens when I stop touching it.

"But this is very confusing, because the idea of an idea is so loose. How did you learn about these things? Are they subjects you studied in school? Who is Locke?"

"Locke was a philosopher in the 17th century. What I told you, I learned gradually. Locke and Addison were not subjects in my high school. It's the kind of thing you can study in college, and it's the essence of a liberal arts education. What you don't know is what you don't know because, as Locke might say, you haven't experienced it. But think of all of the experiences you've had that I haven't."

It was at this point that Nina came to realize how fully taken she was with Red. He knew a great deal. He grasped immediately the complexities she talked about. She wondered whether she would shock him if she talked about the specifics of her life. She decided to risk it.

"For example, I know a great deal about sex because of my extensive reading. But not having experienced it, I don't know what it feels like." And then she waited to see how he would react.

At first he just looked at her wide-eyed, at a loss for words. She thought she detected a slight blush. But he recovered quickly, and said something about the difference between knowing about lobstering and actually doing it.

He wondered why she had used sex as an example, but was hesitant to ask her. To talk about it with her felt like it would be handling a loaded gun. He didn't want to risk losing her by saying something offensive or stupid. He certainly didn't want to reveal he had sex on his mind. Suddenly she was no longer just pretty. She was vibrant and wise and someone he really wanted to be with. Now he was seeing her with more clarity. Her enthusiasm for everything and her total focus on him sent him over the edge.

He had a hard time describing her to himself. She carried herself confidently. She had an intelligent look in her eyes. Her facial expressions were kind, and when she smiled at him it conveyed such genuine pleasure that it dissolved him. He loved how her ponytail waggled. When they were working together, he had exerted great restraint not to swish it. He thought of her as a goddess, and felt honored that she wanted to spend time with him. He dreaded the day she would leave the Island, and there was no question in his mind that she would. He wondered if there was any possibility they could go to the same college.

Red had never talked about sex. That she initiated it gave him courage. He told her he hadn't read much about sex, nor had he experienced it, but he was curious. "We gossip about it on the Island, but no one talks about how it works, or the impact on people's feelings. Basically, all I know is what I can do for myself, and I realize that isn't knowing much."

He turned red and waited nervously to see how she would react. And then the words, "I can't believe I said that" escaped from him before he could pull them back. He thought he had doomed their relationship and stopped breathing. The pause while she tried to figure out what to say to put him at ease was so stretched he didn't know if he could live that long. Her reaction surprised him. "I bet I'm the first person you've ever told that you masturbate. And you thought that I'd be horrified. What would surprise me is if you didn't." With that, he began breathing again. He felt as if he had just been in free fall and her reaction saved him. This was another aspect of what an unusual person she was, which gave him the courage to risk asking her why she had used sex as an example. She replied that she wanted to plant the idea in his mind.

He couldn't believe she meant what he thought she meant. He was afraid to ask her to clarify what she'd said, but after a stammer, he said, "Are you hinting that you'd like to have sex with me?"

Even though Ogie had assured Nina of how Red felt about her, and even though she had seen the signs of it herself, she hesitated before saying, "Red, I like you a great deal. I know raising the sex question is premature, but I haven't had boyfriends and don't know how to go about suggesting we become closer. I apologize for bringing it up so soon. I don't know what to say next. I'm afraid to ask you how you feel about me."

Red felt as if he were in a fairy tale and had been given any wish he wanted. He was so overwhelmed he couldn't think of how to answer her. By the time he did, she was in an agony of suspense. Knowledgeable as she was about so many things, in this she felt like the rankest beginner.

Finally, he said, "I can't believe this." His reply didn't comfort her until he went on. "It's too good to be true. I'm afraid to tell you how I really feel because you might think me foolish."

She gave him an open look and an unsure smile and said, "Please risk it."

"I've been worshiping you since I first met you. I've done my best to conceal my feelings from you because I thought it would scare you off."

Nina said, "I know this is going to sound odd, but I need time to absorb what has happened between us before we go further. Next time, let's pick up from here and try a kiss."

"I don't want to rush either," Red replied. "But could we start now with a kiss? I think it will sustain me until we're together again, even though I now know a kiss is only an idea."

Nina smiled. "And not a bad one," she agreed.

But both of them were inexperienced and feeling awkward, so the kiss was a chaste one.

"The next kiss will be more serious," Nina promised.

CHAPTER 7

Nina

———

WHEN THEY MET AT THE Jenny T the next morning they both had a sense of relief from the tension of their uncertainties about each other. They felt more relaxed and assured, and at the same time unsure. There was the deliciousness of knowing what the other felt, and the tension of not knowing what would happen next. Red bowed to Nina in a way that conveyed both his feeling of loving her, his sense of humor, and his self-consciousness. She joined in the game by curtsying and holding out the ends of an imaginary skirt. Her smile was broader than Red had ever seen. The skit broke the ice, and they began the work of getting underway.

The day passed smoothly, with the exception of a pot line that was tangled. Nina was impressed with Red's patience in dealing with it. He asked her to steer and pull pots while he worked on it. She couldn't do it with the smoothness that he and Russ did. She needed to learn how to lever the pots and coordinate that with the motor-driven hauler, instead of trying to use brute strength. As the day went on, she got better and was very pleased to hear Red say, "You'll do." He was reverting to his Maine style of spare speech, but she had seen enough of him and the Islanders to know that "You'll do" was high praise.

When some friends of Red's came alongside to chat for a few minutes, she was surprised to see Red become a foreigner. Their conversation was technical, abbreviated, and their speech strongly regional. It made her question whether or not she understood English.

She reflected back to her times in France when she was talking with rural people who also had regional speech and were discussing the details of their work and other matters about which she had no context. At those times, even though French was her mother tongue, she could hardly understand a word.

Nina's mother had grown up partly in France and partly in the U.S., and had insisted on raising her in French. Nina had fought it every inch of the way, and it wasn't until she was deprived of her mother that she realized what a rich gift her mother had given her.

When she was forcibly separated from her mother at age eight, Nina had a child's vocabulary in French, albeit that of a very bright child. Later, when she was in France with Seth, she was able to enlarge her vocabulary. She was fluent enough and bright enough to immediately recognize the meanings of new words in context.

She was doing the same in Maine English. With lobstering and other interactions with Islanders, she had the context to learn Maine speech. She hadn't tried using the Maine accent and speech rhythm, thinking it would be pretentious, but she thought she could pull it off if she needed to.

Back at the mooring, it started to blow like mad. Red said they had better wait until it calmed down before they returned to shore in the dinghy. The bouncing was horrendous and they retreated below, where they braced themselves on the bare bunks to avoid being thrown around by the motion.

Red asked Nina, "Where do we go from here?" and when she replied, "Ashore," he said, "I didn't mean that."

"Red, I want you to know me more completely, and I want to know you more before we go further. I'm honored and flattered by what you said yesterday. But I think it could be tricky for us to become sexually intimate before you see who I really am and vice versa."

"Nina, when I asked you where we go from here, I was thinking about more than sex. Not that I don't think about it with you, but I feel as if we're in a kind of limbo. Yes, I know we've shared strong feelings about each other, but there's something missing."

"That's exactly what I meant when I said we need to get to know each other better."

"How do we go about it?"

"What we're doing now—spend time together. I would love to meet your parents. They must be super to have raised someone as nice as you. And don't you have a sister? What is she like?"

"My parents aren't as open as Russ. They were surprised to learn that he had taken you on as a sternman. It doesn't fit in with their idea of what women do. I think if they knew how we felt about each other they wouldn't be happy. Also, while they haven't said anything directly, I think they're suspicious of Ogie and David. What they suspect, I don't know. For one thing, my parents don't see any women around, so they wonder if David and Ogie are gay.

"They want to know why you don't go to school. They think maybe it's because you were expelled or are a truant. It wouldn't surprise me if they thought you were after Russ's money. You're a puzzle to them. I've tried to tell them how nice you are, but I'm just their son and they don't take me seriously. My sister, Amanda, contributes to their unease because she knows now, because of you, that a girl can be on a lobster boat, and as soon as she's bigger she wants to do it. They want me to have a girlfriend, but they don't picture you as the right candidate."

"What can we do about that?" Nina asked. "Do you ever go out as a sternman with your father?"

"No."

"Why not?"

"Because we just don't work well together. Everything I do is wrong. He becomes impatient, and then I make more mistakes. He can't understand why Russ wants me to work with him."

"How sad it must be for both of you. I know it isn't unusual for fathers and sons to go through things like that. Seth told me what he and my grandfather went through. But it got better. I promise you it will change."

"You wouldn't say that if you knew my father."

"Even so, I would like to meet him and your mother. Can we do that? How about I invite them over for dinner at Ogie's?"

"I don't think it would work. They never go out and I think they would be too uncomfortable. Russ will be back tomorrow. I'll tell him I think we can get more done if you come along. Do you want to?" He surreptitiously held his breath, hoping she would.

"Yes, I'd like that. What do your folks think about you working with Russ?"

"My guess is they think he's a bad influence, because he gives me ideas they don't approve of. On the other hand, they're loyal to him, and I guess they figure he's my grandfather, so he won't do me too much harm."

"What are the ideas they don't approve of?"

"Well, college for one. They don't think it's necessary. They think you can earn a good living lobstering. Also, Russ encourages me to do things that interest me. I like after-school drama and they think it's a waste of time. I also like to play the flute and they feel the same way about that. They don't like the music I play and they think the flute is really a girl's instrument. They also think I'm wasting my time learning a foreign language, and that English is good enough for us."

"Then why do you stay with French?"

"Well, Russ says that foreign languages expand the mind, but I'm having a hard time seeing how it does."

"I guess it's an uphill struggle for you to raise them—your parents, that is."

Red laughed. "I never thought of it like that, but I guess you're right. I don't know if I can be successful in bringing them up, but I'll keep trying."

CHAPTER 8
Renee

———

AT THE COMMUNITY DANCE, NINA approached Red's father, took his hand and led him onto the dance floor. He was so taken aback by her putting his arm around her that it would have been awkward for him to refuse. "We haven't met," she said, "and I think you should know who's spending time with your son and your father." Even though she did this without batting her lashes, her charm and beauty had the same effect. "You Fessenden men are really something else. I can't make up my mind who is brighter and nicer, your son or your father. How have you managed to keep that line going?"

Even though Russ Jr. knew Nina was only sixteen, she had the assurance of a grown woman, and he didn't react to her as if she were a child. He was embarrassed about having his hands on her, and also about his dancing.

"Well, you have completely captivated both of them. Neither of them can stop talking about you," he said.

"And what do they say about me?"

"They tell me how smart you are and how fast you became a good sternman. They couldn't believe it. I have to thank you for helping my father out when he needed help."

"You're welcome. It has been a pleasure, and I appreciate the chance to learn how to do it. I gather from Red that it has inspired Amanda, which might make things difficult."

"I guess we'll have to get used to women feeling they are entitled to do whatever they want. When it comes to lobstering, I don't know how the territories will work out, because they're always passed down the male line. It's kind of a law.

"I find it interesting that neither my father nor Red said anything about how pretty you are."

"Maybe they thought it was beside the point. I'm glad they saw me for who I am rather than a pretty package."

"I think it's time for us to stop dancing. I see my wife isn't looking happy about it."

"Do you think she would believe you if you told her I forced you?"

"I think it would make it worse."

"How about you introduce me to her?"

"I don't think now is a good time." And then he turned and walked toward his wife.

Right after Red's father walked away, Renee Liegeois came up to Nina. "*Bonsoir, mademoiselle. Comment ça va?*—Good evening. How are you?" While Nina had never met Liegeois before, she knew immediately who he was.

"*Bien, monsieur, Et vous, ça va?*—I'm fine, and how are you?"

"*Red m'a dit que tu parlait avec lui de la mécanique quantique, et que tu parles français avec ton frère à la maison*—Red told me you talked to him about quantum mechanics, and that you speak French with your brother at home."

"*Oui, c'est vrai*—Yes, that's true."

Their conversation continued in French.

"I see you really are a francophone. Now I want to know why you are trying to deprive one of my students of his hold on reality."

That took Nina aback. Red had told her enough about Liegeois that she knew he couldn't be serious, but she wasn't certain. And then it came to her. He was talking about what she had told Red about John Locke and how man only has indirect knowledge. With that, she said, knowing full well who he was, "And you are *qui?*—Who?"

which gave Renee pause. He knew she had to have known who he was because she must have known Red wouldn't have told anyone else about quantum mechanics.

"*Je m'appelle Renee Liegeois, mademoiselle,* as you already know."

"Ah, yes, but I only have indirect knowledge from a source, I might add, who speaks highly of you."

"While I'm not asking you to reveal your source, I suspect I have the same source who regards you as a goddess who has condescended to grace this Earth with your presence. I suspect my source of bias."

"*Oui, monsieur,* and why is that?"

"Because there isn't a human being who has so much virtue, intelligence, and beauty that my informant described. While my source didn't use the word goddess, he might as well have. I knew he must have encountered someone otherworldly."

Renee, having heard so much about Nina, had been anxious to get to know Red's ideal woman for himself. Once he satisfied his curiosity about her, he decided she might well be the answer to his problem. "And now, *mademoiselle,* I have a request. Our French teacher is pregnant and has been told she has to be on bed rest for the next few months. I need someone who can teach her classes. Would you consider it?"

"*Monsieur Liegeois, savez-vous que je n'ai que seize ans?*—Do you know I'm only sixteen years old?"

"Red gave me the impression that you were in your twenties and had finished college."

"He knows how old I am."

Renee replied, "He is so in awe of you that he thinks there is nothing you don't know, which must be why I had gotten the idea you were older and more mature than sixteen. Nina, if I may call you that, would you consider taking on the French classes? You have already shown me you are quick-witted and fast on your feet. If I put an adult aide in the classroom, do you think you could do it? And if you need more help, I could spend some time there ensuring *bon comport-ment*—good behavior."

"I don't know. If I did it, I wouldn't do the traditional lists of vocabulary and rules of grammar and pronunciation."

"What would you do?"

"I'd have to think about it. But the first thing would be some math that went from the concrete to the abstract in short order. Then, if you could supply me with *flûtes à bec*—recorders, and the means for copying the music for the whole group, I would teach them to play. I would absolutely refuse to say a word in English. Further, I might do some basic physics."

"You left out quantum mechanics."

Nina smiled, but didn't miss a beat. "It's a little advanced for the first semester. I would save that for the second semester. If there is time, we'll take on John Locke."

"I attributed Red's glowing description to his having a crush on you. What is your status? And why aren't you in school?"

With mischief in her eyes, Nina said, "Aha, here comes the truant officer. You may not believe this, but I was eased out of high school three years ago."

"What do you mean 'eased out'?" Liegeois said, chuckling.

"I drove some of my teachers and some of my fellow students crazy. They thought I was a know-it-all. It was a relief to them, and me, to have me out. They did it politely by graduating me."

"Why aren't you in college?"

"For the same reasons that high school was a problem. I'm too young, and I thought it important to have some worldly experience before I went."

"How sensible of you. I know I'm the supplicant, but I have to ask you this. What makes you think you could handle teaching a class of teenagers, some of whom are your age or older?"

"Because I have death ray eyes," Nina replied. "It drove the kids in my high school running and screaming when they tried to tease me. They would try it once and then figuratively, and sometimes literally, run away. They called me the voodoo kid. It caught on with the teachers, and they said it behind my back. I worked on perfecting it because it was the only way I could protect myself. Yes, there were some kids and teachers who were nice to me, but the atmosphere on the whole was unpleasant."

Liegeois asked her to show him her death ray eyes. She tried and said, "I can't do it properly without having the feeling behind it."

"OK, OK, I'm convinced. Do you know your IQ score?"

"I do, and you wouldn't believe it if I told you. I don't believe it."

"Well, I'm desperate. I have a good feeling about you and I'm willing to gamble. I would hate to see us lose ground in French and, for that matter, possibly lose it altogether. Do you think you can manage with Red in your class?"

"I'm very fond of him. He's a dear, wonderful person. I don't think he would give me any trouble and I certainly wouldn't want to make his life difficult. I won't let it get in my or his way."

"I don't know how I can pay you, as you are not a qualified substitute. Maybe we can pay you as an aide."

"Don't worry about it. It's a challenge. Just provide me with the materials I need."

"The only aide I can spare is Red's mother. Will that work?"

"Let me think about that. I haven't met her, but from afar I have the feeling she disapproves of me. It was plain she didn't like me dancing with her husband. While Red hasn't said it directly, I think I would be at the bottom of her list of choices as a girlfriend for Red."

Renee said, "I've known her since she was in high school. If I ask her to go all out to help you, she will, even if she doesn't like it. I'm guessing that she will find herself charmed by you."

"If she's willing to throw herself into what we will be doing, it should work well.

"You said something about coming by to help with behavior. I'm going to ask you to not introduce me and not come in until after half of the first period of my first day is over. Listen in on the speaker to check, but I think it will work better if I take charge immediately. Please say nothing to the students before the first class."

"Wow, you don't lack self-confidence. Can you start Monday?"

"Yes."

"I wish you the best. I will support you as much as I can. Let me know what I can do."

After Renee left, Red sidled up to Nina and asked her to dance. "What was going on with you and my father?"

"I dragged him onto the dance floor and made him listen to me about what a great guy you are."

"He must have loved that," Red said sarcastically.

"Actually, he took it very well and he thanked me for helping his father. I got the evil eye from your mother. He ran off to escape my clutches. I suggested he introduce me to your mother but he didn't think it was a good idea. The irony is, I just learned that I'm going to be working with your mother, although she doesn't know about it yet."

"Was that what you and Liegeois were talking about?"

"Yes. He asked me to substitute teach in your French class on a temporary basis and said he would have your mother help me with it. How do you think that will work?"

"My mother doesn't speak French. Also, does he know how old you are?"

"Yes, I told Liegeois how old I am. He's doing this with his heart in his mouth. He doesn't want his students to lose out on French. I think I reassured him. As for your mom, I know she doesn't like me, but if she gives me half a chance, I might be able to change that."

"Are you sure you can handle this?"

"Some professional bullies in my high school learned that even though I was a runt, I was not easy pickings. I think I can make some of that work here. You'll see. I hope you'll help me by letting me know how you and some of your friends think it's going. Suggestions will be welcome. I also hope my doing this will not interfere with our relationship."

Red had been looking worried. "I'm relieved you said that. I was afraid I would lose you. I can't tell you how much I value our friendship and how unbelievable it is that you feel so loving toward me. I assume we'll have to be more discreet than ever."

"Yes, but I don't think we have to be extreme. I don't like the idea of our relationship being public property, regardless of whether or not I'm teaching but I don't want to always have to hide it."

Nina was anxious to set the stage for her teaching by using surprise to preempt negative reactions. "Please don't say anything to anybody, including your mother, about what I'm going to be doing. I'll talk to your mother before class starts, but I think it will make more of an impression on the students if I face them unannounced. I'm going to need all the drama I can muster to make this work."

CHAPTER 9
Nina

———

MONDAY MORNING, BEFORE CLASSES STARTED, Renee Liegeois introduced Nina to Pearl Fessenden, who had just heard from Liegeois what she was going to be doing. She didn't look happy. Nina suggested they go to the classroom. The first thing Pearl said was, "I didn't ask for this and I don't like it. I don't speak French and I think it's crazy for a sixteen-year-old child to be the teacher."

"I think I can understand how you feel," Nina replied. "What do you think you can do to make the best of it?"

"I have no idea."

"Let me ask you to throw yourself into it. I know the kids will have an advantage in French, but they will respect you for wanting to learn. When the students enter, I would like you to sit in the back of the room with me. Please don't say anything for the first ten minutes. You'll see what is happening. After that, I'd be very happy if you decide to participate."

"I told you I don't know French."

"If you keep an open mind, you may surprise yourself."

As the students entered the room, they looked for their teacher. Instead they saw Pearl Fessenden and the girl who lived with Owen sitting in the back of the room. Nina wore a simple A-line dress, unusual in a school where all the girls wore jeans. The students began to ask each other if anyone knew where Mrs. Tyler was. Nina waited for what she hoped would be just the right moment.

She walked to the front of the room as if she owned it. She looked into the eyes of as many students as she could, and in a quiet voice said, *"Bonjour, mes amis*—Hello, my friends." When there was little response, she repeated it while giving them a stern, expectant look. A few then said, *"Bonjour."* Nina waited for the rest to respond. When they had quieted down, Nina spoke in a louder voice.

"Maintenant nous allons deviner un numéro entre zero et dix— Now we're going to guess a number between zero and ten." Most of the class was quiet and watching. A few had not fully settled down and were finishing conversations. Nina stopped and looked at them with her evil eye. The students who saw her stopped talking immediately. The others couldn't figure out why it became so quiet so quickly. Nina then went to the blackboard, and as she said the numbers from one to ten in French, she wrote them down.

Nina asked in French for someone to choose a number. Red, who had been primed by Nina, walked to the front of the room and behind Nina's back, wrote the number eight on the blackboard. When the students had seen it, he erased it thoroughly.

Nina then asked in French for someone to count the questions. No one volunteered because they didn't understand her. She then took a boy by the hand, gave him a piece of chalk, led him to the blackboard, and told him, *"Reste debout ici*—Stand here." She then said to the class, *"Vous répondez oui ou non*—Answer yes or no," and used head motions to illustrate. She pointed to the numbers zero to five on the blackboard and asked in French, "Is the number between zero and five? *Oui ou non?"* She then walked to the side of the room and chose a girl who said, *"Non."*

Nina went to the boy holding the chalk and said to him, *"C'est une question. Fais une marque*—That's a question. Make a mark." He didn't understand, so she took his hand with the chalk in it and made a tally mark.

She then asked, *"Est-ce que le numéro est six, sept, ou huit?*—Is the number six, seven, or eight?" At this point, several hands went up, and the student she chose said, *"Oui."* Again, she had the boy at the blackboard make a tally mark.

Her next question was, *"Est-ce que le numéro est six ou sept?—*Is the number six or seven?" After the *"non"* answer she said, *"Le numéro est huit. Combien des questions est que nous avons utilisé?—*The number is eight. How many questions did we use?" She pointed at the tally marks until one of the students responded with the correct answer.

She repeated the process several times, with different students writing the number on the blackboard and others making the tally marks. Soon the students were able to generalize that it took three to four questions to determine the number. She then asked them to guess how many questions it would take to find the number if it was between zero and a hundred, zero and a thousand, or zero and ten thousand, all the way up to a million.

Nina only had to use her severe look once, because the class had become so wrapped up in the process. The kids were anxious to answer the questions. She conveyed to them that she was not only anxious to hear what they had to say, but she was interested in them personally. The way she looked at them made them feel unique. She gave off a feeling of liking each one. Her prettiness enhanced her acceptance, particularly for the boys.

She was one of those rare teachers who could make a subject magical. The interest and involvement were so intense that Pearl, who had no intention of participating, was intrigued. Nina noticed there were several times when she started to raise her hand and then forcibly controlled herself, remembering that she wasn't supposed to like any of this.

At the end of fifty minutes, the class was jolted when Nina said, in English, "What happened to you just now?" They had only associated Nina with French and were shocked to hear her speak English. They eagerly replied.

"I didn't know you spoke English."

"I didn't know I could want to say something in French."

"I've never been in a class where the time went so fast."

"I understood almost everything you said in French. That's never happened before. You made me feel as if it would be easy to speak French."

Nina spoke again, "This will be the last time I say anything in this room in English. If you want me to talk to you in English, it has to be outside of the room. When we're in class, if you don't know a word or a phrase, you're welcome to say it in English. I know you will try to stay in French."

Then someone asked, "What will we do tomorrow? One to a billion?"

"No," Nina replied. "I have some other ideas. It will probably be either physics or algebra." At which point there was a groan from the class. "It won't be any more difficult than it was today," Nina assured them.

After the class left, Nina approached Pearl and said, "Thank you for going along with me. I appreciate that you don't approve, but you didn't show it and I thank you for that."

Pearl replied with some chagrin, "It wasn't bad. You held their interest. I wanted to answer some of the questions but didn't think it was fair to the students." Nina graciously accepted this at face value.

"Mrs. Fessenden, if we show our enthusiasm for learning, we're giving the students an important message. Please feel free to take part."

"I now understand why my son and my father-in-law like you so much. Just keep your hands off my husband."

"You should know that I dragged him onto the dance floor. He was uncomfortable and politely tried to get away, but I wouldn't let him."

"Why did you do that?"

"I knew both of you were unhappy about my relationship with Russ and Red. I wanted to see if I could make you and your husband more comfortable about it and the dance was the best chance I had."

"I see," Pearl said. "How can I help you tomorrow?"

"I don't know yet. I haven't had time to do much planning. In the meantime, if you have any ideas, please let me know."

Renee Liegeois intercepted Nina as she was leaving and asked her to join him in his office. Twenty minutes after the class started, he had slipped into the room. Neither Nina nor the students had taken notice of him.

"I couldn't believe what I saw in there," he said. "You had them eating out of your hand. Even Pearl, who is not the most genial person, seemed wrapped up in it. I would ask you how you did it, but I know the answer."

"I don't know what it is. Please tell me?"

"Magic," he replied with a smile. "It's the only reasonable explanation. If you quote me, I'll deny I said it."

Nina smiled. "*Monsieur* Liegeois, I've never done this before and I appreciate all the help I can get. Is there any other feedback you can give me?"

"First, let's straighten out this *Monsieur* Liegeois business. I'm called Renee by everyone."

Nina said, "How unusual in a public school. I've never encountered that before."

Renee told her that on a small island where the same people are in different roles it was hard to stand on ceremony. "A teacher might also work as a carpenter and a school janitor might also teach a class. There are many such examples."

Then he went on to answer her question, "I'm afraid to ruin a good thing by intellectualizing it, but if I had to use one word, I would say *intensity*, but obviously there's more to it than that. You show the kids, individually and as a group, that you're interested in them and that you care. I think I can be most helpful by saying, continue to do what you're doing, and what can I do to help you?"

"Give me a time frame so I can know how far out I need to plan."

"Materials are relatively easy. We can have them delivered by plane in the regular UPS shipment. Mrs. Tyler will be out until the end of the semester. I was going to find a substitute as soon as possible, but now that I've seen you in action, I'd like to keep you on if I can. Crazy as it is, I will suggest she consult with you with the excuse that you could use her assistance. May I videotape what you're doing? I'd like Mrs. Tyler to see it. However, I can't promise you this will fly with the school board and the video might help with that."

Nina nodded agreement and Liegeois went on: "It's very good that Pearl is coming around. There may be problems in the community with a sixteen-year-old teaching. At least we have a respected, responsible adult in there, and if she continues to enjoy it, she will be good support. While she isn't the easiest person, she is honest and will straighten out anyone who raises questions about what goes on in your class. How did it go with Red in the class, considering that his mother was there, and that you and he seem to have a special relationship?"

"Except for arranging with him ahead of time to write the first number on the blackboard, he didn't get any special treatment. He wasn't acting self-conscious or awkward. As you know, he is very mature and self-possessed and seems to be wise beyond his years."

"That's a perfect description of you, Nina."

"Thank you," Nina replied. "I'm not used to living in a fish bowl and having everyone know what's going on with me. Do you think it will get around about Red and me?"

"It's inevitable, but it doesn't necessarily mean trouble. Much depends on how you handle yourselves. Even though people will come to know about it, I strongly suggest you be discreet. Avoid displays of affection in public. Having watched you today, I know you will be very professional with Red in your classroom.

"This brings up another problem, and I don't know how we will solve it. It's the question of grading the students. Maybe Mrs. Tyler has enough records of their work to grade them, but it wouldn't take into account the work they're going to do with you. I know it's just your first day, but have you given any thought to it?"

"I won't give grades. I'm uncomfortable with grading and particularly uncomfortable giving grades in a situation where I'm asking the students to be open to trying new and difficult things. We haven't discussed the curriculum, but I've just assumed you wanted the best I could do. That best is going to be interactive learning, which doesn't lend itself to conventional grading. I was planning to write a narrative about how each student is doing."

Renee thought for a moment. "OK, let's try that and see how it goes."

"I've just begun to think about what I will teach next," Nina said.

"What are your thoughts?"

"Algebra tomorrow, inventing new number systems, and kitchen physics. If you can get me some recorders, I'll teach them how to play them and read music, using only French instructions."

Renee said, "OK, you've got me there. What is kitchen physics?"

"One example is that groups of students will measure the viscosity of liquids and compare the results mathematically."

"What about the standard curriculum? Why ignore it entirely? After all, there is a need for grammar and structure."

"Mr. Liegeois, how many adults do you know who have studied foreign languages in school and express comfort about using them, now or when they were studying them?"

"Not many, Miss Cartwright."

"Why should people bother to study a language if the result is to make them feel inadequate about using it?"

"I have taken on a first class mind who tells me the Emperor has no clothes on. Nina, you're right, but being right has problems. Let me think about the curriculum issues, and in the meantime, please continue with the exciting teaching you're doing. I think you are super and I hope we can get away with it. If we can, the children will be the beneficiaries."

On her second day teaching the French class, Nina did some basic algebra. Most of them knew it already but were intrigued to be able to talk about it in French.

On the third day, she faced them with a question, "*Maintenant nous n'avons pas dix numéros. Nous en avons seulement six. Comment est-il possible de compter jusqu'a cent?*—Now we don't have ten numbers. We only have six. How is it possible to count to a hundred?"

The answers were all over the place. Some thought it wasn't possible. Red, who obviously knew Nina had something up her sleeve, even though he hadn't figured out what, said, "*Je crois que c'est possible, mais j'ai besoin de plus de temps pour réfléchir la reponse*—I think it's possible, but I need more time to think about how."

Nina went to the board and listed the numbers from zero to nine, vertically. She said the numbers in French as she wrote them. At the top of the column she wrote, *Unités*—Ones. She then asked, "*Que est que ce le nom de la prochaine colonne?*—What do we call the next column?"

The answer came quickly: "The tens" and Nina said it in French, "*Les dizaines.*"

Nina then repeated what she had done with zero to nine, but stopped at five. She labeled the column with the six numbers in it *Unités*. As she was about to ask the name of the next column, Isabelle and Red called out simultaneously, "*Les sixes*—the sixes." Nina was elated that they had figured out how a number system works.

When the bell rang at the end of class, they were up to the six thousand column and speculating about what the larger columns would be called. The enthusiasm of their discoveries was intoxicating.

Liegeois had come in for the last few minutes of the class and had a hard time believing his eyes. He had rarely seen a class oblivious to the end of a period. He wished he could show some of the school board members what Nina was doing. Some had already begun making complaints about Nina teaching the class. He wanted them to see not just the students' enthusiasm for the math and the French, but the quality of their thinking and how she led them there.

He didn't want to miss a single class she taught. Instead, he was going to have to spend time preparing for the inevitable school board meeting about it. Perhaps his first step would be to have a heart-to-heart with Pearl. If she were convinced how good the teaching was it would make a difference in how the community felt about Nina.

Renee had to admit to himself that it was a pleasure to watch this lovely young woman invest everything she touched and talked about with that highly unprofessional term he had used with her—magic. He wished he could have her teaching all day long. He knew she could handle any subject.

Russ Fessenden was on the school board. Renee knew that Nina had been lobstering with him. Maybe when Russ returned, Renee could get him to sit in on her class. Renee thought that of all the board members, Russ would have the vision to see the intellectual excitement Nina brought to the class.

Russ was a gruff man and one of few words, but his words carried weight. He had opposed building the school addition, contending that it didn't have enough space for their coming needs. He had been right, and now it would cost more to build a second addition than it would have cost to make the first one bigger to begin with.

On the fourth day, Nina's plans immediately went awry. She was planning on teaching her students how to play the recorder, instructing them only in French. She had done considerable preparation to ensure it would go well. But before she could get started, Isabelle asked, "What would happen if people had twelve fingers instead of ten? What would our number system look like?" Nina could see that several other students had seen that as a problem and wanted to know the answer.

It took Nina a moment to think through whether she should abandon her plans, and she quickly decided there was no good reason not to capitalize on their interest.

"*Est-ce que c'est possible?*—Is it possible?" she asked, knowing full well how a number system based on twelve could work. This would be a good challenge for the students. She listed the numbers in the "one's" column, stopping at nine, then asked, *en français*, of course, "What do we do next?"

A reflective time descended upon the class as they wrestled with the question. One student suggested using one with zero touching it, like the sound œ. Another suggested using the Roman numeral for ten. Still another came up to the blackboard and made a vertical line with two horizontal lines through it. When he was cheered, he did it again, but put three horizontal lines through it. The class agreed that those symbols for ten and eleven would work.

At this point, they were so used to Nina's approach of leading them to the next question that several said in unison, "*Quel est le nom de la colonne suivante?*—What do we call the next column?" And from there, they took off, jumping to the symbol for two elevens next to each other and then, without Nina saying a word, they named that column. They were just getting to five columns when the bell rang. As they rose to leave, Nina said, "*Fantastique!*" and she had the intense satisfaction of having enabled her students to invent something.

Nina's whole body felt the power and gratification of what she had done. How wonderful that she could stimulate their thinking, have them be enthusiastic about it, and have them take the lead because they understood it so well. It was a physical feeling that went through her body.

Speaking of her body, she was impatient for an opportunity to be alone with Red. She knew it would come, but she didn't like waiting. She felt as if she had been postponing her first sexual experience forever.

CHAPTER 10

Board of Education

———

RENEE PUT THE QUESTION OF Nina's age and qualifications on the school board agenda for the next meeting. He knew the board chairman would raise the issue and wanted to preempt him. It was going to be a challenging meeting. The agenda had been posted on the community bulletin board a week in advance and had stirred things up. The sourpuss cranks were talking about how they planned to put a stop to the ridiculousness of a child teaching the French class. Remarkably, most of the parents of students in the class had contacted Renee directly. They wanted him to know that not only did they support Nina, they wanted to ensure that nothing interfered with her continuing to teach. They had been delighted by the enthusiasm of their children and planned to be at the meeting en masse. Renee told Nina that the meeting could be ugly and it might be a good idea if she didn't come. Nina said it didn't scare her, but didn't commit to being there.

Renee, unbeknownst to the board members, had already been in touch with the State Superintendent of Schools, who had been so curious about the situation that she came to visit and brought a foreign language specialist and an accreditation specialist with her. Liegeois, wanting to keep the situation low key, requested that the visitors not identify themselves by their titles.

The visitors balked at the thought of giving a sixteen-year-old who had not been to college teaching credentials. But after they observed Nina in the classroom and interviewed her, and learned she had taken advanced placement courses, they had a change of heart. Nina answered the French specialist's abstruse questions about the language, and then she asked him about aspects of French of which he had only the vaguest knowledge.

When the accreditation specialist asked about teaching techniques and educational theory and practice, Nina convinced her as well.

Facetiously, the educators toyed with issuing Nina an Advanced Certificate, but settled on an Emergency one.

When Henry Olds, the school board chairman, called the meeting to order, he was so anxious to get to what he had referred to as, "The craziness that Liegeois was up to," that he asked for motions to dispense with the reading of the minutes and old business.

Henry wanted to sink his teeth into Liegeois, whom he had never liked. He had an inkling that a few members of the community thought highly of Nina, but he didn't think this would sabotage his agenda.

If Henry had to sum up his feelings, he'd say that Renee was too nice and too relaxed. That he had been a successful and beloved principal on Megantic for seventeen years was beside the point.

When the Lord boy had defied his teacher, because he was under incredible pressures at home, Liegeois had counseled the boy and his parents and readmitted him two days later. That was only one example of the crazy things Liegeois had done. This Nina business was Henry's best opportunity to get rid of him. Fortunately, the last school board election had given Henry a second spiritual brother. This would give him three votes, which was all he needed on the five-member board.

However, it took unanimous consent to change the order of business. Russ objected, so Henry had to control himself while they went through old business, which included an interminable review about contracts.

When the innocuous-sounding item, "Qualifications of the substitute French teacher" finally came up, Frank Lyon moved "That Nina

Cartwright be dismissed from her temporary teaching assignment because of her lack of qualifications."

Henry lashed out with, "Renee, what the hell were you thinking when you appointed Nina as a teacher? She's only sixteen, doesn't have a college degree, and can't have finished high school. Additionally, how can someone that age control a class and have the respect of students? Have you even thought of the legal liability?"

Liegeois pointed out that Nina was a substitute, not under contract, and there was an aide in the room. Further, he mentioned that all of Nina's high school classes had been for college credits.

When Renee started to tell the board about the visit and decision of the State Superintendent of Schools, Henry interrupted him.

"Be it moved that, because of policy and philosophical differences, this board will not renew the contract of Renee Liegeois as of July first."

Fred Fellowes, the third member of Henry's triumvirate, quickly seconded the motion.

Frank asked for all in favor, but before he finished his sentence, Russ asked quietly whether this wasn't an issue that needed discussion. Frank said that he might reconsider if Liegeois dismissed Nina. The vote to dismiss Liegeois was over quickly.

At that point, two unusual things happened. The first was that Russ, who normally spoke sparingly, said, "I think you will find you have overreached yourselves."

The second was that several parents of children in Nina's class let out a collective gasp.

The board then voted to close the meeting. Russ Fessenden and Jonathan Logan, the fifth member of the board, were outnumbered and couldn't stop the process. The onlookers didn't have a chance to make a comment, except among themselves. It was clear they weren't happy, and they wondered what they could do to reverse the board's actions.

The next day, almost no children showed up for school. Parents picketed in front of the houses of the three board members responsible for the dismissal motion. No one could remember picketing ever happening on the Island before. Henry's call to Liegeois to bawl him out for inciting the picketing gave Henry more aggravation yet. He learned about the mass absenteeism and that what happened was as much of a surprise to Renee as it was to Henry.

Renee gave Henry another shock when he told him that State money would be lost because of the reduction in average daily attendance. One day of this might be survivable, but if it continued, it would badly impact the school's operating budget.

When Renee said that letters addressed to Henry, Frank, and Fred had been delivered to the office by a group of parents, Henry's disquiet escalated. Russ's words from the previous night echoed in Henry's mind, and he wondered whether Russ had instigated the protests. Somehow, it didn't seem in character for Russ, but then he really didn't understand any of this nonsense.

Henry's calls to Fred and Frank added to his worries. They too were upset by the letters and the pickets. Henry hadn't looked in his mailbox yet. When he did, and read the copies of the letters that had been delivered to the school, he had to sit down. There was nothing polite about the letters. They said in unequivocal terms that the board action regarding Liegeois had to be reversed or the strike would continue.

As the day progressed, the bad news continued. When Henry went by the town clerk's office, Jonathan, the town clerk, handed him a photocopy of the petition that had arrived earlier to recall Henry from his elected position. It had been signed by 70 percent of the voting population of the Island.

Henry felt his world was coming apart. He didn't know where to begin rectifying it. Ironically, he thought the person he most detested was the one person who might have some answers for him, and he stopped by to see Renee. Renee couldn't have been more courteous, which only added to Henry's agony.

"What should I do?" Henry asked.

"What do you want to do?" Renee replied.

"Damn it, Renee, you know what I'm asking. I need more than that."

"What could I possibly tell you that you don't know already?"

"How about you tell me your thoughts."

"Henry, this is a political question. My job is to run the school district and the school. If I go into politics, I step out of my role as a professional educator. If I do that, how can anyone trust me?

"I will tell you that the school district is severely threatened by student absenteeism and the resultant loss of funds. Resolving the issues to stop that loss should be the highest priority. How it is done is up to you because that is your role."

"Jesus, Renee, I don't know what the hell to do. I feel as if I'm going crazy. I never thought it would go this far. Last night, after the meeting, my sister came over to talk to me about what Nina has accomplished with her twins. She begged me to change my mind about Nina because her girls had learned so much in such a short time and loved the class. She convinced me I had been wrong about Nina. How can I make things whole again?"

"Well, I had no intention of asking Nina to stop teaching, so that leaves you with two worries. The first is if she is willing to continue, considering what happened last night. The second is whether my successor would want to have her continue to teach. And then, of course, we don't know when and if Mrs. Tyler is coming back."

"What do you mean, 'my successor'?" Henry asked.

"Wasn't there a motion passed last night that established a vacancy in the principal's position?"

"Oh, yeah," Henry replied. "My sister weighed in heavily on that subject too. She didn't make me a convert, but she did make me think about it. Is it true you've been spending your own money for school materials, for food and medicines for some children, and a number of other things?"

Renee said, "You weren't supposed to know about that. I've tried to keep it quiet, but I suppose in a small community it's almost impossible. My doing that should not influence you in your decision about my employment."

"I have come to see a lot that I didn't before. My sister worked me over about how you've made the school so good and how much you've contributed to the community. To be frank, I still don't like you. But I see that this has to go beyond my personal feelings. I would really like to work with you to repair the damage. How would you react if I could get the board to reverse its decision about your employment?"

"Henry, I'm not stalling when I say this, but I need to do some thinking about it before I give you my answer. Last night was a shock to me. One question that occurs is, can this happen again if you and the other board members decide you not only don't like my decisions but don't even want to hear the reasons I made them?"

"Renee, these recall petitions may resolve that. I don't know if I would win a recall vote, and I don't know if I want to."

CHAPTER 11
Nina and Red

———

ON SATURDAY, NINA JOINED RED and Russ on the Jenny T. She'd missed their company and wanted time with Red. Russ greeted her with a grin and said, "You sure were the cause of a lot of turmoil around here. It was a needed shakedown for the board. I suspect that some of them don't know what good teaching is or what good sense is. I would love to know how you learned to teach so well."

After unloading their catch and dropping Russ off at the dock, Nina and Red took the Jenny T back to the mooring. It was a windy day and the wave tops were being blown off into their faces. Once again they had to wait in the cabin until it calmed down.

Even with the protection of the harbor, the boat was bouncing violently. Nina and Red were exhausted from the day's work and the beating of the sea. Nina's inexperience with teaching necessitated an extraordinary amount of planning. Even though she was only teaching two classes a day, she had to work hard at it. That and the controversy had exhausted her emotionally and physically.

Many of the parents of her students had praised her teaching, but gratifying as teaching was, it was time consuming and tiring. She had also been working hard with David on the construction of the nude Vermeer. She looked forward to a day on the Jenny T as a way of relaxing as well as having time with Red. The rough conditions made making out impossible, so Nina asked Red, "How are you? I've missed you. We really haven't seen each other except in public."

"Nina, it feels like it's been forever since we've been alone. I was worried you'd changed your mind about us. I've missed the conversations we had together. I'm thankful you came out today.

"I can't believe how lucky I am to have someone who is so bright, so smart, so good a teacher, so well liked by so many and, of course, so pretty as my girlfriend. I know you talked about us having sex, but for me just having you as a close friend is great."

"I hope that I can be more than your close friend," Nina said. "I know the term boyfriend covers a lot of ground and frequently describes superficial relationships, but I really do want you to be my boyfriend."

"I adore you," Red replied. "I was so worried that you wouldn't want to continue."

"Red, I can't promise you we will be together forever, but I'll never end our relationship without telling you why."

Nina wondered whether Red had reservations about having sex with her, and if so, what they were. She had a sense of his possible reluctance. "Red, do you want to have sex with me?"

"Oh, Nina, of course I do, but I don't know how to say it."

"Just tell me what you're thinking."

"There are so many thoughts, I don't know where to begin. How could I not want to be that close to you? But I don't want to have sex with you if it threatens us being close friends. And where could we do it and not have anyone know? My parents would be very upset, and it's against everything I've been taught in church. I don't know much about birth control. I'm also afraid I might hurt you, and I might be clumsy."

Nina wanted to address what was worrying him the most. She decided on the practical aspects, and told him that David was going to be away for a few weeks on business. He wanted her to continue some work for him, take care of the house, and feel free to use it. She told Red she had bought condoms and an anti-spermicidal gel on her last trip to the mainland and the combination should take care of things.

Nina said that while she had done a great deal of reading about sex, she too lacked experience with a partner. If they took their time and proceeded carefully, they might avoid awkwardness.

Then she addressed the religious issue. "I'm reluctant to tell you to ignore your feelings about the church, but let me ask you a question. What are the most important rules in Christianity?"

"The Ten Commandments," Red replied.

Nina then asked, "Where in the Ten Commandments does it say that unmarried people should not have sex?"

"Well, I was taught that adultery and fornication are synonymous."

Nina said she supposed that was one interpretation of the seventh commandment, but added that there were conflicting interpretations of adultery. The ancient Hebrews viewed it as a married person having sex with someone they weren't married to, and that was also the dictionary definition. She asked Red if he really felt that sex between two unmarried people who cared deeply about each other was sinful, and did it occur to him that Russ leaving them alone on the boat wasn't entirely accidental. She finished by telling Red she wanted him to think about it carefully. As much as she wanted to have sex with him, she didn't want to if it made him uncomfortable.

It was apparent that Red was giving it much thought. He said to Nina, "I agree with the ancient Hebrews, but I don't know if my agreement is intellectual or self-interest."

Nina asked Red to think about how he would feel about it after they had sex together. She asked him, "Do you think you will feel you have done something wrong?"

"I can't picture that happening." And with that and the wind calmer, Nina suggested, "How about a kiss?"

"Gee, Nina, I don't even know how to do that, except when I kiss my mother or my sister."

"Red, I haven't kissed anyone romantically either. Let's experiment."

Once the classic nose problem was solved, it began to work well, and they were surprised at how nice it was. The awkward part for Red was where to put his hands. He was afraid to touch Nina in the wrong place because he didn't want her to think he felt free with her body. She sensed the awkwardness and guided his hands around her so they ended up on her back and her bottom. Even with permission, he was still uneasy about touching her so personally, so she took both hands and firmly planted them on her bottom. She asked him if that bothered him, and he said he didn't want to assume anything without knowing if it was OK.

After a brief discussion of how satisfactory the first kiss had been, they tried it again. Nina wanted Red to know that more physical intimacy would be welcome, and asked Red to put his hands on her breasts. Nina had only recently begun to think about herself as sexual. She realized she had pride in her body—she wasn't ashamed of any part of herself.

"Nina, do you really want me to do that?"

"I want you to learn how to be comfortable with me and my body. Starting with my bottom and my breasts is a good beginning. You've been respectful, and I appreciate it. You may think I know what I'm doing and am in a hurry, but I'm just as scared as you. If you'd been putting your hands all over me immediately, we wouldn't be here. Because you're so thoughtful and careful with me is one reason why I care for you so much and want to be intimate with you."

She continued, "But I want to go slowly, and I want us to get permission from each other about what we're doing. Permission can be in words or in how we respond to tentative touching. Slowly, slowly, slowly is what I want, because anything else would scare me and I think it would scare you too."

For Red, having his hands on Nina, even through her clothing, was a revelation. He had never touched anyone in a sustained way. His family wasn't touchy, and at first it felt odd to have his hands on her. But Red was a quick study, and he went from the strangeness of it, to feeling good, to something else he had no way to describe. Completeness was the best word he could think of. Her reaction was making it better. She had started out tense and then loosened up. All of the sensations were new. He was surprised at what her breasts felt like. She didn't wear a bra because of their smallness. They had a soft hardness—neither soft nor hard described them. He'd imagined Nina having a hard body because of the way she handled the traps and the way she moved. To find softness in her body was unexpected.

He'd never imagined the kind of pleasure he was having touching her. When her hands started to explore his body, at first he tensed up, just like she had done. It took him awhile before he could relax. Then he was embarrassed to find himself with the stiffest erection he'd ever had. He backed away from Nina in order to avoid having her notice it.

"The surprise would be if it hadn't happened," she said. "It's the first time I've personally encountered that reaction and I'm flattered to have been the cause of it. Is it OK for me to feel it?" This flummoxed Red even more. He didn't know how to react, but Nina did, and pulled him against her. He embraced her enthusiastically and kissed her with his newly learned passion for kissing.

Finally Nina pulled away. "I hate to leave you in that state, but I want our intimate time together to be in better circumstances. I want to know how you're feeling about what happened just now. Has it changed your thinking and feeling?"

"There were so many new sensations!" Red said. "It felt good, but I have nothing to compare it with. It really felt like you care about me. I still have to pinch myself that you do. I want you to know that my slowness to touch you physically is because of my adoration and my fear of hurting you. I worry I'll lose you because I might scare you or do something stupid. I never dreamed I could get close to someone like you who is so bright and has so much magnetism."

"For the next two weeks, David will be gone, and I hope you will agree to meet me there."

"I will. What should I bring?"

"You, and a willingness to experiment and go slowly. I'll provide food, and ideally it will be for a whole day. I promise you I won't leave you like you are now."

"Nina, you're very solicitous of me. Are you going to show me what I can do for you?"

"When we're at David's, I would like us to spend a lot of time exploring each other's bodies before we try intercourse. That's where I will show you what you can do for me. I know how to take care of myself, but I don't know what someone else can do for me. I hope I'll be able to do things to you that will feel good."

"Now it's my turn," Red said. "I want to hear your feelings about what happened."

"I also have nothing to compare it to, but it felt good!"

The wind had eased enough to go back in the dinghy, but the water was still wild enough to be tricky. Nina was in awe of the way Red anticipated waves and wind and managed the rough passage well. She realized that while there were gaps in his knowledge of the kinds of things she knew, the same was true for her about Red's world.

Renee greeted them at the dock, having watched their progress from his house. His comment about Red's boat handling reinforced Nina's conclusion about how good he was at it. But Renee was there for more than social chitchat.

With a twinkle in his eye, Liegeois said he had a serious matter to seek their advice about.

"If one of my teachers was having an affair with one of her students, what would be the appropriate thing for me to do?"

Red and Nina were worried. Both realized the implications. Liegeois was surprised to find Nina inarticulate for the first time since he'd met her. The confirmation of having thoroughly penetrated their shells came in their simultaneous stammering.

Nina recovered first. "You wouldn't," and then, "It hasn't happened." Then she realized that Renee was comfortable enough with both of them to tease them about the normal things that went on among teenagers on the Island—things that other adults were not willing to discuss openly.

"How do you know who I'm talking about?" Renee asked. Nina was mute for the second time.

"Well, if it hasn't happened, then I'm free to talk with you about taking on more teaching. Are you willing and interested?"

Nina recovered from her surprise and said, "Not if it means that I can't sleep with Red."

Renee was interested to observe that Nina was no longer the slightest bit embarrassed, but that Red was uncomfortable. He said to Red, "This conversation remains with us. There's no reason for me to repeat it to anyone. And in keeping with how politicians handle sex scandals, I would deny that I heard or said anything about it."

Renee could see Red's relief, but he also saw that Red was still uncomfortable. Well, it couldn't be helped. There was no way that their close relationship would not become public knowledge.

"Nina, our math teacher has just accepted a job at a company that will pay him three times what he's making here. He's going to remain here for two weeks or until I find a replacement, whichever comes first. Would you take on one or two of his classes? Do you feel up to it, and are you willing to do it until the end of the semester?"

"Which ones are you thinking I should do?"

"Whichever ones you would be most comfortable doing."

"I would have the most fun teaching advanced algebra or calculus. However, I would love to be able to give beginning students a good feel, if not a love, for algebra. But I have conditions, which I told you about before. I don't believe in—nor will I give—grades. I would be happy to tell or write descriptions of what each student can do, or alternatively I'd have them demonstrate what they can do, but I'm not giving exams or grades."

"I'm not sure how to handle that. In any case, the state exams have to be given at the end of the semester. We have no choice about that."

"Have there been any problems about my not giving grades in French?"

Renee conceded, "No, in fact I've had positive feedback about the anecdotal reports you've written."

"Couldn't we do the same thing with algebra?"

"A comment about 'his accent or his comprehension' wouldn't seem to describe what is learned in algebra."

"Why not? It's the same thing. If someone comprehends, they comprehend, and I can describe what it is they comprehend. Isn't understanding polynomials specific enough?"

"How many parents are going to understand that term?"

"How many parents understand what a letter grade means? An 'A' could mean a bright student who never worked, or just studied for the test, or it could mean someone who plugged away diligently and turned herself inside out to learn."

"What is hardest for me to deal with is that I know you're right, but I also know there are political limits to what we can do."

"Mr. Liegeois, I will work with you on reporting to parents, but that is as far as I will go. The rest is up to you."

Nina had become very sure of herself from her accomplishments teaching French. She also knew that Renee valued her highly and wasn't the kind of person who would stand on ceremony. It was that element of Renee not getting worked up about unimportant things that irritated people like Henry and his cohorts.

"OK. I will double check with the state certification people to see if they will go along with this, at least on a temporary basis. I don't think they will give any trouble. Both the certification specialists and the Superintendent were dazzled by you. And by the way, I think it's time for you to start calling me Renee."

"As long as I don't have to give grades, I will, Renee."

CHAPTER 12
Melanie

———

JUDAH WORTHINGTON, THE OWNER OF the Island Art Gallery on Megantic, told Melanie Wright that he wanted nothing more to do with her paintings and packages. A few weeks ago she'd assured him that all he had to do was give a letter to whoever asked for it and not reveal where it came from. She also said, "If Sanford Black comes by, give him the painting." Instead, two men from the Secret Service had come and not only taken the letter, but grilled Judah and taken the painting. He didn't dare refuse them. But his fear of Melanie was greater than of the Secret Service. The one thing he didn't do was tell them who gave him the letter and paintings.

What Judah didn't know was that Melanie thought the man in the painting was her father. She'd found a painting of her mother and a man who she recognized as Sanford Black. She painted a copy of it. Her mother didn't know she had found that painting and Melanie didn't want her to know.

Judah had wondered why Melanie wanted to work in his gallery when she had David Chenoweth's studio to work in. At first he simply enjoyed her company. She was a cynosure for his eyes. She soon became one for his hands as well, after she convinced him of her anxiousness to have sex with him. He was so intoxicated with her that he believed her when she said she would never tell.

He knew her mother, Marianne, and knew Melanie lived in fear of her. What he didn't know was just how scared Melanie was of her mother finding out what she was doing with that painting. Melanie's mother didn't want Melanie to know who her father was.

When Melanie insisted that she wanted to have sex with Judah, he didn't see any problems with her being sixteen. Now he saw problems. She was furious that he'd given the painting to the Secret Service. She threatened to tell what happened between them if he revealed who had given him the painting.

The stress on Melanie was immense. The Secret Service men were pressuring David to find who made the painting. David had to know she had done it because there was no one else on the Island who would have the interest, ability, or access to the original to do it.

The painting showed Melanie's mother and a man. Both of them were nude. The original had been done before Melanie was born. Her mother had kept it well hidden and Melanie found it by accident. When she saw the painting, she recognized the man because his pictures appeared in the news. His name was Sanford Black. The painting was the clue she had about who her father might be. She thought the painting would be a way to make contact with Black. She never dreamed it would turn into the nightmare it had become. She had no idea of the security surrounding a man who was an Assistant Secretary of Defense.

She knew David was on her side because he hadn't told the Secret Service men about her, but she worried how long he could hold out against them. She was too scared to answer his questions about it. If the Secret Service men came to her, she didn't know what she would do. It would be the end of the world, because her mother would find out what she had done. She couldn't picture her mother pardoning her or having any understanding of why she had done it. Her mother would probably throw her onto the mercy of the Secret Service, and she couldn't imagine that they would understand.

The painting Melanie had copied had been painted and signed by Ogie. Ogie must have known what the relationship was between her mother and Sanford Black. But Ogie and her mother were good friends, and that meant she couldn't ask him about the painting.

CHAPTER 13

Melanie

———

DAVID BANGED ON THE DOOR and without waiting for an answer came crashing into the house where Ogie and Nina sat eating breakfast. "Fuck 'em all, and I don't mean in a good way!" Ogie couldn't believe this was the calm, controlled David he knew so well.

The intensity of David's thoughts made him easier to read than usual. Ogie could see that the Secret Service was bullying him to find out who had done the copy of the painting of Marianne and Black. He had seen an image of it in David's mind a few days ago. He couldn't figure out who'd made a copy of it, or why. And then Ogie saw the rest of the picture. David knew that Melanie made the copy, although she hadn't done it with his knowledge. David knew it was a copy because he could detect slight unsteadiness in its lines. He didn't know how the Secret Service had come into possession of it.

They wanted to know who painted it. To put it mildly, the Secret Service wasn't happy with David telling them he wasn't certain. "David, tell us who you want fucked in a not good way," Ogie asked, knowing perfectly well who he was talking about. David explained to Ogie that the Secret Service insisted on his saying nothing about this to anyone. But he was fed up with what they were doing to him and he had to talk it over with someone. David explained that the painting was a copy of one Ogie had done. Ogie nodded in advance of each thing David said. When David said he was trying to keep the Feds from knowing who did it, Ogie said, "We have to keep them from going after Melanie." David had never mentioned Melanie. Nina realized that Ogie had given away his mind reading, but David didn't notice. Nor did he notice that Ogie was nodding to David's thoughts ahead of his stating them.

Then Ogie said, "They can't be serious about taking you back with them. It's an idle threat." The look on David's face confirmed for Nina that Ogie had guessed or known exactly what the Feds had said they would do.

David knew Ogie's prescience was beyond intuitive intelligence, but he hadn't explored it further. Nina wondered why David hadn't realized that Ogie could mind read. She was surprised when she noticed Ogie doing it because most of the time he was careful not to reveal what he might have read in someone's mind. The worst time for her was when he knew that she had sexual fantasies about Red. She'd denied it, truly believing her denial. But he knew more of her motivation than she did. She didn't realize until later that he was right about her feelings. It was uncanny. It was more than thought and feelings. She had a sense he might even be reading her physical reactions. He grokked her completely. Now was not the time to ask him about it again, but she would as soon as they were alone.

She snapped back to the conversation and heard David ask, "What can we do to protect Melanie? Sooner or later, they're going to find out she painted the copy and sent the letter to Black. I have no idea what they will do when it happens, but shouldn't we preempt them?"

Ogie asked, "Isn't finding her father what is driving her? If it is, maybe we can use that as leverage."

David asked, "Don't you know? You painted the original when Black and Marianne were lovers."

"Yes, but it isn't as simple as that. And I not only don't want to gossip about Marianne's former life, I don't fully understand it."

David wondered what they could do. Ogie said, "If Black is her father, we could compare his DNA with Melanie's and that would answer the question."

"How can we compare their DNA?" David asked. "Do you think it likely Black would give a sample? And how would we reach him to ask? Why not ask Marianne to clear this up?"

"If she hasn't been willing to tell Melanie, why do you think she would tell me?" Ogie replied. "David, have you been contacted by anyone else in the Secret Service?"

"Yes, someone by the name of Bartlett called me. When I wouldn't tell him what he wanted, he said he'd send the agents to follow up and bring back results."

"I have an idea," Ogie said. "Suppose you tell him you can solve his problem if he comes here. Tell him you can give him items that would reveal things about Black that you know he doesn't want the agents to know about."

"What things?" David asked quizzically.

"I'll figure out what we should tell him." Ogie replied.

"But shouldn't we get Melanie to admit why she sent the original letter to Black?" David continued. "If she were willing to come out in the open about this, it would take the pressure off her and make life easier for me."

"She's already refused to do that," Ogie replied. "I think she's scared as hell."

Nina was struggling to figure out what she could do to help. "What if I try?" she said. "I assume she remembers me, and we did get along well."

"How would you approach her?" Ogie asked.

"I don't know, but the first thing I need to figure out is how can I meet her naturally, without it appearing contrived. David, what is her schedule? What does she do for fun? Where does she hang out?"

"During the week, she's in school, although I have the feeling her attendance isn't all that it should be. She's crazy about basketball and there was a time she was going with Roger's son, but I don't know if it's still going on. Why don't you drop in at the basketball court after school?"

"I will, but I need to think of a way to start a conversation with her. I could tell her I've been working with David and have seen how good her work is."

Ogie said, "She may have good reasons for keeping this from us and from Marianne. Things about which we have no idea. Don't pressure her unduly. Remember that officially, she knows me as Owen Cartwright. I've discussed this with Marianne and Marianne has agreed to keep my 'Ogie' identity secret. We both have reasons to have kept our former lives unknown." This was news to David, but he was too discreet to ask about it. He figured that Ogie would explain it later.

And then Ogie asked David, "What is Bartlett like? Do you have any sense of what his weak points are?"

"I've only dealt with him on the phone and he combines a smooth charm with a jet engine's power. He's a hard guy to temporize with. He does his homework. He knows you're here and did the original painting. I suppose being high up in the White House he has all the resources he needs to find anything about anyone. He wanted you to help me. He wants results, with no ifs, ands, or buts."

"Jesus, David, why didn't you say something before this? Bartlett must know there's a warrant out for my arrest. He'll probably use that to pressure us. Did he say anything along those lines?" This was the second brand new piece of information that David hadn't known about Ogie. It was a shock to learn that Ogie was a wanted man.

David had never seen Ogie freak out. He was always calm and took unexpected reverses in his stride.

"No, but he called you Ogie McMaster and made reference to your experience with the Dutch masters. There was no question in his mind that you'd be willing to help. What's with his calling you Ogie? I've heard Nina call you that and assumed it was just a family nickname."

"David, with Bartlett knowing as much as he does, it will soon become apparent why I am living incognito. You have never questioned me about why I turned over the lucrative business of creating old masters to you, for which I'm thankful. For now, let me say that I am trying to stay hidden. The Feds are after me but not because I've been caught with half a dozen bodies or millions in ill-gotten gains. I guess if Bartlett knows who I am, he must really want my help because he hasn't taken me into custody. That means we may have some leverage. Presumably we can use it to shield Melanie. But how?"

CHAPTER 14
Melanie

———

WHEN THE THREE-ON-TWO PICKUP BASKETBALL game was finished, Melanie was bent over, struggling to breathe. Between deep breaths, she asked Nina, "Where the hell did you learn to ball handle like that? I've only seen pros do that. It was just you and Red out there and you creamed the three of us. How did you learn to maneuver the way you do?"

"I've been hanging out with older, bigger kids for years, and the only way I could hold my own with them was to be better. I watched basketball tricks on YouTube until I memorized them. Then I spent hours with a basketball doing the same things slowly, over and over, and then sped them up. When I mastered a new trick, I combined it with the ones I'd learned before."

"I remember you from when we were six. You're my age. Why aren't you in school and how did you get to be a teacher at your age?"

Nina didn't want to answer that question. People had a hard time dealing with a freak who graduated from high school at thirteen. They didn't know whether to be in awe or in fear or both. She couldn't predict how Melanie would react and it was important that she get along with her in order to help her. "I graduated from high school early."

"What have you been doing since?"

"I decided to postpone college for a few years and I've been working on my uncle's farm."

"Well, that explains your physical strength, but it doesn't explain what you're doing on Megantic."

Nina told how she'd missed her brother and wanted to spend time with him. Then Melanie said, "You came down here to find me. Did David send you?"

Nina ignored the question because lying would make it even more difficult to get Melanie to talk. Instead, she asked who the high school team played and how good they were. Melanie told her they played in the Island Basketball League and consistently did badly.

That gave Melanie an idea. "Maybe you could coach the team. We need help and our teacher sponsor never played basketball."

"Is it a girls' team?"

"No, it's mixed. All boys and one girl. Me."

"How will they take to having a girl their age telling them how to play?"

"They're so desperate they even let me on the team, and once they learn what you can do, they'll probably come begging to have you coach them. They might even want you to pretend to be a student so you could be on the team. I'm sure Renee would be happy to have you coach. He wants wins almost as badly as the team does."

Nina thought Melanie would make the boys happy with the coaching arrangement no matter what their sexist feelings were. Behind her pretty face and gorgeous figure, there was a whim of iron. Nina had seen Melanie's effect on the boys in school and the ones she had just played with. Some had a hard time paying close attention to the game because they enjoyed watching Melanie. Having played a lot of basketball with boys that age, Nina knew what their unspoken agenda was. She would have to get them to focus on the game.

If she coached, it would be another way for her to get to know the Island and its culture. She had an unquenchable thirst to learn everything she could about what the Island people were like. While she had spent her teenage years in a rural area, and there were similarities to Megantic, it had a different feel. She had a hard time describing the differences, but they were palpable. There were built in constraints in what you could say or do on the Island, and yet she didn't think the Meganticans she knew felt it. It was second nature to them. She had the sense that they had a clearer sense of who they were in relation to others than people on the mainland. Maturity wasn't the right word, but it came close to describing it. And while the children and teenagers weren't what one could call mature, she had the same feeling about them. Living comfortably in their own skins described it best. She wished she could have that same self assurance and inner peace the Meganticans seemed to have. In addition to knowing Red and his grandfather, and now teaching, this would give her even more contacts with Meganticans.

Part of Nina's fascination had to do with the offshoots of French culture. Nina knew that New England, and particularly Maine, had many French speakers who had come from Canada or Louisiana.

While still catching their breaths, Melanie asked Nina, "What's with you and Red?" Melanie had made it sound like an innocuous question, but Nina knew it was loaded. She had seen Melanie exerting control over the boys they had been playing with and she sensed she didn't like losing a single worshiper. Red was not part of Melanie's stable, but even if he wasn't, she didn't want him attached to anyone else.

Nina decided on a neutral answer. "I go lobstering with him and Russ. We're friends."

"Come on, Nina, there is more to it than that. I have friends in your class. They say that when you're teaching, you work hard not to pay attention to him. Why?"

"Melanie, you're a keen observer of human behavior to notice what doesn't happen. I suppose it's because we're friends from working together on the Jenny T and I'm bending over backwards not to favor him."

Melanie thought for a minute. She'd been having a great deal of enjoyment driving her male schoolmates crazy. She knew precisely what facial expressions, verbal expressions, body movements, and clothing would do it. When she talked with a boy, it was as if he was her whole world. She gave him her full attention with her eyes, ears, body language, and comments. It made the boys feel wanted. She asked them questions about their interests and listened to their answers. The result was that there was hardly a boy in the small high school on Megantic who was not at her beck and call.

Red was the rare exception. At first she thought maybe he was more interested in boys, but occasionally she caught him looking at her or another girl with a hungry look. She was certain he wasn't gay.

Melanie decided to test Nina and asked her, "Why don't you go out with Red. Even if you're a teacher, you and he are the same age."

Nina responded with what was the literal truth, "I'm not looking for a boyfriend. I know he is an interesting, thoughtful person. He is a great basketball partner. He seemed to have the ability to go to where the ball would be rather than where it was. And working with him on the Jenny T has been fun."

Melanie realized she may have made a mistake inviting Nina to coach. It would give Nina exposure to Melanie's retinue of males, and she had the feeling Nina could be irresistible if she put her mind to it. Red had been watching Nina with more interest than Melanie had ever seen him evince in any girl. But if Red was the only one Melanie lost, she could put up with it. Still, Megantic High School was a small pond, and the satisfaction of owning it all was a powerful one.

On the other hand, Nina, brilliant as she must be, lacked the seductive sophistication that she, Melanie, had mastered. What Melanie knew about Red was that he had a very sharp mind. He was so quiet and unobtrusive that almost no one noticed, but Melanie knew his grades were perfect.

Melanie's thoughts came back to Nina. It was obvious Nina loved basketball, but Melanie sensed Nina's real reason for coming to find her. Since Nina knew David, he must have sent her to find out about the painting she'd copied. Well, Melanie wasn't going to reveal that. She had done that painting with the purpose of finding her father. It had been her crusade to find him for as long as she could remember. She was fixated on it. She had learned the painstaking art of Vermeer and others in order to copy the painting her mother had hidden. Melanie wanted it to have a dramatic effect on the man she was certain was her father. That the Feds were here about the painting was a disappointment, because it hadn't provoked her father to come. She did have the satisfaction that it stirred things up enough to get him to send the Secret Service.

Melanie thought for the millionth time how much easier it would have been to pursue her search for her father if she and her mother had stayed in the D.C. area. The move to Megantic had been made against Melanie's violent protests. She felt she was living in a prison of provincialism. The Meganticans didn't know anything. It had been so easy to become the most sought after girl in the school.

She couldn't understand why her mother wanted to move here. Her mother's gallery and art world contacts were left behind, yet she was still able to sell her sculptures for high prices. Melanie suspected the move might have had something to do with keeping her from finding out who her father was. Her mother wouldn't even tell her why she wouldn't tell her who he was. That her father was someone of importance was probably the reason. It narrowed the field.

Melanie missed her time with David. She had learned valuable skills and he'd praised her work. She didn't know if she had it in her to become a good artist, but she certainly had become a superb craftsman. Just being with David opened up a broader world. She'd learned a great deal about art history, literature, and chemistry, as well as about fabricating paints that replicated those of the old masters. And she had begun to see light and color in a new way. It all gave her an added advantage in her schoolwork.

That her mother didn't like David or think much of him was a great plus. He had always remained neutral when she complained about her mother, and his silence made it clear that he didn't want to talk about her. Melanie knew her mother looked down on his occupation and saw it as mindless. Now she had to avoid David because he would ask about the painting she had done. She was afraid he might tell her mother about it.

CHAPTER 15
Melanie

———

NINA HAD JUST FINISHED AN hour and a half session doing ball-handling drills with Megantic's basketball team. She had them practicing how to create space between them and the opposing players when Ogie stopped by to see how it was going. "*Ca va bien?*—Is it going well? Do you think you'll have a good team?" During the conversation, Renee Liegeois came to see his new coach. He heard the interchange between Nina and Ogie and joined in with a greeting in French. He told Nina how much he appreciated her volunteering to help the team. "Melanie tells me you're a superb player and are doing this out of the goodness of your heart. *Je te remercie beaucoup*—Thank you very much." He turned to Ogie and said, "I know you've been on the Island for years, but we've never met. Are you as fluent in French as your sister?"

Ogie searched Renee's mind to see if he were suspicious and didn't find anything to alarm him. What he did see was a very bright, observant person who was curious about a fellow Islander who was hermetic.

After Renee left, Ogie went to greet Melanie. He hadn't seen her since the Feds had come, and he was anxious to know what was going on with her. He saw and felt her terror at encountering him. She assumed David had told him about the painting, and she thought Ogie would expose her. He felt her desperation to find her father, and her fear of her mother finding out what she had done.

Having lived in isolation for the last six years, he wasn't used to reading and feeling that much turmoil in other people. When he was teaching, he became good at diagnosing and solving his students' problems with his mind reading ability; even though he had been unaware he had it. That ability to help his students had gained him a reputation among the parents of the school. It resulted in the principal being overwhelmed by requests to have their children in his class.

But he didn't know how he could help Melanie in this brief encounter. He turned himself inside out to send calmness to her. The effort was the most he had ever done. He began to see the strands of the knot inside her head loosen. He poured energy into her until he could feel the tension draining. She sat down on the bench, exhausted. Ogie knew he had given her a palliative that would only last until she began to think about her life again. He whispered to Nina in French, "Now is the time to talk to her."

The other players left and Nina debated how to begin the conversation and decided she had to be direct. "You do realize you've brought a storm trooper occupation to David's house, and the Feds are about to do the same to Ogie. David and Ogie are sacrificing themselves to protect you. If you don't come out in the open, they could be incarcerated. I understand that you couldn't have imagined the fallout from this. I know you just want to find your father."

"What else could I have done to get him into the open? Do you have any idea of what my life is like?" Melanie's voice was loaded with anger and desperation. Her face crumpled and tears and heaves began. Nina thought the paroxysms wouldn't end. She put her arm around Melanie and pulled her close, feeling the vibrations of her sorrow.

Nina asked what she could do. "Get me my father," Melanie wailed. "I've got to get out of here."

"How should I do it?"

"Call him, write him, tell those bastards in David's house I want to meet him. But please don't tell my mother."

Melanie's sobs had quieted. Melanie looked questioningly into Nina's eyes. Nina returned her look with sympathy. Melanie's furrows and wrinkles began to dissipate and her lips assumed a normal shape. "I know what I just said is crazy. But what else can be done? I've done everything I can think of."

"What do you think would happen if you came to David's house and told the Secret Service agents what you just told me?"

"I can't do that. It is too embarrassing and they would put me in prison. My mother will find out what I have done."

"So what do you think might work?"

Melanie agreed that maybe she should talk it over with David, but wouldn't he then report her to the Feds?

Nina asked her, "Why would he do that when he's been risking everything by not telling them you did that painting? Tell me more about it, and maybe that will help me think of some ideas. There's no hurry—I've got lots of time." Nina made herself look as if she was eager to hear a Bible-length story. Melanie began to talk and didn't stop for two hours. Once in a while, Nina would repeat a significant phrase of Melanie's as a way of prodding her to explore that line of thought. By the time Melanie was finished, she'd told Nina things she never thought she'd tell anyone.

When Nina returned to Ogie's, she was exhausted. She had taken her insides out in order to get through to Melanie. Nina had done a lot of reading about how therapy worked, but using it was something altogether different. She knew that what she did with Melanie was abbreviated and nothing resembling proper therapy, but still, she had been able to draw Melanie out.

Nina explained to Ogie and David that Melanie's drive to find her father was also a way to escape her mother. Her mother insisted on absolute standards for anything Melanie did, whether it was washing dishes or schoolwork. She controlled what music Melanie could play and what she read. She insisted on a daily accounting of every minute of Melanie's time. Nothing pleased her. School, time with David, and being on the basketball team were Melanie's only ways for getting to escape the pressure Marianne imposed on her. Melanie's manipulation of boys was one way she could feel in control. Her feelings of superiority were her way of compensating for the way her mother ground her down.

Ogie commended Nina: "You did a magnificent job of finding out what drives Melanie."

"There's more," Nina went on, "Melanie photographed her copy of the painting and sent the photograph to Sanford Black with a note telling him the painting could be found in the gallery on Megantic. She thought that would get him to come to Megantic. She made arrangements with Judah to let her know when Black came. Melanie told me she didn't realize the amount of protection someone high in the administration would have.

"When I asked Melanie why Judah was protecting her, she told me that she had him under her control. Knowing how Melanie operates, my guess is that she seduced him and then threatened him with a statutory rape charge.

"Melanie is in bad shape. She's scared shitless of the Secret Service coming after her, and of her mother finding out what she's done."

Ogie told Nina she had worked wonders. "David, do you know why Bartlett asked for my help?"

"I suppose Black recognized the painting and of course knew you had done it," David replied.

Ogie addressed David again. "I think you should talk with Marianne."

"How can I approach her? I dread the thought of talking with her."

Ogie thought for a minute. "OK, I'll talk with her. We also need to figure out how to deal with Bartlett. I suggest we find ways to lean on him."

"How the devil can we do that?" David asked. "He has all the cards—the Secret Service and the Patriot Act and I suppose the whole Defense Department if it comes down to that."

Ogie laughed and said, "We have something he doesn't have." There was a puzzled silence. The first one to break it was Nina, who said, "Oh, I see. If he's coming, then it's because we have something he wants."

"Exactly," Ogie said. "There must be more to this because of the resources they've put into it. Bartlett's too important to fly up here and waste his time with something inconsequential. That painting must be threatening them in some way. They must not want the painting to go public. It could ruin Black's political career."

Nina said she was looking forward to watching Ogie make Bartlett squirm. Ogie quickly pointed out that Bartlett was much too dangerous to fool with. Bartlett could send him to prison on the outstanding charges. Nina had to be kept out of it in order to not be accused of aiding and abetting a felon.

CHAPTER 16

Ogie

———

IT WAS A HOT DAY. Being located forty miles off the Atlantic coast made hot days unusual for Megantic. The heat drove Ogie to take a swim in the harbor. The water surrounding Megantic was colder than that of the notoriously cold nearby Maine coast, but the protected harbor was more tolerable than the ocean. The narrow entrance prevented much exchange of water with the Atlantic and thus the harbor water could retain some heat.

The cruising sailboats visiting the harbor had to pick up one of the many mooring buoys available. There wasn't room to set an anchor and leave enough scope. The buoys were attached to heavy lines that ran across the bottom of the harbor. The plastic bottles attached to the buoys had a note inside with the cost per night. Boaters put money in the bottle. Most of the time there were enough mooring buoys for the visitors who made the offshore voyage. On the occasions when too many sailboats arrived, they were faced with the unpleasant choice of either departing and spending the night at sea, or rafting up with someone else if they could get permission. It wasn't a comfortable arrangement because there was so little room to swing. It became worse if a strong breeze was blowing.

Ogie decided that cooling off in the water was worth the risk of encountering the small amount of effluent from the visiting boats. He did several laps across the harbor and was floating in a semi-trance when he began to receive strong thoughts. He searched for where the thoughts were coming from and focused on a Morgan 34 named Sloop du Jour.

The thoughts were particularly clear. Not only was he "hearing" them, he was seeing what the thinker was seeing. The thoughts were coming from a man who was drawing a woman who was reclining on a bunk and reading. She wore underpants but no shirt. Ogie had never had a clear visual image through someone else's eyes. This went way beyond hearing thoughts. His ability to read was expanding to visual images. He was curious what skills would evolve next.

The man was struggling to sketch the woman. Ogie could feel the pen he was using and even the cramping in the man's hand. Feeling someone's physical sensations was also new. The artist in Ogie made it difficult to resist trying to move the man's pen. It felt as if he could. He didn't know if it would work, but he decided it would be too tricky to try, much as he was tempted.

He could feel the man's powerful desire to have sex with the woman. The man had felt it for days. Ogie couldn't understand why he didn't do anything about it. And then, as if the man heard Ogie's question, the response was in Ogie's mind. *"I'm always initiating sex and most of the time she turns me down. It hurts. I can't face it again. Here we are in this idyllic place with no children, no work, and no stress. If ever there was a time for her to let me know she wanted loving, this would be it. We've been alone cruising for a week. I'll be damned if I will go through being turned down again and being a supplicant, or even worse, have her agree grudgingly. What I can't stand the most is her reluctance makes me focus on sex, which pushes me to be someone I don't want to be. The result is I start thinking about it out of the context of loving and just as an act of physical relief. And it justifies what women accuse men of, which is that all they want is sex. I know there are other women who don't feel that way, but are there many of them?"*

Ogie wondered if this man was so crude in performing sex that he turned his wife off. And then he received an answer, again as if the man had heard his question. *"It doesn't seem to matter to Bonnie how we do sex. We can go slow. I love giving oral sex, but Bonnie puts up with it for no more than a minute. She's impatient with foreplay. I'm gentle. But if we do anything but the missionary position, she says no. She wants it over with quickly and pretends that she is coming. I don't know if she's ever had an orgasm."*

Ogie thought that if ever a man would have an affair, this guy was a candidate for it. He could not understand why he put up with Bonnie's nonsense about sex. The man's psychic pain was more than his sexual urgency. It had gone on for years. Ogie put himself deeper into the man's mind and looked around. It was new for him to be this deep in someone else's mind. The man's name was Brian. He hadn't been with other women but had been tempted. Several women had given him signals of willingness, but he couldn't be certain he was reading them correctly and he wasn't going to risk suggesting it. Ogie was turned on by his eavesdropping. It had never occurred to him to satisfy his prurient curiosity by reading others' minds before. There were so many more questions he wanted to probe for but didn't know how. He kept coming back to why had Brian put up with this treatment from Bonnie? He could read that every time Brian had tried to discuss what bothered him about their sexual poverty, Bonnie had shut down the conversation quickly. When they had tried a therapist, if he raised the sex question the same thing happened. She decided not to continue with the therapy. Ogie couldn't figure out why he stayed in the relationship.

Bonnie was reading a book. Her thoughts weren't as clear as Brian's—his overwhelming sex drive was a stronger signal. Looking at Bonnie through Brian's eyes, he observed her closely and intensely. Then he poured himself into Bonnie's mental space. Her slight start surprised Ogie. She must have felt something and he wondered if she was conscious of it. He would have to be careful. She returned to reading her book. She wrote it off as Brian's restlessness, which had momentarily distracted her. She was washing him out through her complete absorption in her book. She was thankful she'd brought so many books with her because she went through them so fast. Her reading was a deep pleasure, which Ogie could see. He couldn't see what else gave her satisfaction until she happened to think about her children.

Ogie searched for a way to get her thinking about Brian and what she thought about sex with him. Trying to get someone to think about something was also new and he didn't know if it would work. First he decided just to sit still in her mind and follow her thoughts. It might give him a clue. He found himself reading her book. It wasn't the same as when he read a book, but he couldn't describe the difference. It was a Jane Austen. Even though there were romantic relationships described in it, sex never entered Bonnie's mind. He couldn't understand how it didn't. His own thought, as he experienced the book through her mind, was when would the protagonists become intimate? After fifteen minutes, Bonnie still hadn't had one thought about sex. Ogie thought it was incredible. He knew he would have had sexual thoughts several times. He wondered whether Bonnie was asexual. How typical was she?

At this point, Ogie became so cold being inactive in the water that he had to break his concentration and swim for shore. Once there, he went back to Bonnie's mind to see what was happening.

Brian had jumped in the water and Bonnie hoped it would cool his ardor. She knew he wanted her to initiate sex, but the thought of it made her flinch. Ogie saw that she was uncomfortable with Brian if she didn't have her underpants on. But it was more than that. She didn't want him to use his mouth on her genitals. She felt too exposed when it happened and agreed to it rarely. His very anxiousness to do it made it worse for her. And her further thought was that if she initiated sex it would encourage Brian to want more and more. There was no satisfying him. He might even want sex three times a week. This made Ogie curious about the frequency with which they actually had sex.

She was used to not thinking about sex. She abhorred revealing herself emotionally and physically. She felt that if she did, she would not only lose control of herself, she would lose control of her relationship with Brian. And there was the ick factor in having sex. Ogie came to feel sorry for her. He wondered how much of her uptightness was nurture and how much was genetic.

Ogie was concentrating on Bonnie so intensely that he wasn't aware of Brian coming out of the water and sitting beside him. It startled him. He was being intimate with this man's wife! It took him a moment to realize that Brian had no way of knowing what had been going on. Brian said, "Hi." Ogie responded, "Hello. Where are you from?" When Brian pointed to the Sloop du Jour, Ogie commented how pretty she was.

"Which boat are you on?" Brian wanted to know.

"I live here."

"Oh, you don't give that impression."

"What impression does a resident of Megantic give?"

"Well, my guess is that they rarely swim, and you just did a considerable amount. I assume you aren't a native."

Ogie didn't want to talk to Brian. He was interested in Bonnie and didn't want to give up seeing how her mind worked. He wanted to know what Bonnie was doing and whether he could continue to influence her. He couldn't talk with Brian and focus on Bonnie.

He had no choice with Brian sitting next to him and talking at him. Maybe he might learn more about Bonnie's peculiarities. But he didn't know what to talk to Brian about. No subject felt safe. He worried that any talk would give away his guilty mind-peeping secrets.

"What do you do here?" Brian asked.

"I paint."

"What kind of painting do you do? Are you able to earn a living here?"

Ogie was uncomfortable with Brian's questions. He didn't want Brian to know about his painting or anything else about him. It could end up revealing who he was. But being evasive with Brian would just stimulate his interest. Brian was fascinated with the Island and life on it. Ogie could feel Brian's desire to come see his paintings. He could read Brian's mind and knew he felt that buying one of Ogie's paintings would give him a sense of cachet because he had discovered the artist and dealt directly with him. Additionally, it would have the romance of coming from a small Island and contributing to supporting someone on it.

"Come on out to my boat for a drink and meet my wife," Brian said. Going out to Brian's boat was the last thing Ogie wanted to do. Plus he was able to read in Brian's mind that Bonnie was not enamored of uninvited guests. However, Ogie was tempted to meet the woman with whom he had such an odd relationship. He knew he would be on edge, and saw it as dangerous, but his curiosity to see this woman for himself—her body language, facial expressions, and other nuances—was strong. It was also a way for him to verify the accuracy of this new skill of seeing things through someone else's eyes.

They swam out together and settled down in the cockpit. "Bonnie, please come up. I want you to meet someone." Ogie could read her reaction, *"Here we go again with no notice and not even asking me. Who is it this time? There is no stopping him."*

Ogie was startled to see her in person. She was both what he imagined and something else entirely. It was as if he'd seen a sketch of her with clear outlines, but the three-dimensional Bonnie had color and energy he hadn't pictured.

She went below to fix drinks. When she settled on deck, she asked, "Where do I know you from?" He could read that she was haunted by a feeling of knowing him. And then he saw her associating him with the school her children had attended—and where Ogie had taught. "What did you say your name was?" He told her, "Owen Cartwright." It didn't satisfy her. "Have you lived on Megantic all your life? What do you do for a living here?"

"I'm a painter."

"You are that Owen Cartwright! Brian, he's well known as a contemporary realist. His work sells for astronomical amounts of money because his watercolors transcend the genre. He's a younger version of Jamie Wyeth and is obviously living a similar life on an island in the Atlantic. He's mysterious, because no one knows where he lives and he appeared on the scene out of the blue. I assume the mystery has made his work more valuable. Well, Mr. Cartwright, your game is over." Bonnie smiled at him flirtatiously.

"Well, Mrs. Hackworth, I hope it's over for you," Ogie countered. "I'd very much appreciate it if you and Brian would keep it to yourselves. It isn't a matter of maintaining my market value. It's a matter of privacy. I enjoy my life without the interruptions of living in the public eye. It gives me more time to paint. Painting is my passion. I live here modestly, and if my fellow Islanders know that I'm well known, they certainly don't bother me with it. People here view you in terms of what kind of human being you are and not in terms of fame or money. There are a few well-known national figures who have houses here and they are treated with neither stilted respect nor in a demeaning way. That they are here is hardly known outside this community. The Islanders are not anxious to be invaded by sightseers and publicity seekers. They keep their mouths shut about who lives here."

"OK, but at least tell us how you came to be so good so young. Jamie and Andrew Wyeth each had the advantage of growing up with accomplished artists. Did you?"

"No, I had passion for it when I was young. My parents stayed out of my way and were knowledgeable enough to know how to reinforce good taste when I exhibited it. They were supportive emotionally. When I had problems, they were able to say, 'What might be the first thing to do to figure this out?' They knew about art in general but knew little about its technical aspects. They exuded confidence in me. When it was clear I would make this my career, they didn't blanch, even though they knew how few people can earn a living painting.

They had modest means and I knew I would have to earn a living doing other things until I could establish myself."

Suddenly Bonnie interrupted him. "You went into teaching! You taught at our children's school. I don't remember your name, but I remember seeing you and hearing about you. You must have had a different name. I was hoping to have our children in your class. I knew parents who swore that you had solved their child's difficult problems and had accomplished magic with them. They couldn't believe anyone could have done those things."

This was what Ogie had feared. Someone knowing him from before and making the connection that he was a wanted man. There had been newspaper accounts of the trial and his escape, and he could see Bonnie was on the edge of making that connection. He had to stop her. He looked into Bonnie's mind to see whether she was picturing him when he was teaching at her children's school. Her image was a little fuzzy, which is what you would expect of anyone's memory of someone they didn't know well. That gave Ogie the idea of trying to plant a slightly different picture than the one she had of him.

He began by zeroing in on individual features. He had straight hair, so he worked at making her "remember" a curly-haired man. He waited for her to make the changes in her memory. Then he changed her memory of his physique so that she remembered someone much shorter and stockier than he was. He stirred up her memory to see if she had any sense of what his voice sounded like and couldn't find any trace of it. He gave her an impression that his brown eyes had been a deep blue. When she turned to look at him, she realized that she was confusing him with the teacher she had known. "I guess it wasn't you after all," she said.

Ogie had been fascinated to hear her impression of him as a teacher. He knew he'd had the successes she described, but when he was doing it, he couldn't understand what was happening. Now he knew that much of his success was due to his early mind reading. Those days of teaching were intensely satisfying. Helping his students feel better about themselves and their abilities was pure gold. When he looked back at that, his mind pulsed with joy. It was a profound satisfaction.

However, the deeper he had delved in exploring, experimenting, and learning painting skills, the greater his fulfillment became. It took over his whole being and made him give up teaching. He often felt guilty about being so self-absorbed and not giving himself to helping children learn and solve their problems. He loved the process of painting as well as the things he painted, whether they were water scenes, old structures in France, or landscapes. He had become their owner in a deeply selfish way. Nothing he could buy could give him the same pleasure. But the gap between the two was a chasm. It was like the difference between sex and swimming. Both were sensual and wonderful, but so very different. There was nothing that could compare to the pleasure he had when he had helped the children he worked with master things they were struggling to understand. He could hug himself when he thought about that. But his involvement in painting was so complete that it excluded everything else.

Ogie still wasn't certain whether Bartlett and his thugs knew his real identity. He couldn't afford to have Bonnie reveal who he was, either deliberately or inadvertently. He thought Bonnie, who was so sure of herself and proud at having discovered a scurrent art mystery, wouldn't be able to be quiet about him. The word would get to the Feds. If he could be certain that Bonnie would forget her association with him as a teacher, then she wouldn't make the connection that he was a wanted man. Of course, if Bartlett knew who he was, it was pointless.

Bonnie interrupted his thoughts. "How about a trade, Owen, if I may call you that? We keep mum and you show us your works in progress."

Ogie felt he had no choice. "It will be worth it if it means no publicity. Did you know that Jamie Wyeth paints in a large cardboard box in order to keep the visitors at bay? I don't want to live like that."

"Do you know him?"

"No, but I know and admire his work. I've learned a great deal from his work."

"When we come to your place, would it be possible to buy one of your paintings?"

"Normally, I don't sell directly. Everything is done through my dealer and I'm reluctant to sidestep him. He's been supportive in keeping me out of the public eye. He hasn't insisted on my attendance at the opening of shows and all the rest of that hoopla."

Ogie saw the excitement in Bonnie's mind about visiting his studio. She knew enough about his work to feel he was going to be in the league of the Wyeths if he wasn't already. She was turned on by the possibility of being able to buy one of his paintings. She felt the *élan* of associating with a successful painter and was thinking that if she held his painting for a few years it could yield an extraordinary profit. *"I wonder if I seduced him whether it would convince him to sell one of his paintings,"* she was thinking.

This startled Ogie. He didn't need involvement with someone who wanted to use him. It was more than being used. It was the idea of being intimate with someone he didn't care about. It was repulsive. He could fantasize about having sex with her beautiful body, but he knew the reality would be different.

That she could think of having sex with him while at the same time having a desire to avoid sex in general was puzzling. How could she reconcile the two? He looked harder into her mind and all he could find were her thoughts of the prestige of associating with him. It didn't make sense. He was curious about what she would do if the opportunity came.

This started a train of thought about his mind reading potential. He was reading minds much more completely now, and not just thoughts of the moment. His ability to read things people had thought and experienced previously gave him powers he hadn't dreamed of. It would mean he could be assured in his approaches to women. He would be able to tell how far he could go. If he applied it to financial situations, he could be a frontrunner trading on the stock market. But none of this mattered because he kept his time on the mainland to a minimum for fear of being caught, and he had no need for more money. Except for not being able to have an intimate loving relationship, he was living an ideal life. He constantly thought about Sashi, the woman he'd been dating when he was arrested. Even with the years of separation from her, the loss hadn't become easier to take. There wasn't a waking hour that he didn't feel the pain of knowing he couldn't ever be with her.

That he was able to implant memories in Bonnie even more effectively that he had done with Meganticans suggested he could do it with other people. It could certainly help him avoid being rearrested. It opened up a new world, but it was ironic that he wasn't interested in the possibilities. There was so much about his present life he was satisfied with, although the strain of living with his false identity was a heavy burden.

The dark hole in his life was the lack of intimate relationships and having to not be himself—the self he had to keep hidden. Traveling abroad was a major problem. He wanted to get back to France to paint, but even with his professionally forged documents, it was too risky. Perhaps he might be able to straighten out the injustice of his conviction with his newer mind reading and idea planting skills, but he would need to improve them.

Ogie thought he could bribe and distract Bonnie by making a painting of Sloop du Jour. He decided to do the painting monochromatically. He didn't know if the Hackworths would go for it, but few people can resist a painting of their boat. Many major artists over the centuries had done monochromatic paintings, and he thought it might appeal to Bonnie and Brian.

The question in his mind was what would be the dominant color? It was always a struggle to paint using mostly one color, because there was the constant temptation to paint things with their real colors. The obvious choice would be blue, because the sky and the water lent themselves to it. While Ogie was a realistic painter, he did have a streak of wanting to exaggerate and a strong urge to do nonrepresentational work. Of course, it was necessary to exaggerate hue differences in a monochromatic painting.

He asked Anita Hall to give the Hackworths a note when they came into the store. It was a request that they stop by his place. When Bonnie showed up by herself, Ogie knew she was preparing to work him over. She said Brian's back had gone out and he was disappointed, because he had been looking forward to the visit. Ogie went into her mind to see what she was thinking. Indeed, she was thinking she would try to get him into bed if she could. Her motivation was curiosity, plus a sense of pretentiousness. He saw she didn't think she could pull it off the first time they met alone. She was feeling self-conscious about flirting, being out of practice, and about the condition of her body. She knew she was reasonably pretty and had exercise and nature working for her. But she also realized that her age didn't give her a Miss America body.

Ogie took her on a tour of his studio. He showed her what was in process and had her look through a stack of his watercolors. When she came upon the harbor scene with their boat in it, she stopped with an intake of breath. After a few minutes of studying it she said, "I never realized how pretty a painting can be when it's mostly one color. It catches the special blue in the sky and the ocean here. It wasn't until I saw this painting that I realized I don't see the slight murky tinge in the air that is almost always present on the mainland. No wonder you love it here."

"Strictly speaking, it isn't one color. Of course there are different hues of blue, but there are also touches of other colors. The hull of your boat, for instance, and the flowers along the shore. But they take up a very small percentage of the painting."

"May I buy it from you? What would it cost?"

"I do hope you can afford the price, because I won't bargain about it."

"Well, I don't know. We don't have unlimited resources."

"I need you to promise that you will not reveal where you acquired it, when it was done, nor from whom you purchased it. That is my price."

"That's a hard bargain. Much of the fun of owning it would be the cachet of getting it from you."

Ogie started to put the painting away and Bonnie went to take it out of his hands. "You're a hard bargainer. I agree to your terms."

"Convince me that you and Brian will live up to them."

"How about I say we bought the painting from your dealer? Would that work for you?"

"I don't think it will. That's a start, but I need to hear more from you to be assured."

"What else can I do? Should I swear a blood oath? I really want that painting."

"I'm listening."

"I don't know what will convince you. You're being inscrutable and won't tell me what you want."

"On the contrary, I made it clear what I want, and now it is up to you to make it clear to me how you will live by my conditions."

He could see she was confused and was thinking he wanted a chance to have sex with her. But when she looked at him carefully, she didn't see any signs of his hungering for it. Still, she thought that doing something seductive might give her the answer, and of course, Ogie saw her thoughts. He stepped back to keep distance between them. He enjoyed watching her struggling to figure out what would work. It was critical that she think of some way to guarantee his continued privacy. He had no idea what she would come up with. Then he saw she had an idea she was pleased with.

"How about I write you a check for fifteen thousand dollars? You deposit it and hold it for one year. If your location or the other things you are concerned with haven't been revealed at the end of the year, you send me back the money."

"OK. Eighteen months."

"OK, but I must say you aren't a trusting person."

"My lifestyle is too important to risk it."

"Now that you have been so generous in giving me a painting, may I choose one to buy? There are many that I love."

"Before we go there, I have another problem for you to solve. What are you going to tell people who see the painting in your house and ask you about it?"

"I hadn't thought about that. What do you suggest?"

"You need to figure it out. I have to be reassured."

"Let me consult with Brian about that and the deposit for your security. In the meantime, may I take a picture of the painting of our boat to show him?"

"Yes. And you can also photograph the painting you'd like to buy."

When Bonnie came back later that day, Ogie could tell she was loaded for bear. She was wearing short shorts and a tight shirt that emphasized the shape of her breasts. What was worse, their shape was to his taste, gentle mounds with the curve of the Alexander III Bridge in Paris. He could tell from her attire and reading her mind that she planned to use sex to get what she wanted. And what did she want? There were so many things that Ogie couldn't sort them out. He knew Bonnie would be likely to crow about her friendship with him. She felt it would be even better if she had sex with him. He was tempted, not having had sex with a woman for years yet turned off because he knew her repugnance for sex and her desire to use him for her ego trip. Island life was wonderful, but it had its drawbacks. One of them was that it was impossible to have an intimate relationship with someone who lived on the Island. It couldn't be concealed. Married women were out and there weren't many single women over eighteen. He knew from his mind reading that there were several married women who were tempted by him, but the repercussions weren't worth it. Intimacy with someone on the Island could reveal his identity.

"We came up with an explanation for having your paintings. It's simplicity itself. They were given to us by a relative."

"That sounds believable."

"Brian goes along with the fifteen thousand dollar deposit."

"Good."

"I showed him the photograph of the painting I wanted to buy and he wants that painting too. What's the price?"

"Thirty-five thousand."

"That's too steep for us. Is there any way we can work something out?"

"What would you suggest?"

"Do you need a model? I could model for you."

"That would be years of modeling. Do you think you could stay here that long?"

"How about a trade of services?"

"What kind of services do you have in mind?" Ogie asked, knowing what she was suggesting because he was reading her mind and her body language.

"Well, there are all kinds of modeling in the nude. Do I have to spell it out?"

"No and No."

"Aren't you tempted? How about we do it not for one of your paintings? Just because I'm attracted to you. As far as I can tell, you have no love life on this Island. My guess is that your opportunities for it rise out of the sea with the frequency of mermaids."

"Would it be fair to say you like the idea of collecting me in bed as much as collecting one of my paintings?"

"Just because you would be in my collection doesn't mean we can't enjoy ourselves." Ogie was surprised by her frankness.

Ogie asked her, "How do you explain that you would feel more comfortable having sex with me than with your husband?"

It took a few moments for Bonnie to grasp the meaning of what Ogie said. As it sank in, her color dissipated and she looked as if she had just been punched in the stomach. She collapsed in the nearest chair. Ogie was able to see the confusion and devastation in her mind. He winced at the havoc he'd caused. He handed her a glass of water and when she caught her breath, she sipped it.

Ogie read a mélange of emotions in her. Primary among them was pain about herself and her feelings of inadequacy. This was followed by anger about how Ogie could have known how vulnerable she was. Then she went into a rage, thinking that Brian must have told Ogie about her sexual disinclination. She focused on Ogie and demanded, "How could you attack me about something so personal?"

"You suggested we become intimate. Isn't that extraordinarily personal? If I were to have sex with you, I would need to know I can trust you. The discrepancy in your feelings scares me and makes the prospect of intimacy dangerous."

"How did you know I have those feelings? Did Brian talk to you about them?"

"Brian didn't tell me anything other than he was anxious for you to see my work. I can't explain how I know your ambivalent feelings about sex. When painting portraits, I look for the inner person, and that's what I did with you. I was able to sense things between you and Brian." Ogie fervently hoped his explanation would satisfy her. "I don't think Brian understands what is going on with you, and if he does, he isn't at a stage where he could articulate it to himself."

"What makes you so smart you could know that?"

"Let me ask you something that won't be easy for you. May I?"

"You're already terrifying me with what you know about us. Now I understand why you wanted me to come up with a way to guarantee your privacy. You don't trust me."

"What do you mean?"

"My first idea for explaining to people how we have your paintings was facile and didn't ring true. Obviously, you're a genius at spotting lack of authenticity. I'm afraid of your next question, but my curiosity is so great I can't help wanting to hear it. This ability of yours is just like what Ogie McMaster had with his students. Are you certain you aren't him?"

"Are you asking me if I know who I am? You still haven't answered my central question. If you chose to sleep with me, with or without a painting in exchange, I ask myself why? It's curious, because you know so little about me. How could you trust me emotionally, let alone in a physical way? After all, you are someone who is frightened of exposing herself, and I am someone who is potentially dangerous. Is this a need you have satisfied before? Am I making sense?"

"I don't understand what you're saying."

Ogie was able to read in her mind that she had slept with the governor. It confirmed his theory about her seeking cachet, but he wondered how she reconciled it with her feelings of shame about sex. "My guess is that you have slept with one or more prestigious men. To repeat, what does this do for you that sleeping with Brian doesn't?"

Ogie had confronted her with the meaning of her affairs. When she saw that her sleeping with important people was a way to feel better about herself, she didn't like what she saw. She was in agony, and he searched for a way to ease her pain.

Ogie could see she was having what he would call mind cramps. He couldn't think of a better term for people conflicted the way Bonnie was now, and Melanie had been before. He knew what to do for muscle cramps, but what do you do for a brain or emotional cramp?

And then it hit him—that was exactly what he had done for the children in his classes. Without knowing what he was doing, he must have unknotted their mind cramps when they were feeling blocked or frustrated. It accounted for much of his success.

He realized he had done it with Melanie as well. Maybe he could do it with Bonnie. He consciously entered Bonnie's mind and looked for a place to massage. He focused all his energy on sending soothing thoughts to the part of her mind in turmoil. At first he saw her resisting what he was doing, and then she let go.

She flashed back to when she was with the governor and had just finished having sex with him. She thought sex was disgusting, but that sleeping with important people made it OK. It was a new insight for her. When Ogie stopped comforting her mind, she emerged from what felt like a long nap. She asked Ogie, "What happened to me? It was as if I was asleep and had a dream. I feel changed, but I don't know how to describe it."

Ogie was fascinated to hear those details. "Tell me more about it."

"You asked me to explain why I would want to sleep with others and not with Brian," she replied. "I relived an affair just now and figured it out. When I saw my motivation, it was painful. My affair with an important person gave me permission to enjoy myself and not be embarrassed about who I am and about the undignified things one does while having sex. It was as if my image of his dignity and prestige were infused in me. Understanding what my feelings were then changed how I feel now. I don't understand how they could have changed so rapidly. Doesn't it take years of therapy for those changes? What have you done to me?"

"What have you done for yourself? I asked you some questions and apparently you gave them serious thought and came to see things differently. I'm impressed."

"But you must have done more than pose some questions. Whatever it was made me go deep into my feelings, but why would those questions have caused me to feel so differently about who I am?"

"Bonnie, there are things that happen to us that are inexplicable. Perhaps I had some impact, but you did the work. All I did was provoke you to think about things. Now why don't you go back to your home afloat and reflect on what has happened to you?"

With that, she tore out the check from her checkbook, picked up the boat painting, and left. It would take time for her to absorb what she had learned about herself. She couldn't believe Owen could have learned so much about her in such a short time. Was she that obvious? Had Brian told Owen about their relationship or was Owen a psychic? It was spooky.

After Bonnie left, Ogie sank down in his most comfortable chair. He was exhausted from the effort of helping her. He thought about his new skills and how he might use them. First he needed to get the Secret Service agents to ease their harassment of David. Next he wanted to clear his name so he could stop living incognito. Then maybe he could do something to free his mother. His increased mind reading abilities might enable him to pull it off.

CHAPTER 17

Bartlett

———

DAVID APPEARED SHORTLY AFTER BONNIE left. He could see that Ogie was spent and looked a question at him. Ogie replied, "Nothing serious now. I'm brain dead."

"What have you been up to that has wiped you out? Whose wife would be foolish enough to exercise you so your brains die?"

"David, I'm heartbroken you think so little of my capabilities and don't see my attractiveness. But you look as if you have something more important to say than building your ego at my expense. However, if it makes you feel better and at the cost to my self-image, be my guest. Never let it be said I don't support my friends in their hours of need, no matter what the sacrifice."

"The Feds are back and forth on what they want. This time, Bartlett himself is coming to talk to me and he wants you there."

"Why me? What does he want from me?"

"You know how closemouthed they are. When I pushed them, they wouldn't tell me. If I had to guess, since Sanford Black knew you did the original painting, he put two and two together and guessed you are here. But the clowns riding herd on me don't know much about that. Their boss is coming in this afternoon and your orders from the troglodytes are to be at my place at two o'clock."

When Ogie arrived at David's house, he was greeted outside by a man who wore an elegant, dark gray, single-breasted suit with a pink shirt and coordinated tie. The last time Ogie had seen anyone on

Megantic wearing a tie was a visiting clergyman for a funeral. The man flashed a White House badge.

"Hello, Owen, I'm Bradley Bartlett. Thank you for coming. From what David said, your presence came in the form of an order, for which I apologize. The Secret Service lads are under pressure to get results. Owen, I'm particularly delighted to have a chance to get to know you. I'm an admirer of your work. I know your gallery in Georgetown and I own several of your paintings. Le Brun says you are 'unavailable' to the public. He's so discreet, he wouldn't even tell me what state you live in and I don't think he knows. Your paintings strongly suggest a New England coastal island. When I heard you had been involved in the 'difficulties' with the Agents, I couldn't resist asking to meet you. I thought you might help us."

Ogie could tell that Bartlett was walking a fine line. He was used to having his orders followed because of the power he represented. But this situation called for finesse in order not to expose Black to scandal. Even though he had learned of Owen's real identity and that he was a wanted man, he could still be dangerous if he wasn't careful. He knew the charges against Owen/Ogie had been contrived. He was also aware that Ogie had access to Robert Hatfield, who had the potential for pulling the administration down.

"That's very nice, Mr. Bartlett, but who are you and what are you here for? All I know from David is something having to do with reproduced Vermeers. Are you here because someone sent you or are you on your own? While I know forgery is in the province of the Secret Service, I thought they only dealt with currency, not legitimate copies or creations of old masters."

"Let me answer one question at a time. I can see that you're put off by the peremptory ways of the Secret Service. I apologize again. Yes, normally the Secret Service is involved in false currency and financial matters. This Vermeer business has to do with national security. We're concerned because it involves a potential blackmail threat to someone senior in the administration. I'm concerned because I'm on the White House staff. It's because of David's expertise and your former work in the field that we've been asking for David's help and now yours."

Bartlett's alluding to Ogie's previous work with Dutch masters was a smooth move and made it clear that Bartlett knew who he was. It made Bartlett more dangerous. But that he mentioned it at all suggested there might be room to negotiate. Bartlett seemed to have compartmentalized so well that Ogie had a hard time seeing in his mind what else was involved. Bartlett was talented in his ability to deal with difficult and complex situations without giving much away.

"What is it you want from me?" Ogie asked. "I'm not nearly as skilled in this as David, and I know considerably less about Vermeer and his contemporaries. What can I do for you?"

"Ogg...Owen, I believe you are overly modest about your abilities. In checking David's background, I found that he apprenticed with you. When I saw the photographs the Secret Service took of you on their last visit, I recognized you. Because of your experience making Vermeers, you can be David's sounding board. He will be looking for the odd things about the Vermeers. He will need to think aloud and bounce his ideas off someone knowledgeable. You must trust him a great deal because you seem to be comfortable with your sister posing nude for him." Ogie was mystified at first by how Bartlett knew that. He realized the Secret Service guys must have gone through everything in his house, as well as David's. But he did read that Bartlett knew more about the painting of Marianne and Black than he was saying.

Bartlett was trying to charm him, but Ogie couldn't figure out why. Bartlett handed him the photograph the Secret Service had picked up at the Island Art Gallery. Ogie could tell immediately it was of a copy of the painting Marianne had commissioned him to do years ago. Bartlett wanted the original and any copies to protect Sanford Black. Why Bartlett didn't want to be in touch with Marianne, who owned it, Ogie didn't know. It puzzled him because he must have known of

Black's prior relationship with her. He knew Marianne wouldn't use that painting to harm Black, but it was the copy that was scaring Black and Bartlett. With the copy loose, there was no telling where the original was, and that was why they wanted both. Ogie could sense Bartlett's fear of Marianne, but he didn't know why. He could also see that Bartlett thought he would be eager to help and would be a push-over because he was a wanted man. Bartlett was relishing the idea of pressuring him.

Ogie knew Bartlett's slip of the tongue about his name was delib-erate; Bartlett did not invite Ogie to this meeting by accident. That he had not yet had him arrested was a good sign, but it was indicative that he wanted something from him.

Ogie was tired of dancing around the problem. "OK, it's time to stop the games. How about you tell me what it is you want to know about the Vermeers? And while I'm asking questions, why David? We both know there are many experts in Vermeer who have more experi-ence than David. There are people who have spent their whole pro-fessional lifetimes doing research about Vermeer and Gabriël Metsu and that period of Dutch painting. Mr. Bartlett, what you really want to know is who is responsible for the photograph and who made the copy of my original painting of Black and Marianne. And you want to be certain that it won't go into the public realm. Right?"

"Yes, that simplifies it," Bartlett replied. But Ogie could tell there was something else on Bartlett's mind.

Ogie took a chance. "Mr. Bartlett, before I help you, I need promises."

"Hold on, Mr. McMaster. You're in no position to make demands with an outstanding warrant that can send you to prison for life."

"OK, then arrest me."

"Ogie, you're bluffing."

"You know who I am and because of that, I have nothing to lose," Ogie replied. "If I'm headed for prison, there's no incentive for me to cooperate with you."

Bartlett hesitated. It was apparent he wanted to prolong the discussion. He was desperate to find out who could ruin Black's career by releasing the painting, or copies of it. Ogie read that Bartlett's people had worked Judah over mercilessly to find out who had given him the photograph and the letter with no results except to leave him in so much turmoil he could barely talk. Judah must believe Melanie's threat to reveal they had sex together, even though Melanie had much to lose if she said anything about it.

Ogie went on. "Mr. Bartlett, that painting, if publicized, could cause harm to Black and the administration. Black was a married man when he had the affair with Marianne Wright, but he's made his reputation as a moral man. We can prevent it being made known, but there has to be a quid pro quo."

"What do you want?"

"Withdrawal of all warrants against me, a presidential pardon, a reversal of my conviction, and no difficulties to be inflicted on anyone on this Island who has a connection with this, including Judah Worthington."

"You think you have enough leverage to demand those things?"

"Mr. Bartlett, are you serious about keeping Black out of trouble?"

"You haven't offered me enough, Ogie. I can keep Marianne's affair with Black quiet without you. You can make it easier, and if you don't, we can put you away on your outstanding warrant. Who would take you seriously as a convicted felon? All I'm offering is not putting you back in prison."

"You don't get it. I'm not interested in exposing Black. I just want justice for myself, and my friends."

"Why would I agree to your demands?"

"Think about these people and what their stories could do to you and your administration: Hatfield, Schoenberg, McAllister, Goldberg, and Moffit, to name a few."

"What can you do? Tell their stories? They're all officially nutcases."

"When I was visiting my mother at Karl's so-called sanitarium, I photographed the ledger entries for Hatfield and the other political prisoners you keep there. Conveniently, there were remarks about why they were there, for how long, and how much the third parties were paying for it. Guess who the third parties are? Would you like to know who authorized many of the payments?"

Ogie could feel the shock in Bartlett's head and his struggle to conceal it. If Bartlett wasn't the actual hatchet man who had arranged for those men and women to be locked up at Karl's, then he was closely connected with it. His name on the ledgers could severely damage the administration. It could free Hatfield to publish his account of 9/11, and once it was made clear that the World Trade Center was brought down by prearrangement, it could reopen the question of how the twin towers came down.

Ogie knew that Bartlett, beneath his smooth, sophisticated front, was slime. Reading Bartlett's mind confirmed that he sent political prisoners to Karl to keep in his sanitarium, and that Bartlett had taken slime to unimaginable highs—or lows, depending on your point of view. It took all of Ogie's self-control to avoid showing his complete disgust. This man had either contributed to, or was responsible for, the deaths of thousands of people by promoting our involvement in the Middle East, and his only concern was not being revealed. Ogie couldn't detect the slightest bit of remorse or conscience in him. Maybe later he could expose Bartlett. First he had to get himself out of danger.

"I knew that information would be useful," Ogie continued. "I fantasized that I could use it to clear the faked charges against me. I just didn't know how. I also knew it would be dangerous for me to be the only one who had it. Mr. Bartlett, I assume you know of the magazine *Evénements de France*?"

"Yes. How does it relate to this?"

"Do you happen to know who the publisher is?"

"What kind of nonsense is this?"

"It's in your interest. What is his name?"

"Pierre Didier."

"What else do you know about the Didier name?"

"The family is very influential in France. Now come to the point."

"Pierre and I are old friends, as well as cousins," Ogie said. "I discussed the problem of freeing my mother, his aunt, with him as well as sharing the information I gathered at Karl's showing how and why he was keeping people who disagreed with the administration prisoners. He saw it as a great scoop for his magazine. I had to persuade him to postpone coming out with it. I was worried about how it might affect my mother. What would you do to her if I caused trouble? You have the Patriot Act behind you, and that gives you the right to imprison anyone you want without cause or trial."

This was the first time Bartlett showed vulnerability. Ogie could see it in the hatred in his eyes. Finally, Bartlett said, "OK, I agree to most of what you want. I can't be certain I can get your conviction reversed, because that is up to the judges, but we can try. Quashing the warrants can be done quickly, but a pardon will take time. There's a procedure specified by law for it. But nothing will be done unless you can guarantee that neither you nor Pierre will reveal anything about what's in Karl's ledgers."

That Bartlett could go as far as he did told Ogie there was definitely more to this than recovering the original painting. "Not satisfactory," Ogie said. "I don't want to continue living with aliases. You know perfectly well that my conviction was arranged with Karl. Your Attorney General could easily go to court to get a reversal. What I can promise you is that neither Pierre nor I will say or do anything to reveal this if I have written proof of your assurances of what you will do to clear me. Until that happens, we won't turn the painting over to you. But we will stop the person who instigated this. I want a letter signed by the President saying he intends to pardon me as soon as possible and that he knows a miscarriage of justice has occurred. I want a press release to that effect. I also want a letter of intent from the Attorney

General, telling of his plans to clear me. And I want one from Black, acknowledging that he knows my conviction was a fraud. As soon as I have those, you will be in the clear."

"You don't have much trust, do you?"

"Why should I? Why would I trust high government officials who collaborated in my false conviction? Why should I trust people who ruin careers out of spite? You do remember Valerie Plame and Susan Lindauer, don't you? It's why I believe in the truism that you should run away as fast as you can when someone says, 'I'm from the government and I'm here to help you.' Look at the millions of people whose deaths we are responsible for in Viet Nam, Iraq, Afghanistan, Libya, etc., when we told them, 'We are here to help you.' Look at the horrors we created and perpetrated in Chile, Guatemala, and Iran by overthrowing their legitimate governments. Look at the so called 'help' we gave Panama by killing many people under the ruse of going to arrest one man—or look at the deaths in Mexico because of our drug laws. And then there were Osama Bin Laden, Saddam Hussein, and Qaddafi, all of whom we supported and then turned against. Do I need to go on?"

Bartlett was annoyed. "I want to know who is responsible for this copy of your painting. Without that, I won't do anything for you."

"I know who did it, but they don't understand the whole picture. And before you say, 'just tell me,' you need to know it's not simple and the ramifications could threaten you and Black. To help clarify who is responsible for the copy of the painting, have some DNA tests done on Black and the photograph of the painting. I will send you a DNA sample in case the photograph doesn't have enough DNA to be useful to determine who made it. I suggest you compare it to Black's DNA. You want to be certain the people who do the lab work are trustworthy, because you really don't want the results to leak out. The tests will give you a good idea of who the culprit is. But before I give you that sample, I want the evidence of the good faith I asked for."

"OK, Mr. McMaster. It's time to play hardball. You already know too much to be on the loose without assurances you will behave. You know what your buddy Hatfield went through because he knew too much, so you know what I can do to you. In addition to your present sentence, we can add charges because you helped Hatfield escape from Karl's sanitarium. If I thought you knew where he was, you wouldn't be a free man. You're lucky you don't know. You two were clever enough to make contact indirectly without knowing where the other one was. I know the charges against you were bogus, but you're a wanted man and I won't hesitate to use that to get what I want."

Ogie focused on Bartlett's mind again and saw he was thinking of more ways to threaten him. His mind was sharper than any Ogie had gone into before.

Ogie was fed up and made it clear, "Your heavy-handedness with us has been counterproductive. You could have achieved your purposes with a lighter touch."

Bartlett surprised Ogie by saying, "I apologize. You're right. The pressure on us is considerable with the next election coming up. It's the original you painted years ago that we want, as well as any copies."

Ogie sensed Bartlett's unease. Bartlett was feeling guilty, but Ogie couldn't identify why. He decided to prod him to learn more. "Have you talked with Marianne about the original painting?"

"I did. She refused to give me the painting. I wonder if you might be successful with her."

That's it, Ogie thought. There is something about his dealings with Marianne he is ashamed of.

As innocently as he could, Ogie asked him, "I wonder why she refused to…" He hit pay dirt. Bartlett's mind reacted as if he had been walloped. His barriers were down. Ogie saw that Bartlett was embarrassed because Marianne had dismissed and threatened him. Ogie searched for a way to get Bartlett to reveal more. He had to have more leverage in order to get Bartlett to leave David, Melanie, and Nina alone. He went deep into Bartlett's mind to find his wince areas.

He decided to work on Bartlett's strong feelings of embarrassment about what he had said to Marianne. "You said something to set her off. If I'm going to help you, I have to know what it was."

The smooth-talking, slick, and facile Bartlett started and stammered, thinking, *"How the hell did he know?"* If it wasn't so serious, Ogie would have laughed, but he suppressed it.

"I requested the painting on the assumption she would sympathize with Sanford and want to reassure him that it wouldn't be publicized. She said she had no intention of making the painting known. I said that if anything happened to her it could get into the wrong hands. She wouldn't budge. I offered her ten thousand dollars and then fifty thousand but she didn't waver in her refusal. Then she told me to get out and if I continued she would let the papers know about it. Now you know."

"No, Mr. Bartlett, I don't know. I don't believe she threw you out because of what you said." Ogie knew Bartlett was still covering up. "If what you've done with me is an indication of how you work, then you must have threatened her in some way. What was your threat?"

"How can you be certain I threatened her?"

"OK, I'll demonstrate. You still haven't given me enough information about your dealings with Marianne to help me help you. Go away."

Bartlett was enraged, "Ogie, I'm going to have the Secret Service arrest you on your outstanding warrants. You can go straight to hell."

Ogie saw Bartlett's memory of the threat he had made to Marianne and Ogie watched him flinch. Finally, and with an infinitesimal degree of chagrin, he acknowledged Ogie's point. He couldn't figure out how Ogie seemed to know everything he was thinking.

"OK, I threatened to take her into custody and she threw me out. Now can you help me?"

"Not yet."

"What do I need to do to get your cooperation? There are many tools at my disposal. I can do things in the name of the President that could end your troubles with the law. Money could be a problem, but that could be solved."

"Well, Mr. Bartlett, you're beginning to see the light. How about you see what you can tempt me with. And while you're at it, you might think about what you can do for David to make him a more cheerful customer. It's in your interest to do so."

"If I agree, you will owe me a great deal. Your demands will take time to accomplish, particularly vacating your convictions. If you take my word for it, I will begin the process."

Ogie, reading Bartlett, could see that the waiting period for a pardon was not a bluff, and that Bartlett did intend to have the Attorney General reverse the conviction.

Ogie didn't see any way he could do better with Bartlett, or that there was a better way to guarantee Bartlett would follow through.

"Yes, if you come through with the letters that contain the elements I insist on and show me the Attorney General agrees to help. The President has to sign it, it has to be witnessed by someone known to me, and I have to have the original copy. Further, I want you to write a letter now describing what you are going to do and sign it with your title. You will leave it with me."

"I will get the letters for you. But I won't hand it over until I get the things I've asked you for." Without another word, he walked out of David's house. Ogie assumed that he was used to dispensing with the social niceties of greetings and partings.

After he left, David said, "How can you be certain you can get Marianne to give you the painting? I wouldn't want to take her on."

"I'll figure out a way. Remember, I knew her years ago and we got along well. If nothing else, she will hear me out."

Marianne

———

BARTLETT CALLED THREE WEEKS LATER. The first thing Ogie asked was what progress had been made in rectifying the miscarriage of justice. Bartlett told him, "It's under way and a press release about the President's commitment to clearing you should be in the local paper, if not a national one, in a few days. The AG has agreed to cooperate fully—in fact, when he learned of the judicial swindle he became anxious to prosecute the people who did it." That last statement was so outrageously false that Ogie didn't bother to respond to it.

Bartlett told Ogie that initially Black wouldn't agree to any testing done on him or on any specimens of his. It wasn't until Bartlett told Black that Marianne was living on Megantic with a child of sixteen that Black agreed. He was thunderstruck at the possibility that he could be that child's father without having known about it, even though he thought his paternity was unlikely. The first report Bartlett received from the geneticists comparing the unknown person's DNA with Black's showed a very close family relationship. But the picture was muddied by something called methylation, which confused the issue of whether Sanford Black was Melanie's father. Bartlett consulted with more geneticists and received the same answer. The father of the unknown person was probably related to Black. The geneticists knowing Black's family history suggested a more refined test be done in Europe by Eurofin. At first Black refused because they wanted a sperm sample. Fortunately, the blood sample you sent satisfied them. Black finally agreed to provide a specimen.

"When I told him about the genetic results, he grilled me for all the details. We believe that Marianne's daughter, Melanie Wright, is the one who made the copy of your painting and sent the photograph to Black. But you probably knew that already." What Bartlett was not saying and must have become apparent to him when dealing with the lab people was that Black had had a brother.

"Black is concerned about Melanie as if he were her father. I will not do anything until you have talked with Marianne. Now it's even more urgent that you talk with her and get that painting."

Ogie knocked on Marianne's door. He knew Melanie would be in school. He had waited to contact her until the genetic tests were done. Marianne was startled to see him. Even though they'd been living on the same island for years, they didn't see each other much. When they had both lived in the Washington, D.C. area, they had been friends. When Marianne arrived on Megantic, Ogie had asked her to keep his former identity a secret, to which she readily agreed. Ogie's appearance was a surprise. Marianne was wearing a dirty smock and her hands were covered with remnants of clay. "Well, Ogie, what can I do for you?"

"Marianne, the question is what can I do for you?"

"Don't tell me Melanie is in trouble again."

"Yes. Can we sit down while we discuss it?"

Marianne wasn't happy to be interrupted, but Ogie was an old friend and she knew he wouldn't have come to see her without a good reason. She invited him in and offered him something to drink. Ogie looked at the *objects d'art* in the room, fascinated by what Marianne found interesting and aesthetically pleasing.

"Come to the point, Ogie."

He told her what Melanie had done with the painting and the photograph of it. He also mentioned that Black had sent the Secret Service to investigate, and then had sent Bartlett to bludgeon David and Judah into telling who had done it. "We refused to tell Bartlett because we wanted to protect Melanie."

Marianne interrupted, "She is still searching for her father and she must have assumed it was Sanford Black when she saw that painting."

Ogie couldn't help himself. "Why don't you tell her who her father is?"

Marianne's answer dumbfounded him: "Because I don't know."

"Bartlett compared Melanie's DNA with Black's and found that Sanford is not her father but is closely related to her. Now you know Alan is her father."

Marianne's breathing stopped and she stared at what appeared to be nothing. To Ogie, it was an eon. He didn't say a word. Marianne took a breath and explained. "You know, I had a spectacular relationship with Sanford's twin, Alan. I had never been so close and so in love with anyone. Then came the accident that killed him. I was destroyed and paralyzed. I couldn't think or move or do anything for myself. Sanford came by and nursed me through it. He came twice a day to literally spoon feed me, leave me groceries, pay my bills, and do everything he could think of. I don't think I could have recovered without him. In my fog, I came to see him as a savior and worshiped him. My feelings of gratitude were overwhelming. I saw him as a god, and as his brother. Sanford merged into Alan. I found myself hugging Sanford in appreciation. I wanted to give him the gift of myself, and I desperately needed to feel real again through physical loving. Looking back at it, I can see he was torn and tempted and didn't want to hurt me by refusing. I had put him in an intolerable position, because he is a moral person. I hope he hasn't suffered as a result, but to avoid inflicting more torture on his conscience, I haven't had any contact with him since then." Marianne took a deep breath, as if she hadn't had one for days.

"Until you told me just now, I didn't know who Melanie's father was. I didn't want to find out because it would have been too painful for both of us if she was Alan's and too cruel to Sanford if she was his.

I realize it has driven Melanie crazy, and I know she is angry because I have refused to tell her why I won't tell her. Black's stress about it, the pressure Melanie is under, and the problems it has caused you and David make it past due that I tell her who her father is. The irony is that Bartlett hadn't known about Alan and that I had been involved with him. He knew, of course, about my relationship with Sanford and was doing everything to protect him from publicity about it."

CHAPTER 19

Sashi

———

Natasha Aleksandra Lebedeva worked in le Brun's art gallery. She did it for pleasure, as relaxation from her full time job in intelligence. It didn't pay much except on the rare occasions when she received a commission on the sale of a painting. That wasn't often, because she spent so little time there. But handling paintings, talking about them, deciding how and where to hang them, and everything else that went on in the gallery gave her deep satisfaction. She enjoyed and was good at hostessing the openings, and sales on those nights were sky high. The paintings she talked about with clients had an added luster because of her involvement with them. She was that rare bird who was fluent in three languages, with a fair amount of ability in another two. Her friends called her Sashi, even though it was not a diminutive that Russians would use.

Her beauty stopped people in their tracks. They had to catch their breath when she gave them her full attention. She became art in their eyes. She was beyond the age when she thought of her beauty as increasing her worth as a human being. She had achieved that maturity early and the result was a quintessentially decent person. That decency showed within a sentence or two of conversation with her. She avoided personal relationships with any man who gave the slightest hint of not being inclined to treat her with a humanity and dignity that matched hers.

The gratifications of her work and her relationships with her parents and friends obviated any need she might feel for going with or living with a man. Her wants were easily satisfied by what she earned. She had a sufficient sense of who she was and how effective she was at her work to have no worry about job security. Once her coworkers and bosses came to see beyond her beauty and natural elegance, they found a keen mind that tracked everything around her. She was able to suggest solutions to problems that hadn't yet been anticipated.

One of her passions was running. The nature of her work in intelligence made it incumbent upon her to avoid publicity, so she entered marathons under an assumed name and deliberately didn't finish among the leaders. Her satisfaction was in knowing she could do well in them.

What she loved about working with le Brun was his unfailing good taste. He had come to see that she was his match in aesthetics, and so he gave her a free hand arranging things in the gallery. When they disagreed, it enabled each of them to gain insights and share new ways of looking at things.

Sashi had met Ogie years ago in connection with his one-man show at the gallery. She had been amazed to learn how young an artist was going to be featured, until she saw his work. One of the very few affairs she had had was with him. It had been satisfying and inconclusive. While they were very much in love, they had concerns about the extent to which their relationship might harm other parts of their lives. It was particularly important for Sashi, because she was doing highly classified work.

She and Ogie were beginning to sort out how permanent their relationship would be when Ogie was arrested. After his arrest, he had been insistent on separating, because he had to go into hiding, and he wanted to protect her from being tainted by association with him. She was willing to take the risk, but he was adamant about the danger to her. He had told her the whole sordid story about his stepfather, and she knew that what had been done to Ogie was a miscarriage of justice. Le Brun and Sashi were among the very tiny circle of people who knew that "Ogie on the run" had become the successful painter Owen Cartwright, doing a different kind of painting.

The message Ogie left with le Brun for Sashi was a simple one: "Please call." It was followed by a phone number. Sashi postponed calling. She had adjusted her emotional life to living without Ogie and had learned how to be content without him. She had no idea what Ogie had in mind.

Finally she realized that delaying was not going to make it easier. She heard a young woman's voice answer. Her first thought was that Ogie was in another relationship. She swallowed, said who she was, and was startled by the warmth of the response. "Oh, you're Sashi. Ogie has told me so much about you. I'm dying to meet you."

"And you are?"

"I'm sorry. I was so enthusiastic to hear your voice after all of the wonderful things Ogie has told me about you that I forgot my manners. I'm Nina, Ogie's sister."

Sashi dredged her memory and remembered that Ogie had talked about his sister, who was then a little girl. Sashi had never met her. Nina bubbled over with excitement, "I'm so glad you called. Ogie has been on edge, hoping you would. I can't tell you what a relief it will be for him to hear from you. For me too, because now he will stop driving me crazy with his worrying. You must be a terrific person, if half the things he says about you are true. When are you coming here?"

"Nina, slow down. I haven't been invited yet."

"Well, if Ogie won't invite you, I will. I hear from him over and over what a beautiful person you are and that you have a great aesthetic sense as well. That you did wonders arranging his first show at le Brun's."

"Ogie has a tendency to exaggerate when describing me. It's dear of him, but he overdoes it. Tell me, Nina, how old are you? What are you doing with yourself?"

"I'm teaching French in the high school and substituting as a sternman on a lobster boat. I'm helping Ogie with a project he's working on, and I'm working for David. I don't know how long it will last. I'm sixteen."

"What is the project you're helping Ogie with?"

"I wish I could answer that, but I've been sworn to secrecy. Maybe Ogie will tell you. He's off with David again and will be very upset to have missed you."

"Who is David Again?"

"Not David Again, just David."

"I'm sorry, Nina. I couldn't resist," Sashi said with a friendly chuckle.

Nina laughed too. "David copies Vermeers to sell or creates new ones."

"He does what?"

"You must know something about it, because Ogie used to do it and you handled them at your gallery. It's all above board. There's a market for well-done copies of Vermeers and invented Vermeers. I'm certain you know more about them than I do.

"Occasionally, David will do copies of other painters. Gabriël Metsu is one of his favorites. I've been posing for David and making suggestions for new Vermeers and now some new Metsus. But I'm going on and on about things, you know."

"Nina, you sound very knowledgeable."

"Well, it's one of my passions. I was so lucky to find someone like David on the Island who would let me collaborate and participate."

"What is it like living on that small Island?" Sashi asked. "Are you bored? Do you feel constrained in such a small place? Is the community accepting of outsiders?"

"I grew up on a farm with my uncle. I'm used to small town rural living. Yes, this is more intense small town living than on the mainland. But I don't have the feeling of being rejected because I'm an outsider. It's more a feeling that people don't know me well. You know close relationships take time to develop, and I haven't been here long."

"That's a very perceptive observation coming from someone so young."

"Thank you," Nina said. "If you come up, I think we could have a good time together, if I can steal you away from Ogie. We have much in common in addition to art. Am I too forward if I say we have Ogie, whom we both love?"

"No. That does describe it. But my relationship with him is not clearly defined. As you know, much turmoil has prevented that. Our separation may have changed things."

Sashi went on, "I haven't even met you and here I am telling you about my love life with your brother. I can tell that you're emotionally trustworthy and mature after a very few minutes on the phone. Normally I don't talk about my feelings and relationships except with people I know well. You must be an extraordinary young person.

"How is the school on the Island? Have you had trouble fitting in?"

"I graduated from high school three years ago. I have been asked to substitute teach French and algebra and I've been coaching the basketball team, and from what I can tell, the school is amazingly good for its limited size and isolation."

"Nina, how did you manage to graduate at thirteen?"

"I think they decided I was too much of a problem and the easiest way to solve it was to graduate me."

"All right, you have successfully dropped my jaw. I'm looking forward to meeting you."

"Ogie has just returned. Before I go, let me say again how anxious I am for you to come here. Here he is, and if I delay handing him the phone, I can't be certain of my safety. Bye." Nina handed the phone to Ogie and discreetly left the room.

Ogie was so tense that all he could get out was a garbled, "Er row."

Sashi was feeling much the same way and her greeting wasn't much better. They both started speaking the same words at once: "Well, this is awkward..." and then laughed. Ogie said, "Where do we begin?"

"Ogie, I'm returning your call. Did you have something in mind?"

"Sashi, I have some amazing news. It looks like the charges against me will soon be dropped."

This was one of the rare times since becoming a proficient mind reader that Ogie missed being able to use his skill. The distance was too great.

"Sashi, there is so much I feel and want to say. I don't know whether you want to hear it, and if you do, I don't know where to begin. Our long time apart has made me feel you're a stranger and yet I have such loving feelings about you. I would love it if you could come and visit here. It's a beautiful place, and we're on the water, which is always a marvel to gaze at. If you came, it could give us a chance to get to know each other again. In our years apart we've changed and we probably see things differently."

"Ogie, that is lovely, but I'm missing something. I don't quite know how to put it, but you don't sound very delighted. It's more as if you are arranging for relatives to come."

"Sashi, I'm frightened. I want you so badly. Because of so much time apart, I'm scared I've lost you. I certainly didn't want you to think I assumed you would want to be with me again. I was worried that if I was too enthusiastic you would think I was taking you for granted. I'm afraid to ask how you feel about me."

"Ogie, I have to be honest. I have mixed feelings. The ones from when we were together couldn't be more loving. But I've had to work at putting aside those feelings, because I didn't know if we would ever be together again. Neither of us made a commitment other than to say 'Let's see what happens.' I do want to try, but I can't promise you what will happen."

"Would a visit here work for you?"

"Ogie, let me think about it.

"Nina and I had a great talk before you got on the line. She sounds like a very bright, perceptive person with a delicious mischievous streak. I gather she is very knowledgeable about art. She is so young and yet she has a very mature outlook. How long has she been with you?"

"She's only been here two months and it already feels as if she has always been here. She already knows more Meganticans than I do. She's been helping my friend David with his artwork, as well as working on a lobster boat. I've always known how capable she is, but I hadn't seen her for eight years. What a surprise it was to find her an accomplished young woman. She graduated from high school at thirteen and decided to put off college for a while. Seth did a magnificent job with her."

"Nina must be very unusual to have fit into your life and Island life so readily."

"Yes, I'm lucky to have her here. I hadn't realized how awful it was to have no family until she arrived. It's been painful to have been separated from her for what felt like forever. She took the initiative to get herself here. If I had known she was coming, I would have stopped her, so I'm glad I didn't know. She convinced Seth to let her go and she managed to charm le Brun into telling her where I was. She is a powerhouse."

"Ogie, I'm reluctant to ask this, but what is the situation with your mother? Is she still in Karl's clinic on the west coast?"

"Yes. If the charges against me are dropped, I can start figuring out how to deal with Karl."

CHAPTER 20

Nina

———

Nina had taken the article from an inside page of the *Bangor Free Press*, enlarged it several times, stuck it to the glass of the entry door facing outwards, and circled Ogie's name in orange. There was no way Ogie could enter without seeing it. Underneath, she had drawn a male and a female figure wildly dancing.

"AP, Washington, D.C. June 5, 2012. Ogie McMaster of Megantic Island, Maine, is on the newly released list of Presidential pardons. McMaster was found guilty of kidnapping his mother and sentenced to 25 years in prison. He was sentenced to an additional ten years for escaping during his sentencing hearing. The Attorney General is seeking to vacate his convictions on on both counts. What is particularly unusual is the active interest the President has taken in this case. The President's press secretary when asked about this would only say that there will be a follow up by the Attorney General.

"McMaster has no known address and we were unable to contact him. Roger Burgess, the resident Sheriff's Deputy on Megantic, an Island of 725 people off the coast of Maine, said, 'I don't know of anyone by the name of Ogie McMaster on this Island.'"

After her initial whooping, shouting, and whirling around in the empty house, Nina realized the extent of the tension she had been carrying. She let her body go and collapsed on the couch. The relief for Ogie would be wonderful. She thought about what it meant for her as well. Now she didn't have to measure and weigh every word and action for fear of sinking their world. There might even be a chance that her mother could be freed from Karl.

The good news started Nina thinking about her time with her uncle Seth and how living with him hadn't always been easy. Seth had made her think her problems through. It had strained her emotionally. At the time, she felt he was cruel, but it taught her to be her own therapist. It saved her sanity, by giving her the ability to understand her emotions and motivations, and the tools to find solutions. While he wasn't her mother, he enabled her to keep her equilibrium after her grisly experiences with Karl, her separation from her mother, and her father's death.

She often wondered how Seth knew exactly what to say to her to help her gain insights about herself. He wasn't a trained therapist. She wanted to ask him how he'd made judgments about how much she could figure things out on her own. It had been inspired of Ogie to send her to him. At the time, she'd felt Ogie had abandoned her, but now she understood.

She thought it was important for Seth to know that Ogie had been pardoned. It was time to call him, because even if the phones were tapped, there was no longer any danger. He must be worried. She didn't know whether he knew where she was.

When Seth came on the phone, she could hear in his voice how glad he was to hear from her. "Aren't you taking chances calling me?"

"Seth, you haven't seen the article that appeared in today's Bangor paper. Ogie is going to be pardoned! His sentence for escaping is being vacated! Supposedly, the Attorney General is delving into the reasons for 'the miscarriage of justice.' Ogie is out, and I don't think he knows about it yet."

"I can't even picture how much relief you and Ogie must feel about this. Nina, what are you doing these days? I don't know where you are or where Ogie lives. I'm amazed you found your way to him. How did you do it?"

"We're on Megantic Island, about 40 miles off the coast of Maine."

"Well, Ogie certainly found an out-of-the-way place to hide. What are you doing there, and what is Ogie up to?"

"Seth, you must come and see us. It's beautiful here. Ogie is painting watercolors that are super good. They're unlike anything he's done before. They have a life to them you wouldn't believe could be conveyed with watercolors. I think he's on a par with Jamie Wyeth, and I'm not the only one who thinks that. He has an arrangement with le Brun, who sells his paintings under a different name, and they sell for enough for Ogie to live comfortably."

"What are you doing, Nina?"

"My new life feels unreal. I started out helping Ogie's friend, David, who took over Ogie's work of creating Vermeers and Metsus. I helped him design some new ones and I do some modeling for him. I also volunteer as a sternman on a lobster boat, which gives me entrée to Island life. I was asked to substitute teach in a French class. I never dreamed I could have so much pleasure teaching. The thought of doing it scared me, but the principal is supportive. My students and their parents love what I'm doing, which is very satisfying. There was a ruckus on the school board about a sixteen-year-old teaching, but the State Superintendent gave me a temporary teaching certificate. Was I nervous when she visited my class!

"Renee Liegeois, the principal, also asked me to teach a beginning algebra class. Enabling my students to master difficult things has given me an unbelievable sense of confidence and self worth. Many of the girls in my classes talk to me about their personal problems, and that's also been very gratifying.

"Seth, you are responsible for this great life I'm living. You hung in there with me when I was coming apart. You made me ask myself questions I couldn't bear to look at and didn't even know how to think about. There were times I hated you for forcing me to face myself when all I could see was blackness. But I learned, and the tools you gave me helped me get to where I am now.

"The skills of facing myself you made me acquire also enable me to help my students, who often don't know which end is up and don't even know there is an up to look for. I've been very careful to do what you did for me, which is to only ask them questions and not give them advice. To see how they have learned to sort things out and find clarity makes my whole body feel good. It's hard to believe just talking with someone can do that."

"I'm so proud of you, Nina," Seth replied. "That you have come out of all this such a positive, well-put-together person is amazing and fantastic.

"Tell me more about Ogie. How has he been holding up under the strain of hiding out? It must have taken a toll on him. I assume he hasn't had contact with Sashi, and that has to have been difficult."

"Seth, you wouldn't believe the oddity of what has been going on here, but Ogie put pressure on someone high up in the government to get his pardon. While we didn't get word about the reprieve until today, he decided to take the risk and be in touch with Sashi a few weeks ago. They had a long telephone conversation, but I don't know where they stand. I had the opportunity to meet Sashi on the phone when she called. I really liked her. I invited her here and I hope Ogie discussed a visit with her.

"I can hear Ogie returning. Let me say goodbye and celebrate with him. We will be in touch."

"Nina, have him call me when he's ready."

Much to Nina's surprise, Ogie didn't appear to have a reaction after reading the clipping, other than looking thoughtful. "Ogie, isn't that wonderful news?"

"I'm not certain. From the point of view of not being in danger of going to prison, yes. But a pardon is not a vindication. It's only being forgiven for the crime. I'm still legally guilty of it."

"How will that handicap you?"

"It probably won't make much difference in what I can or can't do. However, it still leaves Mom a prisoner of Karl and leaves us with no standing to prosecute him and free her."

"But Ogie, didn't you see where the Attorney General is going to do more?"

"Yes, but we don't yet know what that is and if he really will do it. It's a good start, though."

"I just called Seth with the good news. He would like you to call him."

When Ogie called, Seth's first words were, "I got a call from Karl today—he asked if I could help arrange a meeting between you and him. He says he has a 'lucrative' proposal for you."

"If Karl wants to see me, he must be running scared. He has to have gotten word that my conviction may be reversed. If so, he probably realizes that puts me in a position to have him prosecuted. That explains the 'lucrative.'"

When his conversation with Seth was over, Ogie told Nina what Karl wanted him to do and went on to say, "I always assumed Karl was keeping Mom a prisoner because he didn't want her to expose his spa fraud. But I'm starting to think there is more to it than that. Could there have been something else Mom knew about? And why did he question you? Could you have known something important? See if you can remember anything he asked you."

Ogie's train of thought continued. "Will we need protection while Karl is here? I wonder if I should ask Roger Burgess to help with this. To be safe, it would be wise to keep you out of Karl's sight."

"Ogie, as much as I detest the idea of being with him, I think I could be helpful in figuring out his motives."

"Nina, I don't think you should be near him. He's dangerous and clever. It's not worth taking a chance."

CHAPTER 21
Karl

———

OGIE DECIDED IT MADE SENSE to confide in Roger and asked him to be at the airport when Karl arrived. In spite of having been deceived by Ogie in his fugitive role as Owen Cartwright, Roger had a soft spot for him. Nina had also won his heart, because he had a child in her classes. When he realized that Ogie's felony conviction was a miscarriage of justice, he forgave him for deceiving him. It wasn't the first miscarriage of justice he had encountered. He offered to stand by in case of trouble.

"I would appreciate it if you would check to see that no one is on that plane when it leaves who didn't arrive here," Ogie said. "I don't think he'll try anything, but with Karl, you never know."

Ogie pondered the question of where to meet with Karl. He didn't want him in his house, and there wasn't a public place with privacy. He asked David if he would be willing to host them and be a witness. David agreed, and Ogie asked him to put the painting that Nina had modeled for out of sight.

Roger was at the airstrip when the jet landed. He and Ogie helped pull down the boarding ramp.

Ogie was shocked at Karl's appearance, even making allowances for not having seen him for years. He appeared gray all over, smaller, and wizened. His movements were those of a much older man, and his face was lined with anxiety. When Karl saw Roger in uniform, Ogie read his thinking. *"He's called a policeman to arrest me. Can we take off immediately? I knew coming here would be dangerous. That's why Ogie insisted on no extra people on the plane. He didn't want anyone protecting me."*

Ogie motioned for Karl to get in the car, which made Karl uneasy. But he realized that even if Ogie did something to him, he'd never get away with it. As they drove, Karl made some comments about the beauty of the Island. Ogie didn't respond.

David, not having Ogie's history with Karl, was more polite. He welcomed Karl, offered him tea, and showed him to a comfortable chair.

Ogie got straight to the point. "OK, you're here. What do you want?"

"Ogie, I want you to know that I truly care about your mother. She has been in desperate need of psychiatric care and is doing much better."

"Karl, I suggest you try that on someone who doesn't know your history with my mother. If that's all you have to say, let's return to the airstrip."

"I'm here because I want to make things better for her and for you and Nina. Has Seth told you what I'm suggesting?"

"Not really."

"Well, I feel that Nicole has made enough progress that it would help her if she could be with you and Nina. She hasn't seen either of you for years and she has been desperate to be reunited. I know she hasn't been happy with me, having been in the dual role of her therapist and her husband. And to be frank, it has worn me out taking care of her and running my clinic and often not being able to separate which role I am in with Nicole—that of therapist or husband. I recognize that there will be costs associated with taking care of Nicole and I am prepared to take care of them."

As Karl was struggling to put a good face on the cruelty he had inflicted on Nicole, Ogie was reading his mind. Ogie saw that the two million dollars Karl had offered was a small portion of his wealth. Even though Ogie was not interested in Karl's money, he wanted to learn more about the extent and source of Karl's riches. He decided to bargain with him. "Karl, you were quick to suggest two million dollars. It makes me think we should receive more."

Ogie saw in Karl's mind that he would leave the country if it looked as if charges would be brought against him. He had established another identity and bought property in a country without reciprocity. He would prefer not to give up the life he had, but if it was that or prison, the choice was easy.

Karl cheered up a little. He was thinking that maybe Ogie would agree to the bribe. *"I will have to be careful in what I offer next,"* he thought. *"If I give in too easily, there will be no limit to what he will ask for."*

"Well, I don't have unlimited resources, but Ogie, what do you think would be a reasonable figure?"

Suddenly Ogie saw an image in Karl's mind. Coins with roosters on them. He recognized them as French 20 franc rooster gold coins. His mother had shown him a few when he was a boy. He concentrated harder and saw what looked like a wall in a cellar. Were the coins in the wall?

Hoping to trigger some answers, Ogie replied: "Karl, if you own that jet, which I assume you do, because it has your name and logo on it, you can readily offer us more. I can't believe your institute is earning that kind of money. How did you become so wealthy?"

Ogie could feel Karl flinch. "I inherited some money," he replied.

Again, Ogie could see in Karl's mind the image of the wall and the rooster coins. This time, he could see that Karl had learned about them from Nicole. They were in a house that was Nicole's family property in France.

Things began to fall into place for Ogie. He remembered stories about his mother's parents. They had been part owners of the French-Italian Citronelli car company. His mother made few references to it because she didn't know that much about it and she preferred not to live in the past.

The company had been taken over by the Germans during World War II. Nicole's parents escaped from France a few days before the German invasion, with the clothes on their backs and a handful of the 20 franc gold coins.

CHAPTER 22
Nina and Red

———

NINA AND RED'S LONG-AWAITED DAY came Saturday. David was off-Island and Red arranged a day off from lobstering. When his mother asked, Red said he was spending the day with Nina. Pearl objected, but Red pointed out that it was time he had a Saturday for himself. She knew he had strong feelings for Nina, and it was pointless to try to stop it. Her last objection was, "But she's your teacher."

As much as Red was looking forward to this day, he had qualms. He was unsure of himself and worried that he would disappoint Nina.

When he arrived at David's, Nina said, "Red, if we're going to be sexually intimate, we must talk it through. It's not the most romantic way, but if we don't, it could be awkward and possibly physically painful for me."

She jumped right into it and asked him about his masturbation and how quickly he came. Wow! He knew they would be talking frankly, but the reality was a surprise. He was slow to answer because it embarrassed him. When he did, Nina replied, "Most women don't come as quickly as that. I know you know that we're built differently, but most boys don't understand how completely different we are sexually. It's a rare girl who has an orgasm from intercourse alone. When I masturbate, I don't have orgasms that fast. Do you know how to help a girl have an orgasm?"

Again her frankness startled him, and he paused before he answered her. While he had heard his friends talk about it, he knew he really didn't know. "I'm not sure."

"Have you read about how sex works for girls?" Red shook his head and Nina went on to say, "Can I tell you about it?"

"Yes, I want to learn from you. I love you and I want to make sex good for you. How can you be so relaxed talking about sex?"

"I don't know. I've read enough to know a lot about how women's bodies work and how frequently they're unsatisfied having sex with men. I don't want to have sex with you if it's painful, awkward, or doesn't give me pleasure. That's why I want to talk it through.

"It may also have a lot to do with how I was brought up. I lived with my Uncle Seth through my traumatic times. When I was feeling depressed, he would ask me questions that made me think about what was really important to me. It helped me see what was bothering me, and deal with sensitive situations frankly.

"I know how strong the sex drive is, and I know many people, if you'll pardon the terrible pun, screw up the sex act from lack of knowledge and not caring deeply enough for each other. I don't want that. It will work better if you know what I want and vice versa. We'll both have more pleasure that way.

"You probably know from your male friends that it's usually a quick in and out and maybe a little oral sex, but the pleasure is short-lived. You can relate it to how long it takes you to have an ejaculation when you masturbate: feels good, and over quickly. My guess is that it's rare when any of the girls having sex with boys have an orgasm."

"Why do they put up with that?"

"Because they don't know they have a choice. They worry that if they fuss, the boys will lose interest. With luck, some girls are taught how to make babies and the anatomy of sexual intercourse. They're almost never taught how to have sexual pleasure or that they are entitled to it. For boys it seems to come—again, pardon the pun—so easily that there isn't much to learn about how their sexual parts work. And the real shame is that the girls' mothers, and their mothers going way back, have felt uncomfortable talking to their daughters about it."

"How do you know this?"

"I know that a lot of younger girls want babies, but are scared and even disgusted by the thought of having a penis inside of them, and sometimes this attitude carries on even when they are older. If their mothers had talked respectfully about the pleasures of sex, the girls would have gotten a different message. The mothers would also have stressed that a penis and labia were useful for beautiful things, and not just for peeing and making babies. You also see this attitude in the affairs men have, and the sex they buy."

"I don't understand."

"Well, how do you think men feel when they have sex with women who are indifferent to sex or would really rather not have sex? They probably don't feel loved and then try to meet their needs elsewhere. I've read that most married women initiate sex maybe once every ten times. The message men get from that isn't a pretty one. They think they aren't cared for, or that their wives don't like sex, or both."

Red then put his arms out for Nina and told her how glad he was that she wasn't like that. It delighted her that he made the first move, because she worried about his shyness, and whether she dampened his enthusiasm by talking about sex so academically. She pulled him against her as her way of agreeing with him. "Let's start by taking a shower," she said.

Nina naked in the shower surpassed the most beautiful art he had ever seen. The curves at her waist, her bottom, and her breasts were exquisite. He had to pinch himself to believe how lucky he was. They washed each other, and Red's excitement was so great that when Nina was washing his genitals he ejaculated. Nina assured him that it was normal, and their intimate time wasn't over.

When they were out of the shower, Nina told Red she wanted to explore his body first, so she could show him how she wanted him to touch her.

While Red was stretched out on the bed, Nina began using her hands and her mouth, checking in with him about how it felt on each part. Even when she was far from his genitals, he found to his surprise that he was excited again. He couldn't believe he could become excited so quickly after just ejaculating.

When her hands came near his penis, he tried to control his trembling. Nina asked him to show her what he wanted, and he took her hand and placed it on his erection. She gently massaged it and then went to another part of his body. When he had calmed down, she resumed gently stroking his testicles, looking to see if it gave him pleasure. Then she took the end of his penis in her mouth and with her tongue stroked the underside just below the ridge a few times. The pleasure was so intense that Red moaned. He knew he couldn't hold out much longer and told Nina so. She paused and lovingly took his hand. "Don't repress the sounds you feel like making—it tells me you like what I'm doing. The noisier you are, the more satisfaction I have. It's a turn on for me."

She resumed licking the underside of his penis, pausing to make sure he didn't ejaculate. He had no idea such intense pleasure was possible. When Nina asked him what he was feeling, he told her, "It's driving me crazy! What happens if I come too soon?"

"It will be the end of the world," she said. When he looked shocked, she grinned impishly, much to his relief. "Remember, there is always the possibility of an encore. Whenever you want, I will take you all the way." He couldn't believe what an impossible choice that was, but the urge to come became so strong that he gave Nina the signal to keep going. She did, with the expected result.

When Nina returned after washing up, Red said it was his turn to explore her body.

"You don't have to use your mouth on my genitals if you're uncomfortable," Nina told him. "There are many other things you can do."

He did the kinds of things Nina had done to him, and as he did, his excitement built up and his enthusiasm increased. When he came close to her vagina, he hesitated and said, "I'm afraid I might hurt you, and I don't know what will please you."

To his relief, Nina asked him, "Would you like me to move your hand?" She took his middle finger, placed it near her clitoris, and started moving it around, and after awhile put it on her clitoris. As her breathing became more intense, he asked her if that was where he could use his mouth. She nodded.

Keeping an eye on her reactions, he licked, sucked, and pushed her clitoris around with his tongue. He had a hard time judging which gave her the most pleasure, and remembering her emphasis on talking things through, he asked her. Her answer was, "Do it all. I don't know yet what is best."

He now understood what Nina meant when she said his reactions turned her on. Her excitement was driving him crazy.

Nina began to tremble and make low moaning sounds. Red was worried and pulled back. She promptly held his head down to continue. She was moving enough that he was having a hard time staying in place. Suddenly she went rigid, which scared him again. Then the tension went out of her body. In an almost religious tone, she said, "Thank you!"

When she opened her eyes and looked at him, she saw he was erect again. With a mischievous grin, she asked, "Would you like to see what happens if you put it inside me?"

At that, Red hesitated. Unschooled in sex as he was, he had some idea of the hymen problem and asked Nina, "If this is your first time, won't it hurt?"

Even though Red's question confirmed what Nina already knew about him as a thoughtful, considerate person, it was comforting. She debated how to answer it, and as was her wont, decided on the truth. "Red, in addition to living a very active life, I have explored my vagina with my fingers. I can't be certain, but I don't think it's going to be a problem if you go about it slowly and watch my reactions."

She brought out ultra-thin condoms and asked Red to lie down while she put one on him. She gave him another to put on top of it. She then squirted some anti-spermicidal gel in her vagina. She climbed on top of Red and guided his penis into her. He let out a sound of pleasure. She began slowly, with uncertain movements. As she found the motion that worked for her, she could tell from Red's expression that it was OK. She tried changing the motion and he nodded. Nina was fascinated by the different sensations.

Holding his condoms in place, she climbed off and suggested they change places. "Gently try a motion that's good for you."

At first, he was terribly tempted to go fast, but realized that if he did, it would be over. He didn't think he would be up for what would be his fourth round, and he couldn't bear the thought that this unbelievable pleasure would stop. It was light years beyond what he could do for himself.

When he realized he was at the point of no return, he let himself go. Nina helped him hold his condoms on while he withdrew.

He couldn't believe it was possible to have so many wonderful sensations in so many ways. He realized that if it had been anyone else, it would have been over in two minutes, and he wouldn't be feeling this much love and gratitude.

It seemed to have worked well for Nina too. Red realized that to be able to give her pleasure was the ultimate satisfaction, both because he loved her, and because her excitement increased his.

From deep inside him came, "Thank you."

Nina was on the edge of tears from the gratitude and love she felt for him and for what had just happened between them. Despite her fears, her first time having sex with a man had been idyllic. What could it be like after they had some experience?

"Nina, I can't believe what just happened. I had so many new feelings I've lost track of how many and what they were. They merged into wonderfulness. You have given me the most incredible gift. Did you have a second orgasm?"

Nina said the one she had was enough and afterwards it was wonderful having Red inside her and experiencing his joy.

"This will sound 'anticlimactic,'" she laughed, "but I'm hungry! Let's eat something." They had been at it for three hours. It seemed as if it had been three minutes.

After lunch, Nina asked Red, "What gave you the most pleasure in what we did this morning?"

"The greatest was when you used your mouth, but being inside you was the most satisfying. It was not only the physical pleasure, but the feeling of oneness, of being a part of you, and of losing myself in you. I wish it had lasted longer. How can I stop myself when I'm so excited?" he wondered aloud.

She replied that they would have to experiment.

"You really did your homework about making sex work for us," he said. "How did you learn so much?"

"Well, like most people, I guess, I'm fascinated by sex. I've read everything I can get my hands on. I especially like books by people like Nancy Friday and other women who described their actual experiences. And then, of course, there are the old standbys of Masters and Johnson and the Kinsey books on male and female sexuality. While they're outdated, they have useful information. I also found a web site called 'Cherry,' where women have frank discussions about their experiences and their preferences. It was one of the best sources, because not only was there factual knowledge, but you got their feelings about what gives them pleasure."

It wasn't easy for Nina to answer Red's question about what was best for her. "Women aren't as focused on one part of our anatomy as men are, yet there are times when my focus was intense. I loved being so close to you and having you inside me because it was you."

She went on to say that there were concentrated pleasures when Red had used his mouth and his fingers. "But, like you, there were so many new sensations I can't sort them out yet. One of the amazing things for me was the pulsing in my vagina after my orgasm."

Being emotionally intimate with Nina was so different from anything Red was used to. It was more than the touching and being physical. There was the verbal frankness about feelings. His parents didn't express their feelings, and he didn't think many people on the Island did.

The more he thought about Nina, the more he realized how different she was. It wasn't just her brilliance. It was everything, from her frankness about sex, to her knowledge about the art world, to her fearlessness in dealing with Renee, his parents, and Russ. It hit him that it was a cultural difference, and he was pleased to identify that. But he also realized that she was probably unusual even in the milieu she grew up in. He felt how lucky he was, and he wondered not only how long it would last, but how long Nina would stay on Megantic.

CHAPTER 23
Sashi

———

Ogie's nervousness anticipating Sashi's arrival was getting to Nina. Nina could not remember when Ogie had ever been edgy with her. Knowing how anxious he was made it easier to take, but it was still tense.

Like Ogie, Nina was looking forward to Sashi's arrival. When they had talked on the telephone a few weeks ago, Nina felt warmth and sisterhood from her. There was a feeling that they were tuned to the same frequency. They had immediately recognized each other's sharpness of mind.

Nina craved intelligent female companionship. Carrie, Seth's wife, had treated her as a child, and another responsibility added to the heavy load she was already carrying with her own children and the always-consuming farm work. While Nina had been embraced by much of the Megantic community, it was a foreign culture. It was hard to find someone to be close to other than Red, and of course Ogie.

Nina felt that anyone Ogie loved would have to be a wonderful person. She looked forward to being able to use Sashi as a sounding board. It would be an opportunity to talk about her relationship with Red with someone besides Ogie, who was uncomfortable knowing the intimate details of her sex life. Another thing Nina hoped to discuss with Sashi was her concern over the extent to which the girls in the school were using her as an adviser. As neutral as Nina tried to be with them, she was worried she might be making mistakes in the counsel she was giving them. She was concerned there could be repercussions in the community about what she suggested to them. Most of all, she longed for a chance to unburden herself with a woman who could understand her on a deep level.

The day of Sashi's arrival, Nina waited impatiently for Ogie to return from the airstrip. She knew deep in her marrow that Sashi was going to be wonderful. When Sashi entered the house, Nina couldn't stop herself from giving her a welcome hug.

Nina sensed immediately that everything was not joyful between Ogie and Sashi. Sashi took Nina's hands in hers to reassure her that she was not the problem.

Nina had found a Julia Child recipe for lobster bisque and served it to them for lunch. She outdid herself in preparing a desert. Much to her pleasure, Sashi asked if all of their meals were as extraordinary as this one. Nina hadn't yet figured out why it was so important to make Sashi happy, but she already knew she didn't want her to leave.

An awkward time came right after lunch, when Ogie asked Nina if it was OK for Sashi to share her room. Nina's facial expression showed surprise, but she quickly made it as neutral as possible. She had assumed that Sashi and Ogie would sleep together. "I'm delighted to have you as my roommate," she managed to say. "It will give me more time with you."

When they were together in Nina's room, Sashi said, "You expected us to be intimate right away, didn't you? It was uncanny, but Ogie knew, before a word was spoken, that I wasn't ready to sleep with him, and he suggested the separation. We've been apart and out of touch for so long, it feels as if we're strangers. He's been living a life of risk and tension, and it has changed him. I need time to get to know this new person."

Because years ago Nina was so young and her contact with Ogie was so intermittent, she didn't really know what was going on with Ogie and Sashi. "Sashi, I want to know about you and Ogie during the time you knew him, before his arrest. What was your relationship like then? How did you meet him? He hasn't told me much about that time and I'm sure he's left out important things."

"Sure," Sashi replied. "I met him in the gallery where I work part time. I couldn't believe the quality of work someone so young could produce. I had studied the Dutch 17th century masters extensively, and there he was making Vermeers, Metsus, and even Rembrandts, better than they did. His compositions were in their style, but it was as if they had matured and become more sophisticated. Somehow he must have gotten his head inside their heads. I can't understand how he did it. He produced paintings in under a month, which, for that kind of work, is the speed of light.

"He was doing this while also teaching full-time. It turned out he was extraordinarily good at teaching as well. Parents said things like, 'He works magic on the children. He seems to know exactly what their difficulties are and then solves them. There are children I've known since they were in kindergarten who were often out of control, and they behave in his class. My son never really grasped math, and now he's doing advanced math and begging for more.'"

"I was attracted to him, even though I didn't want to be. I felt as if he knew my innermost secrets."

That told Nina that Ogie's mind reading skills existed then, and that Sashi was unaware of his ability.

"He was thoughtful of everyone he had dealings with," Sashi said, "and made them feel he cared about them. He didn't defer to anyone, but treated everyone with the same dignity.

"I was living a very contented life not having intimate relationships. I wasn't looking for one, and if the truth be told, I was avoiding them. I had had some unfortunate experiences. My feelings for him surprised me. I was hoping he would pay more attention to me, and yet when he did, I turned him down. At first I thought he was good looking and had a great deal of charm, but I assumed that for all his accomplishments, he was just a pretty boy. His reaction to being turned down was to continue to be as wonderfully decent and good-natured as ever."

Nina wanted to know how it changed for Sashi.

"I came to see the man underneath," Sashi explained. "As we worked together, I could tell he saw beyond my attractiveness to my seriousness and competence. I never had the feeling he wanted me for my body. I don't know how to explain that, because I knew he wasn't sexless or gay. I came to be more and more drawn—pardon the art pun—to him, and began to hope he would ask me out again. Because he didn't, I finally did, and he surprised me by asking, 'What changed your mind?' It was one of the rare times I was at a loss for words!

"We went out for several months and became close friends. He talked about his teaching, and we covered the art world, from cave drawings to Pavel Tchelitchew to children's art. We discussed intimate details of our lives, but we always separated at the end of the evening. He knew I couldn't say much about my work in intelligence, so he would only ask how I was feeling about it. He never suggested sex or even implied it in his actions and conversation.

"After a few months, we still weren't even kissing good night. I wanted more, but I was afraid to initiate something. I finally screwed up the courage to ask him if he would like us to be lovers. And again, he asked me 'Why?' That was a first for me. I'd never known a man who wouldn't jump at that.

"I told him that I felt I knew him well enough to trust him emotionally and in other ways. The answer satisfied him, but I had the feeling he already knew what I was thinking. I challenged him about that. I told him I sensed he knew that I was ready to go further, so why hadn't he initiated it? His answer surprised me. He said, 'I was afraid I would lose you if I made a pass.' He seemed so competent in so many ways, and yet he was timid.

"Your brother is one unusual human being, and I'm glad I have the chance to renew my relationship with him. But I have to say, he spooks me, because he seems to know what I'm thinking before I tell him. It must be the quality that made him such a successful teacher. What is it like living with him?"

Nina knew exactly what Sashi was talking about, but was reluctant to say anything, for fear she would inadvertently tell about Ogie's mind reading. If Sashi was going to learn of it, it should come from Ogie. "There is no question that he is very perceptive and at times he spooks me with what he knows about me. I've reminded him I'm old enough to take care of myself and he doesn't need to micromanage me, and mostly he has stopped doing it."

"OK, Nina, I've told you about my personal life. Now tell me about yours. I gather from something Ogie said at the table that Red is an important part of your life. What's he like?"

"You'll meet him soon and have a chance to see for yourself. He's coming over this afternoon."

"No, no, no, you can't get away with that. I want to hear about him from you. How you got started with him, what attracted you to him, and vice versa. I've shared things with you about my sex life with your brother. You can do no less. Have you slept with him? And if so, what's Ogie's reaction to that? What was your reaction to it? Was he your first?"

"Wait," Nina said. She wanted to know more about the history and extent of her brother's mind reading abilities, and Sashi seemed like her only and best possible source. With her heart in her mouth, she said, "Before I answer, I'm going to risk asking you a very personal question. What was it like sleeping with my brother?"

"Nina, you're right, it is too personal, but I will answer you anyway. He was the same in bed as he was the rest of the time, although more so. Thoughtful, considerate, always ready to change what he was doing to suit me. I've described his anticipating my reactions as uncanny, and when we had sex, he carried it further. It was rare when I had to use words or motions to guide him because he seemed to know what I wanted before I did. It was as if his only goal was to please me. I was having so much pleasure that I would forget about his needs and finally took to asking him what he would like. He convinced me that seeing my pleasure was the ultimate pleasure for him.

"Nina, do you sense his awareness of others' feelings too, or is it my imagination? It's partly why I've been reluctant to commit whole-heartedly to him, because while it's beautiful to be with him, there is something scary about it."

Nina blanched, and thought quickly. "I think you shouldn't be afraid to talk to him about it."

"Yes, I think you're right," Sashi replied.

"OK, now tell me about Red."

Nina proceeded to tell Sashi everything that had happened with Red.

Sashi was impressed. "Nina, how did you manage to organize your first experience so completely? I doubt many girls have much plea-sure their first few times, and you pulled it off beautifully. I'm jealous that you had the smarts to do that. I was very careful my first time, but I didn't have the pleasure you had. I even had mixed feelings about doing it again. It wasn't until I was with Ogie that I enjoyed sex."

They talked about the incredible strength of the human sex drive. When Nina thought about the politicians and other famous people who get in trouble because of their sexual escapades, she realized that was only the tip of the iceberg in what went on with people. How powerful that drive must be if people are prepared to risk their careers and their money.

Sashi was impressed by Nina's perceptiveness and ability to bring logic to such a hormonally driven subject.

Sashi wanted to know how Nina learned to teach. Nina told her how miserable she'd been when she was in school. She'd often thought of ways she could teach better than her teachers. She didn't realize that what was for her a diversion during dull classes would be one of the most useful things she could have done to prepare herself for teaching. An important thing she'd learned as a student was to use the material itself to involve students as the way to keep order. After she'd accepted Renee's invitation to teach French, she'd spent two sixteen-hour days planning her first lesson. For the rest of that week, she'd stayed up until three o'clock each morning working on the next day's plans.

But the effort was worth it. The high that came when she was teaching made her feel as if she owned the world. It was hard to believe the enthusiasm of her students. She had to force herself to keep her feet solidly planted on the linoleum because she didn't want to convey arrogance to her students or anyone else.

CHAPTER 24

Sashi

———

RED WAS NERVOUS ABOUT MEETING Sashi because Nina had told him how sophisticated she was. Sashi had been forewarned about Red's penchant for being intimidated by people "from away," so she put him at ease by asking about lobstering, life on the Island, and Nina.

The questions about Nina caused him to blush. He blushed even deeper after she told him that Nina couldn't stop talking about how thoughtful and gentle he was.

Sashi gave Red her full attention to overcome his shyness. He was swallowed up by her eyes and her charm and soon made the conversion from shy to talkative.

Once he got started, he asked more questions than Sashi had the breath to answer about her work at le Brun's gallery. What kind of people buy handmade copies of paintings? Why did people want them, or new paintings in the style of Vermeer? Why were Ogie's paintings so valuable when most other watercolors weren't? How could one gallery market such different kinds of art? Were all the paintings on consignment, and if they weren't, what was the arrangement with the artist? Could people buy on time? How did Sashi learn to do the work in the gallery? Did she work on commission? He was still going when Sashi said, "Whew, that's enough for now!" at which point Red turned the color of his hair and realized he had been going non-stop and apologized to Sashi. Sashi had been so attentive to Red that it had encouraged his nonstop questions. None of them had ever seen him so animated before.

When Sashi had a moment alone with Nina, she said, "He wants to know everything! It's obvious he's learned a good deal from you and Ogie and hasn't forgotten a thing. My guess is that in his own milieu, he isn't nearly as talkative. You've given him a glimpse of a new world and its culture."

After Red left, Sashi asked to see Ogie's current work. She stopped when she saw Melanie Wright's copy of Ogie's painting. "It's structured in your style but obviously not done by you," she said. "That's what Bartlett must have been talking about. When he came to the gallery and grilled me about you, he didn't believe me when I told him how little I knew about what you were doing. He wanted to know if the gallery had seen or been dealing in any counterfeit Ogies."

"What else did he want from you?"

"He assumed we'd been in touch throughout your time incognito. He insisted on me going to dinner with him. He turned his charm on high and hinted that things could go much better for you if I cooperated with him.

"He talked around the subject of who you had gotten to know in Karl's sanitarium. He was particularly interested to know if you had told me anything about that. He also hinted that he could get me a very senior position on the White House intelligence Staff if I wanted it. He wasn't happy when I told him I wasn't interested."

CHAPTER 25

Nina

———

SASHI STOPPED BY NINA'S CLASSROOM after school. As she entered, she overheard a student asking Nina, "What if he won't do it?" The student hastily excused herself when she saw Sashi come in. As she was leaving, Nina asked her student to think about what she really wanted, and told her they could talk about it the next day.

Sashi's curiosity was piqued and she asked Nina what it was that 'he' might not do. Nina hesitated before she answered. She explained that her student had asked for advice about her boyfriend. "She feels her boyfriend is taking her for granted and doesn't care about her feelings. She says he won't take any suggestions about what they do when they have sex. She wants him to go slowly and make sure she has pleasure. He says he will, but then just satisfies himself. She wants to give him pleasure, but for her, it's more pain and nuisance than anything.

"Many of the girls feel the boys they are with now are the ones they will marry. They can't see opportunities to hook up with other boys because there aren't that many boys on Megantic. They feel it's now or never," Nina continued.

"I ask the girls to look hard inside themselves to find out what are the most important things in their lives now, and five and ten years from now. I ask them if they think the way their boyfriends are treating them will change in time. Many of them, when they think hard about it, realize that if they don't do something, there won't be any change."

Sashi was curious about why the girls were coming to Nina for advice.

"I have good relationships with them," Nina said. "They feel comfortable with me and they can tell I care about them. While Red and I have tried to be discreet about our relationship, they sense it, and they see that he and I are both happy. One girl told me that when she has sex with her boyfriend, he still doesn't seem happy."

"What did you tell her?"

"I suggested she tell him, 'No more sex until we talk about how to make it work better for me and for you.' Most of these boys can't think beyond the immediacy of getting it off. They don't have any idea it's possible to extend their pleasure, and they think girls work the same way they do. They don't understand there are differences."

Sashi wondered if some of that might be unique to being on a small island, but thought much of our society was the same. "I read recently that nearly half of a poll of girls fourteen to eighteen said they had never discussed sex with their parents, while only six percent of their parents said they had never discussed sex with their children. The parents think if they've told their girls 'the penis in the vagina produces babies,' they've covered it. Actually, all they've done is told about biology and not about sexuality. It speaks volumes about our society's difficulties dealing with sexuality. It's a shame, because both sexes are missing out. I'm certain, and the polls support this, that almost no women tell their daughters what pleasure their clitoris can give them. And that gives girls the message that it's not something that should be talked about. While they may find their clitoris themselves, there's something odd or wrong about it because it's 'unmentionable.' And I'll bet that few parents tell their boys that there can be more to it than an ejaculation."

Sashi went on, "It requires as good a sense of self to insist on having pleasurable sex as it does to refuse sex because it wouldn't feel right to do it."

Nina agreed. "Those are the problems I'm dealing with. These girls don't know what they don't know, and it's hard for me to know where to begin. It's both an ignorance of their own biology, and a lack of sexual self-esteem. I assume it's generational, and how do you break that cycle?"

"Exactly. How can they possibly know change is needed if this is the culture, and it has been modeled this way by their parents? I'm certain that if you trace generation after generation of girls and mothers, there'd be an unbroken chain of no one mentioning what the clitoris does, dating back to Eve.

"So what happens if some of the parents find out what you've been telling their daughters?"

Nina said three parents had already talked with her. One of them complained and asked how her daughter was going to get married if she didn't get pregnant, because Nina had provided her daughter with condoms. Another told Nina she should be telling her daughter no sex before marriage.

The third parent said her daughter had become more sure of herself and more mature. It was a dramatic difference, and she asked her daughter what happened. The daughter clammed up and wouldn't say anything. The mother asked Nina if she knew of anything that would account for it. Nina felt weird counseling the mother of a sixteen-year-old, and the mother saw the irony as well. Nina was reluctant to tell her, because of the trust the daughter had placed in her. Instead, she told the girl's mother they'd had serious conversations and to ask her daughter what it was about.

"I advised her to tell her daughter how pleased she was with the difference in her, and to encourage her daughter to keep doing whatever it was she was doing. I also stressed that she treat positively anything her daughter told her about why she'd changed. I was afraid the mother would be angry if she learned what I had discussed with her daughter. I dreaded the mother coming back to see me.

"But she came back to thank me. She told me what a relief it was I encouraged her daughter to take her sexuality seriously. She was particularly happy that I emphasized that if a boy didn't plan birth control with her, it was an indication that he didn't really care about her. She said that if she had tried to say those things to her daughter, it would be just another harangue, with the added problem of embarrassment, and her daughter wouldn't listen."

Sashi advised Nina to tell her principal what was going on. "He sounds like a sensible person, and it's only fair for him to know ahead of time what might cause trouble."

CHAPTER 26

Renee

———

NINA PEEKED INTO RENEE'S OFFICE, and in reply to his look of inquiry, she told him she wanted to talk about sex. He blanched at her question, then replied, "Do you think this is the time or place for it?"

Nina had grown comfortable with Renee. She knew she could be frank and even tease him a little. She said that after his comments to her about sex with Red, it was only fair she should make him uncomfortable.

He visibly relaxed and invited her into his office. "OK, now that you have my interest, what can I do for you?"

Nina explained that many of the girls in her classes were talking to her about the problems they were having with their boyfriends.

"What are you telling them?"

"Do you want to hear the long or the short version?"

"Let's start with the short version."

"Lysistrata with conditions."

"That sounds like good advice, depending upon the conditions. Let's hear the long version."

Nina recapitulated her earlier conversation with Sashi, and for a few moments Renee was quiet as a church mouse. When he'd found his voice, he said, "Your genius is not restricted to French, math, and captivating your students. It also lies in creating unspeakable troubles. Now I understand some rumors I heard and discounted, from both parents and students.

"One was that having someone so young teaching our students might not set a good moral tone. The other was by being who you are, you were making the girls feel so good about themselves that they're not having as much sex with their boyfriends. I didn't take either one seriously until you walked in. I realize that now is one of the rare times in my life when I would rather not think about sex."

"Here are my thoughts," he said at last. "I'm glad you're not conducting a school-sponsored class in sex education. Your being a temporary employee means I don't have to worry about the community reaction for long. How could I stop a teacher from answering her students' questions in private? Isn't a sixteen-year-old entitled to talk to other sixteen-year-olds?"

Renee said he thought the girls were benefitting from Nina's talks with them, and he was happy to be forewarned about what she was doing. He also commented about the irony that teaching girls how to get more sexual pleasure resulted in their having less sex, because they were learning to demand more than "slam, bam, thank you ma'am." Now it was Nina's turn to blanch. Sometimes Renee had to remind himself that she was only sixteen. He was glad she had felt comfortable enough to let him know what was happening.

Nina felt relieved after talking with Renee. He was a down-to-earth, practical guy who saw things realistically. No wonder he'd lasted here so long. She was grateful to him for having given her the opportunity to teach. It was unlikely it could have happened any place else, considering her age and lack of credentials.

Thinking about how it couldn't continue was depressing. She knew she would have to leave in the not too distant future, for college and other reasons. Doing sex counseling could have her run off the Island even sooner.

In the meantime, she wrestled with the problem of how to help Christine. Even though it was confidential, she decided Red might have some insight about Christine's boyfriend, Cal, that could be helpful. She was heartened to hear that Cal had already complained to Red about Christine, "Not giving him any." That would give Red entree to discuss it further with him.

After she and Red had talked about it, Red got a glint in his eye and said, "That reminds me of something."

"What could that be?" Nina put her right palm on her chest with her fingers spread and her eyes wide and innocent. She could play the ingénue when it was called for. Red had never seen her in that role, and it made her more irresistible than ever.

Catching on, he joined the game, bowed and swept his right hand from left to right, and said, "Milady, methinks you protest overly much."

"I will ignore the misquote and agree with the sentiment. Tell me what you are reminded of."

Red told Nina how wonderful the aftertaste was from their time at David's. He'd been playing it over in his head. The richness of it was still there, but it was fading. He said the memory needed renewing and was wondering if Nina felt the same way. She asked him was he certain their time hadn't been painful for him because she didn't want him sacrificing himself for her. He couldn't believe she was serious but he couldn't be certain until he saw the glint in her eyes.

He said, "I think a little sacrifice would be good for my soul. If you are prepared to contribute to the betterment of my spiritual life, I would be much obliged."

"Hmm, I wonder if it would also better mine," she mused. "Let's find out."

Pearl

———

ONE OF PEARL'S JOBS WAS to pick up the school mail at the post office. This morning she didn't have her car and asked Nina if she could use Ogie's. Nina told her to get the keys out of her purse. While looking for the keys, Pearl found a box of condoms. Even though she had suspected that Nina and Red might be having sex, she had successfully denied it. She knew Red and Nina had a date after school, and she knew Red was excited about it. Finding the condoms made it impossible for her to pretend their relationship was platonic. During their lunch hour, Pearl asked Nina if they could talk privately. Pearl loathed the idea of confronting Nina, and was nervous about discussing her son's sex life with her, but felt she had no choice.

Once they were alone, Pearl found herself stammering, rather than being righteous. She could not understand how this sixteen-year-old girl had the poise and dignity of a mature woman. From the first, Nina, without intending to, had intimidated Pearl, while at the same time being completely friendly and solicitous. When Nina gave you her attention, you felt as if you were the most important person in the world and that she thought your every word was vital. It was why her students came to adore her. While Pearl felt the warmth of Nina's personality, she also felt like a child waiting for her teacher's permission.

She was never comfortable talking about sex, and now she had to ask Nina if she was having sex with her boy. She knew it was happening. What could she say if Nina denied it, or for that matter, if she acknowledged it? Momentarily she thought of asking her husband to talk with Red, but rejected it. She wasn't certain how he would feel. He might even be proud of Red.

Then it came to her. She would talk to Renee. He would know what to do. He might even agree to talk with Red and Nina.

What could she tell Nina now that she was alone with her? She had to think of something. She decided to simply talk about the condoms. She suspected that Nina gave them to the girls who came to talk to her. She didn't know how she felt about what Nina did with the girls. It was good she helped them avoid pregnancy, but wasn't Nina encouraging them to have sex? She'd read that where there were sex education programs with birth control information, the frequency of teen pregnancies and maybe even teen sex was down, but she had a hard time believing it.

"Nina, could you tell me about the conversations you have with the girls who come to see you privately? Is that why you have those things in your purse?"

"Pearl, would you be more comfortable not knowing that? I will tell you about it if you want me to."

Pearl had a hard time deciding. But she was curious, and asked Nina to tell her.

"The girls tell me I'm the first person to take their worries about boys seriously. I think they sense that things work well between Red and me, and they want to know how I manage it."

"Do you really give them those things? And why do you do it?"

"I do. This may be hard to understand. I give them condoms in order for them to get the boys to treat them better."

Pearl didn't understand, and Nina explained that many of the boys only cared about sex and had no concern about the consequences. "They don't worry about the girls' feelings or the possibility of pregnancy. I tell the girls that if they really want to change things, they have to stand up for themselves. I explain that if they insist on using condoms, it gives them the opening to insist on being treated with respect. I stress that if the boys don't care about planning sex, the message is that they don't care about the girls. I ask them if they really want to have sex with boys who don't care about them. I think it sobers them. I know there have been situations where the boys were resistant to talking and the girls said, 'Then I won't sleep with you.'"

Then it slipped out before Pearl could stop herself. "And do you use those things?"

Nina looked directly at Pearl. "Do I use them with Red? Is that what you're asking me?"

Pearl turned lobster colored and both whispered and stammered, "Yes."

Nina took her hand, and with a sympathetic voice looked into her face and said, "I can't answer that. It's Red's private business. If he wants to tell you, that's up to him."

Pearl knew there was no way she would be able to ask Red that question. And she also knew, although not for sure, that Nina had just answered it. It was possible that all they were doing was making out, but much as she wanted to believe that, she couldn't.

Pearl went to see Renee that afternoon. Pearl could not believe how Renee turned her head around. She had gone to him seeking sympathy, comfort, and reinforcement for her concerns about Red and Nina having sex. After an exhausting two-hour discussion, and much to her disbelief, she was relating to them and happy for them. How had Renee done that? His questions had been impossibly personal, and yet she couldn't object to one of them. After she'd delivered her tirade about the awfulness and, yes, sinfulness of sixteen-year-olds having sex with each other, he asked her, "Who is being damaged, and how?"

"It's wrong," she began. "They're not married. Nina is his teacher. What does it say to the other girls? What happens if she gets pregnant? What will people think? What if Red catches a disease? Will he go to hell? I don't want to raise another child."

Renee asked her to take one question at a time. "Which one is the most important?"

This stumped Pearl and made her sort through the river of her anger. "But, but, but..." she said, and trailed off.

Renee intruded with the question, "How smart do you think Nina is?" Pearl said she couldn't think of anyone smarter.

He followed up with, "Do you think she wants to have a child?"

"I know she doesn't, at least not yet."

"Do you think she knows how babies are made?"

"Of course she does. She gives the girls condoms." After that, a dawning came to her and she said, "OK, so she won't give me a grandchild. But there are other problems."

Renee asked her to pick the next one, and when she couldn't decide, he asked her, "Can you tell me who will be hurt, and how, by their activity?" When Pearl didn't answer, he asked her, "How many of our high school students have had sex with each other?"

"Most," she replied.

"Are they all going to hell?"

"Renee, you're being ridiculous."

"So all of them are exempt from hell except Red? Do I understand you correctly?" His tone was gentle.

Pearl put her head in her hands and said nothing.

Renee looked at her intensely. "Do you think you're going to hell?"

"Why are you asking that? We're talking about the teenagers."

"Well," Renee continued, "if I remember correctly, there was a time when you..."

With embarrassment, Pearl said, "Yes of course. You knew me then and helped me feel it wasn't the end of the world."

"What do you think of the result?"

"I'm proud of him. You know how bright he is, and how devoted he is to us and his grandfather."

"He is a good human being. What a shame he's going to hell."

"Renee, you're teasing me."

"Who suggested he's going to hell?" Renee chided. "OK, Pearl, let's hear your other reasons for being upset."

"The example that Nina sets for the other girls."

"Is she harming the girls by helping them stand up to their boy-friends and make them use condoms? Is it awful that this year we will have fewer teenage pregnancies? Do you think she's just using Red to gratify her ego and as a badge of her power? Is she planning to trap him into marriage?"

Renee continued gently but with what felt like an onslaught to Pearl, "Is she a bad influence on him by stretching his mind to learn about art and history and French? Is she flaunting her sexuality? Is she flirting and teasing other boys? Is she saying things to undermine Red's relationship with his family? Is it because she insists on using birth control? Could it be that by modeling and counseling the girls to feel good about themselves and not let the boys disrespect them, she is dangerous?"

Pearl shook her head no to every question. But there was some-thing about her reaction to his last question that gave Renee the feeling he had stirred something up in Pearl. He asked her, "Is there something I'm missing about her bad example for the girls? If so, I need to know, in order to ensure that it stops."

"Renee, you think too fast for me. I can't disagree with anything you've said, but it still doesn't feel right."

"OK, that's understandable. After all, he is your son. Try to describe what it is that unsettles you."

"Well, when I was young, we were ashamed of what we were doing and tried to hide it. It's not as if they're boasting about it, or even talk-ing about it, but they don't seem embarrassed or self-conscious. They seem proud."

"Would it make you feel better if they concealed it?"

Pearl felt that Renee turned everything upside down. "I see what you mean, but I'm still stuck with my feelings about it."

"Fair enough. You are entitled to your feelings. What do you want to do with them, and what do you think you should do with them?"

"I want to ground Red and forbid him from seeing Nina."

"OK. Can you tell me the details of how a day will go if you do that? Start with Red leaving the house to go to school in the morning, assuming you're going to let him. Is he going to skip going to French? How about lobstering? Are you going to ask Russ not to let Nina on his boat, or are you going to deprive Russ of Red's help?"

All of his questioning was in gentle tones. Renee liked and respected Pearl, and she knew it. It was why she felt comfortable pouring out her insides to him. That she did not always agree with him did not alter her admiration.

She knew he was right. There was nothing she could do to stop what was going on between Red and Nina without making everyone's lives miserable, including her own. The more she thought about it, the more she realized that Red was lucky to have a girlfriend who was decent, kind, thoughtful, and cared about him. She knew other girls who she would dread him hooking up with. Some of them would want to trap him into marriage. Some would be after him for the family money, because in this small community, people knew what each other's lobster hauls were, and how they spent their money. Red's family had a reputation for saving, and not splurging on expensive, unnecessary things.

Pearl couldn't believe that at the end of her session with Renee, she was feeling grateful for Nina and Red's relationship. Her new depressing thought was that sooner or later, Nina would leave Megantic to pursue her education. What would happen to Red?

CHAPTER 28
Karl

———

"YOUR SHITTY RELATIVE IS ABOUT to land again. He declared an emergency five minutes out. How do you want to handle him this time?" Roger said on the phone to Ogie.

"I guess we don't have much choice. He is an ugly surprise. I hoped I had seen the last of him. Let's see what he wants."

By the time Ogie arrived at the airstrip, Karl's plane was taxiing to the shack. He watched the steps being lowered and saw a woman limping down them. Every step was a struggle and he had to force himself to watch as she slowly moved her hands down the rail to support herself with each step she took. What the hell was Karl up to with this stunt? And then as he came closer and looked more intensely, he realized it was his mother. His knees started to give way and he struggled to straighten them and rush toward her. He had not seen her in seven years because Karl had kept her incommunicado. He knew that regardless of the bargain Karl intended to make, he would not let her go back with him.

He approached his mother slowly because he didn't want to scare her and he didn't know whether she would recognize him. There was no telling what condition Karl had her in. He could see that her breathing was hard and labored as he got closer to her. When she came down the last step, he took her free hand and her upper arm to support her. Her slow turn to look at him was a stab wound. He could see the effects of the drugging she had undergone for years in her eyes

192

and her movements. Seeing her this way, combined with his feelings of guilt at letting this happen to her, Ogie was barely able to support himself, let alone his mother.

The beginning of her smile of recognition gradually became pronounced. Without a word she let go of the rail and pulled Ogie toward her with her free hand. He was appalled at the weakness of her arms and the wateriness of her eyes. And yet in spite of it, he could see the strong and gentle look of his mother. He read her thoughts, *"This is the last of Karl. Even if Karl changes his mind, I know Ogie won't let me go with him."*

It was a relief for Ogie to know Karl had decided to turn his mother loose. Karl must be desperate if he brought her here without an assured quid pro quo. He must have known that Ogie would not let Nicole go again, regardless of the negotiations they might make. That Karl had not appeared yet was the only thoughtful thing he had ever seen him do. He did not look forward to seeing him.

Ogie could see his mother's thinking was diffuse and saw her struggling to concentrate. She was recovering from the drugs Karl had to have stopped a few days ago. What he saw of her thoughts confirmed his worst fears about what Karl had been doing to her. How the courts could have sided with Karl when they returned her to him he couldn't understand. It was so plain he had treated her cruelly and the only explanation he had come up with was Karl had bribed someone to get the verdict he wanted. Considering the amount of money he had offered and ownership of that jet, his bribes must have been huge.

What next? How can I arrange a good recovery for my mother? He knew Nina would throw herself into it and would be a godsend. Karl still hadn't appeared. He wondered what was keeping him from insisting on Ogie helping him out if it came to his being on trial. He guided his mother to the car. He called Nina to warn her what was happening, worrying that it might overwhelm her if they just appeared.

Karl came out of the plane as he was getting ready to go and motioned to Ogie to join him. He did, with reluctance. Karl said, "I know you have to get Nicole to your house, but I must speak with you. Can you get permission for me to stay here for one or two nights? Can we talk tomorrow? It is urgent." Ogie agreed and said he would arrange for permission and asked if there were sufficient sleeping arrangements and food aboard for Karl and his copilot.

As he was leaving, Ogie asked Roger, "Please ask Henry if they can spend a night or two here and let Karl know."

"For someone who can't stand that bastard, you are very obliging."

"Roger, there is more to it. I don't want him here, but I'll explain later. It's important I get my mother home and I talk with Karl. The talk can wait because my mother needs my full attention now."

When they arrived at the house, Nina began shaking and had a hard time getting words out. She hadn't seen her mother for seven years. Her limbs went rigid and she consciously tried to ease them. Her body was reacting to the tension she had been carrying. It was a revelation to her that her body would mirror so closely what went on in her psyche. She knew from the little Ogie had told her on the phone that her mother was in bad shape, but to see her straining to walk was too much. She had to pull herself together. As she came close to Nicole, she saw the same loving smile of recognition Ogie experienced. Except this time there were tears on her mother's face, which triggered more shaking and uncontrollable paroxysms and tears in Nina. Then her mother did something that tore Nina apart. She took Nina in her arms, and with shaking hands patted Nina's back. In a halting, barely audible voice, she said, "My baby." Nina became a pool of liquid. She had held herself together all these years without her mother. It was the first time in a very long time that she could remember that she could let herself go completely. It would awhile before she would lose the constant tension she had been under.

Ogie asked his mother what she would like to do first. "To eat, to sleep, to talk?"

Nicole took a full minute to reply, which was hours for Ogie and Nina.

She said, "Let's sit at the table and have some tea." As they were drinking their tea, Nicole said, "There is too much to say. It will take us years to talk it through. We have time. Tell me about your lives. First Nina, because you were so young when we separated. I am most worried about you."

Ogie answered before Nina could get a word in because Nina was so shaken she could barely speak. Ogie told his mother of the fantastic job Nina had been doing teaching math and French and how her students adored her and how many of the parents thought she could walk on water.

Nicole demonstrated, in spite of the drugs still in her system, that she could be on top of things when she asked Nina, "How can you be teaching at sixteen? And if you are teaching, who are the boys you can go out with?" Nina told her she had already had a relationship before she started teaching. "What's he like?" Nicole asked.

Again, Ogie answered for Nina, who was still a quivering puddle and in any case would give such a biased description of Red that Nicole might not believe it. He described Red so positively that Nicole replied, "No one is that good. That's Ogie's view. What's your view, Nina?"

Nina had calmed down enough to say, "Ogie understated it. Seriously, Red could not be more thoughtful, kind, and intelligent. And he is very respectful of all of us. He's a great student. The principal has him researching quantum mechanics and doing advanced courses on an individual basis. He works as a sternman on a lobster boat with his grandfather, and the two of them have a strong and loving relationship. I feel privileged to be able to work with them." Nina explained she had worked with Red and his grandfather before he became her student. "And when his grandfather has to be on the mainland, I work as Red's sternman. He is one of my best students in French."

Nicole said with a twinkle in her eye that she would check on it herself when she met him. That twinkle brought great relief to Ogie and Nina. She said she would like to go to bed. Ogie thought it would be best if she shared the room with Nina and asked Nina to move Sashi's things into his room, which raised Nina's eyebrows. He said to her, "Enough, little sister. I will sleep in the studio."

Nina could not think of what she could do to make things better for her mother. She helped her unpack. It was impossible for her to interpret the look on her mother's face. It appeared as if it was a combination of joy and sorrow, but there was more. Nina was desperate to ease her pain and couldn't think of how until Nicole invited her to sit down next to her on the bed. Nicole took Nina's hands in a gentle but firm grip and said, "Please stay with me. I need you here. No one has touched me other than to inject awful things in a very long time, and I long for touch." And then she lay down on her side. Nina laid down behind her in spoon fashion.

For Nina, the years of emotional deprivation began to fade. The tension was oozing out of her body. She could feel her mother's tightness and was hoping their lying together would have the same effect on her. They both fell asleep and it was six hours before Nina woke. Her mother was still asleep. Nina got up to go to the bathroom and get something to eat. She told Ogie what had happened and that she was going to lie down with her mother again. "Isn't Red coming by soon?" he asked her.

"Please call him for me and tell him I apologize and I will be in touch with him. Mom needs me and I need her and this is the only way I can think of to be of help to her."

Nicole woke sixteen hours later and felt reborn. Her head felt closer to normal. For all these years, it had been someone else's head. When she realized how long she had been sleeping, she asked Nina, "Have you been here the whole time? How were you able to do that? Your body must have absorbed the poisons in me. Are you OK?"

For Nina to hear what her mother said was a gift from the creator. The satisfaction of knowing how much better her mother felt poured into her marrow. Her reunion with Ogie had felt like that, but this was many times more. She couldn't see how anything else in her life could ever give her this feeling of goodness. It was so much more than joy.

"I didn't think I would ever again have a head that wasn't polluted, fuzzy, and awful. I want to know how you got Karl to release me. What could you have possibly done to move that torturer?"

Nina told her it was a long and complex story. "Ogie maneuvered someone high in the government to get himself pardoned and possibly exonerated and the results made it clear that Karl was the villain of the piece. And once the first pieces of Ogie's reprieve had fallen into place, Karl realized he was threatened and wanted to bribe Ogie and Seth to cover up for him. Ogie's only condition to Karl was your freedom and he never promised Karl that he would help him even if he freed you. Karl is still here and Ogie has gone to talk with him."

Ogie thought joining a pride of hungry lions might be less dangerous and painful than talking with Karl. The thought that Karl had probably killed his father was not far from his mind. And of course that he had held his mother a prisoner and made her a zombie made him feel as if he was going to enter a flowing sewer line.

The first thing Karl did when Ogie came into the passenger compartment of Karl's plane was to hand him a checkbook and forms. He explained that this was a checkbook on an account he had set up for Nicole. Four million dollars had been deposited in it. He reminded Ogie that he had said he would provide two million to him and Nicole and another two million to Seth. The understanding was that neither he nor Seth would testify against him should there be a trial. "I've done it this way because there is no tax on money transferred between husband and wife. Your mother will have to sign the forms to activate the account and she can give money to Seth and you and Nina as she chooses."

Ogie's response was he would have talk with his mother to see if she wanted to accept the money. He asked Karl where the funds came from. He wanted to know because his mother might feel dealing with that money would make her sick. He could read Karl felt strongly about not wanting to answer, which made Ogie more curious. Karl's thinking was disjointed. Nicole's grandparents had been involved in the Citronelli automobile company. They had seen WWII coming and had converted much of their stock to cash and then to gold in the form of 20 franc French rooster gold coins. These had been hidden in several different places on the grounds and in the basements of the houses on their estate in France. Karl had learned of this through a casual and joking reference Nicole had made. She didn't believe the money was there, but Karl had taken it seriously and had gone to France to see for himself. Diligent searching and the use of expensive metal detectors enabled him to find part of the hoard. He had done it secretively, when no one else was around. He realized that he would have to have Nicole's cooperation to retrieve the rest of it because she had inherited part ownership of the estate. This motivated him to find a way to become closer to Nicole. Then Karl stopped that train of thought and told Ogie he wanted assurances that Ogie at least would not testify against him. Ogie said, "I need to think about this and I must talk to my mother before I agree to anything. I will talk with you again tomorrow."

Karl said he didn't have much time and had to settle things promptly. While saying that, Ogie read in Karl's mind that he had many of the French gold coins on the plane. He was preparing to flee the country. The more impatient Karl became, the easier it was to read his mind and he came to see where the coins were stashed. Karl wasn't entitled to this money. While Karl was guilty of horrific crimes, he didn't want to be the person who turned him in, nor did he want to testify against him. Protecting Nina, escaping from the law, finding a way to live, and struggling to bring peacefulness into his life were things he didn't want to risk having to re-live. It had taken a great deal out of him to put his life together after Karl had torn it to shreds. On the other hand, he didn't feel Karl should keep what he had stolen. He felt that his mother had the right to the money.

Ogie suggested Henry collect a landing fee from Karl and keep him and his copilot busy filling out paperwork. Henry was always happy to collect landing fees but didn't always do it. It depended on how the owner of the plane handled himself as to whether he collected a fee. Keeping them busy with paperwork enabled Ogie to board the plane and find the gold coins. Some of them were in locked compartments but a good deal weren't. He had the map in his head of where it was from having read Karl's mind. He was in and out of the plane within five minutes with six sacks that must have weighed a total of 75 pounds. He stashed them in his car. He had no idea of what he would do with the gold. While it was a huge amount of money, he was certain that it was a small proportion of what Karl had recovered from the estate in France. Once again, he was faced with the problem of a ten thousand dollar reporting limit. One benefit he was certain of was that the loss would handicap Karl. There was poetic justice in that Karl had stolen the money from the family and had torn into shreds the lives of at least three of them to do it. While Karl must have a great deal left and who knows what in bank accounts, the loss of some of the gold might handicap him.

Ogie's quandary continued as he thought of the problem of discussing these issues with his mother. It would be difficult talking to her about whether he should testify against Karl. The gold question raised more complexities. He assumed she didn't know about it because Karl had kept her drugged.

When Ogie entered the plane the next day, Karl said in an unpleasant tone of voice, "I see you have helped yourself."

Ogie asked him, "Who owns the property where you found that gold? Did the owner of it give you permission to search for it and take it?"

"I don't know what you're talking about."

Ogie could sense in Karl's mind there was something more he was trying to keep hidden. "How did you get all that gold into the country? There must have been problems with Customs and the IRS." BINGO! That started a new train of thought in Karl, which explained many things that Ogie sensed but hadn't been able to figure out.

Karl worked with Bartlett to avoid customs and tax problems. It was a quid pro quo because Karl was keeping the whistle blowers Bartlett wanted out of the way incarcerated. Karl had used some of the gold to contribute to the election of the President. Bartlett and Karl had done a great deal of one hand helping the other. Ogie wondered how they had originally gotten together.

Ogie asked Karl how he had retrieved the gold. Karl asked him in a defiant tone, "How did you find out about it and what are you going to do about it?"

"Aha, you're the stereotype of the offender being the self-righteous one. I wish you had been more original than that. You are Newt Gingrich accusing Bill Clinton of adultery. It's an act that takes considerably more than one cake. I've always been open-mouthed in amazement at people who could do that, but my amazement at your hypocrisy is mixed with revulsion and horror at the effect you have had on my mother and Nina. Does it matter how I found out about it? It's unimportant. My question to you is how can you restore Nicole and Nina? Can you give my mother back the years you kept her in a fog? Where would you begin with Nina, who has lived with an insatiable hunger for her mother? Did any of your training to work in a caring profession have any effect on you or did it just teach you the opposite? You with your so-called cleverness and self importance don't have a clue nor a care about how to be a decent human being."

"I suppose this means you won't agree to refrain from being a witness against me in court?"

"Karl, I don't want to go to court for or against you. You are an untouchable. The thought of having anything to do with you is revolting. I don't promise you a damned thing other than I cannot vouch for your safety if I should have to deal with you again. I wish I were a big enough person to wish you good karma. I will work on it for my sake."

Then Ogie read in Karl's mind what he had done to Ogie's father. "And to cap it off, you want my help when you killed my father to get to the gold."

Karl was aghast and his first thought was he had let it slip and then thought Ogie was guessing. What else did Ogie know that he had no way of knowing? And with that, Ogie had pictures of the torturing he had done to Nicole while heavily drugged. He described to Karl the details of what Karl had done to his father. Karl felt as if he were going over the edge. These were things no one could possibly know and yet Ogie knew them. But Karl remained defiant. Ogie left him and said that Henry was unwilling to have his plane stay there another night. He advised him Henry was not someone to cross.

CHAPTER 29
Nicole, Ogie, Nina, Sashi

———

OGIE'S HEAD WHEN HE RETURNED home was so full of Karl's sickness he headed straight for his room with barely a word for Nina or his mother. Nicole made a move to go to him and Nina stopped her and explained he had just been with Karl and he needed time to pull himself together. Sashi was reading on the bed and couldn't believe the pain she saw on his face. She came toward him tentatively, afraid he wouldn't want anyone close. She said nothing to him but she took his head in her hands and lightly massaged his scalp. He stopped her fingers and pulled her next to him on the bed. They were on their sides and he rested his hand on her hip and remained wordless. He could read Sashi's knowing that there was nothing more she could do. He was thinking he couldn't have a more ideal partner. She did nothing extraneous and was clearly there and completely for him. He realized he had to start giving her his full attention in order to convince her to become his partner for life.

He fell into a deep sleep and woke with a start when Sashi got up. "How long was I out?" and when she said three hours he said how much he needed it.

Sashi asked him, "What went on?"

"I think it would be better if I told you with Nina and Nicole at the same time. They need to know what happened."

Sashi demurred, "Should I be part of it? I'm not family."

"Yes, you should, because your life was seriously affected by him, Nina adores you, and I adore you and so much want you to be part of my family."

"Hmm, I wonder whether you have the 'adores' in the right order. I have come to love Nina, but wouldn't it have been better strategically to say you adore me first before saying Nina adores me?" When Ogie started to protest, he saw the glint in her eyes and knew he had been had.

Nina had prepared another one of her gourmet dinners, hoping it would help soothe everyone, particularly Ogie. After dinner, Nicole raised the question of what had happened with Karl. Ogie didn't know where to begin. Everything about what went on had a precursor and it was all nightmarish.

If he avoided saying things about what he learned from Karl, it would prolong Nicole's agony. Ogie asked her if she had any idea of why Karl had wanted to marry her. Nicole said in retrospect it made no sense.

"When did he start drugging you?"

"It started after the first trip we made to France to visit the old family property."

"What did you notice about Karl during that time?"

"I hadn't thought of it until you asked, but I realize Karl seemed to have familiarity with the place, which surprised me. Supposedly, he hadn't ever been there before. I thought I noticed someone in the village who acted as if they recognized him, but I assumed it was coincidental."

"On our second trip, Karl wanted me to give him the right to use the property. It was an involved procedure with my cousins and after that, he began to drug me."

Ogie asked her, "What reason did he give you for starting the drugging?"

Nicole explained that she was still upset from the unexpected death of Oliver and Karl was solicitous in trying to make her feel better. She explained she had married Karl soon after Oliver's death because Karl was so attentive and concerned about her. He was taking care of all the problems she had to deal with in connection with his death. She felt marrying him would be ideal. It wasn't until after she had signed over the rights for him to use the property in France that he changed and threatened her with harming Nina if she didn't do what he wanted. He did this pretending Nina was still there at his so-called medical center. He said he kept her from Nicole because Nicole was in no shape to mother her. She didn't know that Ogie had taken Nina away and kept her out of Karl's clutches. Ogie explained he hadn't trusted Karl from the beginning and that was why he had taken Nina out of harm's way.

"Ogie, thank God you did that. What was Karl's reaction? He must have been furious because he wanted Nina to control me."

"Karl was so angry he reported Nina missing in order to have me jailed and out of the way. Fortunately, I had already managed to place her with a friend who was going to get her to Seth's when things calmed down. The police took me into custody and questioned me at length about her whereabouts."

"What did you tell them?" Nicole asked.

"I told them I had no idea where she was. They knew I was lying but had no proof and had to let me go."

Nina broke in, "Ogie, I never really understood why you wouldn't keep me with you. I was hurt you didn't. You explained, but emotionally I couldn't understand it. I guess that's why Seth sent me to school with a different name. I remember before you took me away you attacked Karl when he was with me."

Ogie said, "He was about to drug you, which is why I had to stop him, and the only way I could was to hit him."

Nicole wanted to know how Ogie was so certain that Karl was dangerous to her, but he just replied, "I knew. I can't explain it."

Ogie asked Nicole what else seemed peculiar about Karl in France. She said she had ascribed it to just beginning a relationship and getting to know each other. "But in retrospect, I see now there were things about the family property he was fixated on. Ogie, do you have any idea what that was about?"

Ogie told her about the gold and how Karl had taken her joking about it seriously. "He snuck into the village with a metal detector before our father's death and found some of it. He knew there was more, but it was not accessible without gaining entrance to the buildings. He plotted how to retrieve the rest of it. That's why he needed your cooperation. After he had you drugged, he went back and recovered such a large amount that he has offered us four million dollars not to testify against him. He has an expensive jet, and will still have large sums without the four million. He has property in a country with no extradition to the U.S. and is likely to go there if it looks as if he will be indicted."

Nina broke in with, "If he knew about the gold before our father died..."

"Nina, what are you suggesting?" Nicole asked. "Do you think he might have been responsible for Oliver's death? We knew he had a heart problem."

Nina continued, "Yes, if he was capable of molesting me, drugging you, keeping you a prisoner for all these years, and having Ogie wrongfully convicted, why wouldn't he have murdered our father? What did the coroner's report say?"

Nicole said it confirmed the heart problem and the death was of natural causes.

Ogie did not want to add to his mother's misery. However, if he didn't say anything now, he would just be extending it. What he couldn't figure out was how he could tell about it without explaining his mind reading. Nina had been able to absorb its implications and deal with it, but she was in much better emotional shape than Nicole. "I don't know what the coroner said, but he was murdered."

"Ogie, what makes you certain?"

"Karl told me."

"Why would he have done that?"

"He didn't volunteer the information. I guessed that he had done it. I deliberately said something to him to get him mad and in the same sentence I mentioned his having killed Dad. Karl was already so angry he didn't pick up on that and when he realized I had accused him of murder, he let out an involuntary gasp and then covered it with defiance, 'How the hell do you know that?' His denial was meaningless."

Ogie had kept close track of his mother's reactions. He wanted to be certain she understood what Karl had done. He felt it was crucial to her recovery to understand what Karl had done to her, his father, and Nina.

But Nicole wasn't satisfied and wanted to know, "How did you get him to tell you about the gold?"

"He's desperate. Ever since the announcement of my pardon and knowing the Attorney General would be looking into the case, he has been worried they will find out someone in the U.S. Attorney's office was bribed to indict and convict me. He offered Seth and me millions to get us to not testify against him. I implied that I would agree but I had to hear about everything, including his reasons for keeping you a prisoner. Once he offered so much money, it was relatively easy to needle him to get him to tell how he had acquired it."

Nicole wanted to know how he had deceived the coroner, and Ogie explained that with Karl's medical knowledge, it had been easy. He substituted sugar for Oliver's heart medicine and our father was completely dependent on that medicine to stay alive.

Nicole said, "I need to put all of my energy into my recovery, tempting as it is to focus it on hating Karl."

Ogie said, "There are several things we need to discuss before we can put Karl out of our minds." He went on to tell about the checking account that Karl opened up for her and how much was in it. He asked her to think about how she would like to handle it.

"I don't want it," was her immediate reaction.

"This money is your family's. It really doesn't belong to Karl. It belongs to you and you should use it to help recover and for anything else you want. You should know that in addition to the four million, I took some of the gold roosters from his plane. Unfortunately,

I couldn't get all of it. While I don't want to become involved in his legal mess and assist in his going to prison, I don't think he should be profiting from the crimes he has committed against all of us. And if he has less money, I can harden my heart to his plight. I want you to have the additional money as well."

Nicole said, "I need to think about what to do with it. I don't want to make any decisions now. However, your life and Nina's have been turned upside down by Karl. You have had to give up the work you were doing because of him and you are entitled to compensation for that. I also want Nina to be able to go to the college of her choice, regardless of its cost."

"Mother, please don't worry about money for me. I have been fortunate to earn a good living on my own. It will be a relief to be able to be out in the open and use my real name. I will be able to promote my work, which I haven't been able to do because I was trying to remain hidden."

Nicole said, "OK, I want time to think about it and I want to talk to Seth. He has a good deal of wisdom. He certainly did a good job with Nina. Can you arrange for me to see him?"

"Yes, I can either get Henry to fly you down or I know someone who would be glad to earn the money driving you. Which do you prefer?"

CHAPTER 30

Ogie and Sashi

———

NINA FELT SOMETHING BRITTLE BETWEEN Ogie and Sashi. It was subtle. She heard it in Ogie's voice when he said good night. Sashi came into Nina's room and shrugged. Nina interpreted this to mean the relationship with Ogie wasn't blossoming.

It was confirmed when Sashi said she was returning home. It was a week sooner than she had planned. When Nina asked why, Sashi said there were work things she needed to take care of. Nina knew something else was going on.

"Sashi, I'm not convinced."

"My agency needs me to return."

"If you really wanted to stay, wouldn't it be possible?"

"Nina, Ogie and I haven't become close and it's not changing. Ogie doesn't seem to have the emotional space for our relationship."

"Do you want to have a relationship with him?"

"I don't know. I don't know what he is feeling, and we haven't been close enough for me to know how I feel."

"Why don't you move into his studio and see what happens?"

"He hasn't invited me or even hinted that's what he wants."

"Sashi, I know him, and I know he's anxious for it to work with you. I also know he's scared of pressuring you. He's tiptoeing around trying to see if you really want him."

Nina thought Ogie must have read Sashi's mind and seen her ambiguity. He was blinded by that and didn't see her desire for him.

Nina was certain that the *fait accompli* of Sashi being in his room would help things. How could she convince Sashi, who was just as diffident and self-conscious as her brother?

Nina got up. "I'm going to go talk to him."

When Nina knocked softly on the studio door, his response was garbled. As she came in, he was hastily coming out of a fetal position and using his sleeve to wipe tears from his face.

"Yes? What is it?" Nina left and returned, half dragging Sashi by the hand.

"I've decided to introduce you to my dear friend Sashi," Nina said. "Perhaps you remember her from years past? She said that she would like to renew her acquaintance with you. I tried to discourage her by telling her how busy and worried you are. She was sympathetic, but dubious. I have prevailed upon her to try. I'm leaving her to your tender mercies."

Ogie was nonplussed, but recovered himself enough to say that he had made a grave mistake letting Nina grow up to become a smartass. "Now, little sister, please leave, and thanks you for the reintroduction."

When they were alone, Sashi said, "This is awkward. May I join you?"

"Yes, of course."

Sashi sat down next to Ogie and asked him what was going on. It was rare when he was at a loss for words, but he managed to say, "I wanted your time here to have been better. I wanted to do things with you and talk and give us a chance to know the new people we've become." Ogie shivered, and Sashi tentatively put her hand on his back. "Oh god," he said. "I have so longed for you and your touch and have been afraid to ask for it."

"Why?"

"Because I knew we had to go slowly, and I didn't know how to begin. Where are you?"

Sashi said, "I don't know. I'm confused because I thought we would have come to an understanding. I know why it hasn't happened and it's left me with my feet firmly planted in midair. Your move."

He searched in Sashi's mind. He felt guilty, but asked himself, *"Who writes the ethical rules for mind readers? I do."* He justified doing it as a way to ease their emotional turmoil.

Her head was a mix of thoughts and emotions. *"I don't know where to begin making contact or how to help him. He is a much different Ogie than the one I knew. What he's been through has changed him in ways I can't fathom. I don't know if I can make a relationship with him work, but I want to try."*

He heard her words in his head and it gave him enough hope to stretch out on the bed and gently pull her toward him. He put one arm around her waist and put his hand on the back of her head and stroked. He wasn't being sexual, but she could feel him wanting her through all his pores. She knew this was not the time to make a decision about their relationship. He was desperate, and she was feeling sorry for him. But many of the loving feelings from years ago were still there.

They woke up two hours later. "Would it be all right if I slept with you?" she asked Ogie.

"Which meaning of the verb 'sleep' are you using?" he asked, assuming she meant the less active form. To his surprise, he read that she was considering the other. She wanted to be close and was open to sex. Was he ready emotionally? Did he want to have sex with Sashi if she was iffy about it?

And then she surprised him. She reached down and placed her hand on his crotch, looked him in the eyes, and said, "Maybe this is the best way we can start our renewal?"

It was out of character for Sashi to want sex without all the other parts of the relationship solidly in place. And then he thought, "What have I got to lose? If it doesn't work, it already wasn't working." He reached down and put his hand on hers. "Are you certain? Are we moving too fast?"

"How would we know unless we look at the speedometer?"

"Well, so far the speed is right." Ogie said.

"Don't you think verification is needed?" Sashi said invitingly.

With that, Ogie started to reach down. Sashi stopped him and said, "If you're going to examine the engine, perhaps it would be better to open the hood." She removed her pants and underpants.

During the separation, Ogie had come to accept that he might never again have the pleasure of being with a woman, let alone a woman as wonderful as Sashi. He had become so used to blocking loving feelings that it was difficult to let go.

Sashi asked him what contraceptives he had and was secretly relieved that he had none. She told him she had brought her diaphragm but preferred not to use it, because it was old and might no longer fit properly. Ogie suggested that they help themselves to Nina's condom supply. Sashi said, "I know Nina is anxious for us to be lovers again, but do we really want to make an announcement of it to her? Which of us is going to beard the lioness in her den?"

"I think it best if you do it," Ogie replied. "There's a limit to how much I want to know about Nina's sex life, and she might be more comfortable with you."

Nina was reading, and her first reaction to seeing Sashi was distress that she hadn't stayed with her brother. In the short time of Sashi's visit, Nina had fallen in love with her and desperately wanted her for a sister-in-law or even a sister outlaw. Sashi's clothing was askew and she was flushed. "Is something wrong?" Nina asked. "Are you OK? Ogie didn't...?"

"No, no, everything is all right. I'm going back to join him, but I need something from you."

Nina knew immediately, and told Sashi to open the third drawer on the left and help herself. Sashi was surprised how quickly Nina caught on, as well as by the quantity of condoms she found.

"Before you assume I'm a nymphomaniac," Nina explained, "Remember that I give them to the girls who come to me for advice. I'm so glad things are working out with Ogie."

"Nina, I do love him, but we have a long way to go before I can know it can work."

"Well, what you are about to do..." Nina started to say, and then trailed off.

"I know. I'm glad you pushed me into his studio. He was desperate for love and frightened at the same time. It has to have been a difficult and lonely life for him."

With chagrin, Sashi said, "Well, I'm off to do you know what." Nina and Sashi, who were distinctly not giggling types, broke into nearly uncontrollable laughter.

As Sashi was opening the door to leave, Nina said to her with a mischievous look, "Please keep the noise down. I need my beauty sleep." That started another round of laughter and Sashi said it might not happen after all because she had used so much of her energy laughing.

Returning to Ogie's studio, she found him looking at her quizzically. "I'm not going to tell you what happened, but I did achieve our purpose." She handed him six condoms, to which Ogie gulped. Sashi reassured him that they only needed two at a time, but one did have to keep the future in mind.

"It sounded as if you were enjoying yourselves at my expense," Ogie teased. "But I'm delighted you get along so well, because I love you both.

"Now that we've had a break in our proceedings, should we talk about this?"

Sashi shook her head no.

"Not even to review how to do it?" Ogie asked with a straight face.

"Do you remember how to ride a bicycle?" Sashi asked impishly.

"It takes me a few minutes to get my balance," Ogie replied. "Do you think it's the same?"

The banter was the tension breaker they both needed. They were self-conscious and well aware of the potential for both silliness and awkwardness during sex. When they'd had sex years ago, they'd been very careful about making sure they were both comfortable, physically and spiritually. Strangers might have thought they were talking it to death without understanding the pleasures that came from their complete understanding of each other's wants and needs.

"I've missed you and longed for you for so long," Ogie said. "Could we start by letting me rest inside you for a few minutes? It will give me a fulfillment and peacefulness I've fantasized about since we separated."

Ogie's ability to feel the physical sensations of others hadn't yet developed when he'd last had sex with Sashi. The result was he had a few moments of confusion before he could identify that he was feeling her sensations as well. When he entered, it was most intense for her and that diminished as he went in. He remembered he used to feel the same way. The greatest pleasure was at the very beginning.

Sashi asked him if he'd forgotten how to ride a bicycle. "Are you losing your balance?" she asked.

With pretend astonishment, Ogie said, "You were right. It's like bicycle riding, and I haven't forgotten how to do it. To think I was afraid of falling. However, I don't remember how to stop or turn."

With amusement in her eyes, Sashi said, "It seems to me you just negotiated a gentle turn and a stop without falling. I think your fears are groundless. My fear is you will be too good at stopping."

Ogie told her that being with her, and in her, made him feel whole, and he had been desolate knowing it might never happen again. "I daydreamed about being with you over and over. Finally, to keep from going crazy, I had to discipline myself to stop doing it.

"What I've missed most was the beauty of our unity, more than the sensuous pleasure. But of course I missed the sensuous pleasure too. Thinking of never being together again felt like the end of the world. When I achieved important things in my work, I rewarded myself by thinking about being with you."

Lightening up, Ogie asked Sashi, "And how is your organ with 8,000 nerve endings?"

"My recent count brought it up to 8,009. Do you think you can handle the additional ones?"

"I assume you're questioning my manhood."

When their banter finished, they became serious about giving and taking pleasure from each other. It was heightened by his ability to feel what was happening in her body. He was anticipating exactly what she wanted. Feeling she was beginning to be rigid and the increased intensity of her breathing told him she was about to ignite. He didn't want to distract her from enjoying it with his orgasm and he wanted to relish hers, so he postponed his until she caught her breath.

What a wonder to have felt what she felt. He always had intense curiosity about what women feel during sex. He knew it was more profound because their culmination is felt over much of their bodies. Now he knew it personally. Ogie had never been certain whether the women he had been with had climaxed. How satisfying it was to know definitively. The few women he'd been intimate with were reluctant to discuss details of what they experienced during sex. They acted as if it was a taboo subject. How much did they know about what was possible for them? Did they feel they would lose control by discussing it?

Sashi was gasping for breath and he could feel the afterglow from her orgasm. When she caught her breath, she said, "How did you know precisely what I wanted and when I wanted it?"

Ogie realized that satisfying her wants so quickly risked revealing his mind reading. How should he answer her? Were his rapid responses to her thoughts frightening her? Would it endanger their relationship? If he told her how he did it, would it send her running off? If they stayed together and he didn't tell her, would she be angry when she found out? As their relationship became closer, it would be harder to conceal.

In spite of the great sex, he knew Sashi hadn't made up her mind about their future. Whatever answer he gave her, he knew it needed to be the truth. He wanted to start by making light of it, but how?

"Has it occurred to you that I'm prescient?" he asked. This, of course, was the truth, but not the whole truth.

She thought Ogie was continuing the kidding, and went along with it. "Of course you are. How could I have forgotten?"

Ogie saw her face change expression, as if she was struggling to remember something. "You don't believe I'm prescient?" he asked again. It was the classic ruse of telling the truth but making it seem ridiculous.

She played along with the gag. "Is it genetic? When I went to get condoms from Nina, she knew before I asked what I wanted. You two in combination could make a girl think she was losing her mind."

"Sashi, I'm going to take the risk of losing you entirely. I love you, and if I don't tell you about this, it will get in the way of our relationship. There is no way to sugarcoat it. Please listen until I finish, because what I'm about to recount will strain your synapses to the breaking point."

"Aren't you being melodramatic? And besides, I have very tough synapses."

Ogie told her he had initially been unaware of his ability. "I found I was often reading things in people's minds and assumed I heard them speaking. I was startling people when I commented about their thoughts, and I couldn't figure out why.

"Then I noticed I was "hearing" people when they were too far away to hear their voices. I tried to distinguish what I read in their minds from what I actually heard. At first I thought my hearing was extraordinarily acute. There was even an occasion when I heard the thoughts of a friend with severe laryngitis. Against my better judgment, I thought I might be mind reading. I began to experiment to find out what was going on.

"The problem was that the voices in my head sounded just like people's actual voices. I devised tests. I turned on a voice recorder and mingled. When I played back the voice recorder, I knew I was hearing more in my head than was actually said.

"Next I focused on people in another room. The first readings I received were weak and garbled. After several days, the signals were stronger, and it was evident I was reading people's thoughts.

"Then I observed under what circumstances it was happening. Distance, my familiarity with the person, their mood, and the importance of what they were thinking were all factors.

"My abilities increased. The distances grew longer. I began to read feelings, but not with depth. That ability is increasing. There were times I wanted to know about people's earlier thoughts, but I hit the wall trying to do that.

"Then I had a partial breakthrough and was able to receive someone's previous thoughts. Apparently I'd provoked them to think about whatever the subject was. That was the first time I realized that I could project thoughts as well.

"Recently, I've started being able to feel the physical feelings of others. I wasn't certain at first, because it was weak, but it's growing stronger."

Ogie took a deep breath, and with his heart in his mouth he said, "I'm frightened to ask what you think."

"I'm not sure where to begin," Sashi said. "Why were you so frightened to tell me about this?"

"I thought you wouldn't want to be with someone who could read your mind," Ogie replied.

"You could have read my mind that I was open to renewing our relationship," Sashi said.

"I also read your uncertainty," he said.

"The thought of being with someone reading my mind all the time is pretty weird and it's even weirder knowing you read my physical sensations. I need to absorb this to decide how I feel about it." To Ogie's relief, she added, "And I need to know more."

"I suggest you talk with Nina. When she learned about it, she was upset. We've begun to work out ways to make her more comfortable living with a mind reader."

"Now I understand some of the things Nina said, and avoided saying. Apparently she didn't want to tell me about it because she felt it was up to you, and we had to work it out for ourselves.

"Could you tell me more about how it works? Particularly what happened when we were having sex? Sometimes it felt like you knew what I wanted before I was conscious of it."

"It's hard to describe, because so much of what I did came from physical feelings, as well as images in your mind. My body was feeling much of what yours was feeling. I did things with you and to you without thinking. It was happening so fast, I couldn't stop myself."

"Why would you have wanted to stop yourself?" Sashi asked coyly.

"I didn't want to spook you," he replied tenderly.

"What have you worked out with Nina to make her more comfortable?"

"I'm disciplining myself not to look into her mind. It's been a struggle, because it's like tuning out someone who is talking to you. I have to sort out what I hear her say from what I read in her mind. We've also experimented to see if she knows when I'm in her mind. Now she can recognize when it's happening. This has helped reassure her."

Sashi tested Ogie by sending him a thought question: *"Did you carry on conversations when she talked to you in her mind?"*

Ogie sent these thoughts to Sashi, *"No, because she was so unsettled by my mind reading I avoided that."*

"Sashi, where do we go from here?"

"Well, it has promise for a great sex life."

CHAPTER 31

Nina

——

Renee was trying to find the most tactful way to tell Nina her algebra class had to retake the State Algebra Exam. None of her students had scored below the 95th percentile, and the state thought there had been cheating. It made Renee uneasy, even though he knew the results were due to Nina's teaching. He was amazed at her students' depth of understanding. There were students in her class who had never done well in math. Now they were filled with excitement at solving equations.

Nina could not be a pleasanter person to work with, except when it came to anything implying the slightest slur against her students. Then she was the lioness defending her cubs. He thought of taking the coward's way out and sending her on school business to the mainland while he had her students retake the test. He quickly decided that would be a mistake, because she'd find out anyway.

When she came into his office, he asked her, "Which do you want first, the good news or the bad news?"

She answered the question by making a "come on" motion with her hand. Renee explained the situation, and her reaction surprised him. "Actually, that's good news. It will give me some time off when the tests are repeated, and maybe the state will learn there are better ways to teach algebra. I have one condition. I want Red excused from school that day so he can spend the day with me. When the results are repeated, it will be apparent that the first results were valid. You know from your work with Red that he understands algebra."

Renee figured he was getting off lightly, but couldn't resist teasing Nina. "And just how do you justify Red missing a day of school?"

She looked directly at Renee and said, "He will be getting advanced instruction in several subjects." When Renee smirked, Nina said austerely, "How many pages should the detailed report be?" If the expression about someone being a handful hadn't been in use long before Nina was born, it would have been coined to describe her. Fortunately, Renee enjoyed her when she was at her sharpest.

"Nina, you think the state could learn better ways to teach algebra. What advice would you give them?"

"First, tell the students that the most important rule in algebra is that everything has to be fair. If they remember that, it becomes simpler. I say, 'Consider the feelings of the other side of the equation when you don't give it the same attention.'

"Then I give them a simple equation that can be solved intuitively. For example, $7y=14$. I've already told them that letters and numbers next to each other are always multiplied. Then I tell them to speak the equation as a sentence, and the solution will be apparent.

"In the beginning, I studiously avoid using x as an unknown, because they associate it as a multiplication sign, and I don't want them to confuse the two.

"Once they've figured out $7y=14$ intuitively, I ask them to make up ways to get the answer. They work in groups of three, and they have to convince the others in their group how their procedure works. Sometimes there's competition between groups as to who can develop the most ways to solve the problem. Does this give you the idea?"

"Yes," Renee replied. "It's very clever of you, but I think you've left out something essential. It has to do with your enthusiasm for them and the subject."

"Right, I forgot. The first and most important thing I tell them, and continue to emphasize, is that they are the owners of algebra in an analogous way to their owning English, or a video game. Any time they calculate something to find an unknown, or what they would call an answer, they're doing algebra, whether in their heads or on paper. They're doing it because they have a vested interest in it. They're not doing it for me or for marks or for anything else."

When the results came back from the retesting, Renee told Nina they were the same as before. "The state people wanted to know about your magic, and I promised them I would ask you to see them when the semester is over. I neglected to tell them about your age. However, if the foreign language specialist talks with the math specialist, they may figure it out."

Renee noticed that Nina's eyes were red. "You look upset. Is it the State, or something else? How was your day with Red?"

To Renee's surprise, Nina started to cry.

Renee's heart sank. "Did something happen with Red?"

Nina dried her tears and pulled herself together. "You gave me an extraordinary opportunity, and I've had intense satisfaction from seeing my students learning and being enthusiastic about it. It's been so rich. I have a hard time believing life can be this good.

"What I have to face is that I can't stay here and continue. I know you have to get somebody with full certification and that my age is an impediment to my teaching here. I also feel responsible for my mother. I don't know yet what I need to do for her, but I do know that whatever it is, I must do it."

"What about Red?"

Nina said she'd told Red that she would have to leave the Island soon. "He knew this would happen, but the reality is more than he can bear. I love him. He's wonderful, and even though we've been intimate, he also feels like a brother. I wouldn't rule out that we could end up as a couple, but not now. I dare not hold out hope to him, because it wouldn't be fair to him.

"Red's reaction went beyond crying. It came from deep within him. I had to force myself to watch his raw pain. It was compounded because the day off you so generously gave us was our second time having sex, and it was wonderful. I hope we can have more before I leave, but I don't know if Red can do it, knowing we will part."

"Nina, I'm honored by your sharing your inner life and feelings. You have become a light in my life. I love teaching, and it's thrilling to see it well done. You've done it extraordinarily well. I'm envious of how good you are. I've learned from watching you be so level headed and perceptive about your students and your teaching. I'm with Red in mourning your leaving. You're a Jill of all trades. What can't you do well?"

"What I can't do well is not hurt Red, and that is excruciating. I haven't been able to help several of my students with their personal problems. And I don't know how to help my mom."

Renee gently chided her. "Nina, you have the unmitigated gall to think you ought to be able to solve problems the rest of us have been working on for years. And some of us consider ourselves pretty smart."

"OK, Renee, I get it, but it still hurts not to be able to do better."

"You wouldn't be such a good person if you didn't feel that way. I know your mother is visiting. I would love to meet her. I'll bet she would enjoy watching you teach. It would give me the chance to meet the mother of one of the most remarkable young people I've ever known, as well as a chance for me to talk with another francophone. Why don't you bring her here?"

Nina explained that her mother was recovering from trauma, but that she would suggest it. She liked the idea. It would give her mother a reprieve from thinking about Karl. Nina also liked the idea of having a chance to show off for her mom. And if she talked to her mother during class, it would give her students a chance to observe French being used in a natural conversation.

"One last thing," Renee said. "If you could ever come back to teach, I would embrace that, knowing you could teach anything beautifully."

Even though Nina thought it unlikely, it gave her a warm feeling. She had created a home for herself.

CHAPTER 32
Nina

———

WHENEVER NINA HAD GONE TO the mainland on overnights, Frangelo disappeared, occasionally dropping in for a meal. Nina and Ogie had no clue where he spent his time when Nina was gone. How Frangelo knew she wasn't on the Island was a mystery.

On the days Nina returned, while she was still on the ferry, Frangelo waited for her just outside the door. Ogie would invite him in, but he refused until Nina was in the house. When she returned, he followed her everywhere and climbed under the covers with her. The rare times he came back when she was gone, Ogie would feed him outside and make him feel welcome, but he just ate and ran like the classic rude guest. He would disappear for days and then, without calling, would drop in for a meal. What she didn't want to think about was the relative degree of pain she felt leaving him compared to leaving Red, Ogie, and her students. Thinking of the comparison made her squirm. When the phrase, "He's just a cat" surfaced, she cringed, because he wasn't. When she woke up during the night, she was always startled to see him as a cat. He was a loving presence that she could feel as she felt the loving presence of others. Nina debated whether to take Frangelo with her to college and decided that he wouldn't want to be cooped up wherever she lived. He wasn't ready for a city.

Nina's psychic pain was a ten. It was up there with kidney stones. She felt guilty feeling it. She felt spoiled complaining to herself about leaving Megantic. The past year had been idyllic. She never dreamed her life could be so good. It was the first time she had full control of her existence. There was no way this next year was going to give her a semblance of the warmth and loving she had had for the last twelve months.

She was entering Harvard in unbelievable circumstances. She had not only been admitted, but she had been appointed as a teaching and research assistant. She was wanted by the School of Education and the Physics department. The latter coveted her because on her admissions essay. She wrote a theoretical paper on the archaeology of sound and how it would be possible to retrieve sound from objects. Renee suggested she include it in her essay and Nina had, against her better judgment. It turned out Renee knew what he was doing when he pushed her to do it. She described what she would do in the field if she had access to the people and the equipment in the Physics department. No one had explored that field. When the Admissions Officer checked with the Physics department to verify there was substance to it, the Department Chairman, Agamemnon, went bonkers to ensure she would come to Harvard. He leaned on the Director of Admissions to accept her. Forest Davis, the Director, pointed out there were procedures to be followed, including interviewing. Agamemnon asked him if he really wanted to risk losing a potential Nobel winner. Davis told Agamemnon he could discuss Nina's research with her, but he could not commit the University to accept her until she was interviewed and the rest of the process was followed.

Agamemnon promptly called Nina on Megantic, and after identifying himself, asked her to explain how she would retrieve sound from solid objects. She said she would do it by obtaining the molecular history of an object and had the feeling that Agamemnon already knew about it. He wanted to hear more. With diffidence, she said that it ought to be possible to come up with algorithms that could be used to construct formulas that would make it possible to extrapolate from current molecular behavior how the molecules had behaved earlier. He then asked her how she would be able to read the molecules to identify their behavior. She said that was why she wanted to come to Harvard, because she knew she would need help developing the tools to do it as well as use of equipment.

While Agamemnon didn't want to risk losing Nina by plaguing her with too many questions, his curiosity was aroused so much he couldn't help himself. His next question was, "Once you have the molecular history, how are you going to convert it to sound? And how will you know when the sound was made?"

Nina's answer convinced him she would be a gem in the department. She explained that it would take a good deal of experimentation and a great deal of math to do it, but that logic dictated it would be possible.

Agamemnon wanted to know what she would do with the sounds she was able to reconstruct. He foresaw there were uses that could not only be an abuse of privacy but could also threaten national security. Her answer reassured him when she said she thought it would be great for researching in history, reconstructing ancient languages, and in tracing the development of languages.

He asked her, "What other schools have you applied to?" She mentioned MIT and Caltech. That she might not come to Harvard worried him. "What would it take to get you to come to Harvard?"

"Well, your calling me has been a good start. I sent the same essay about myself to the other schools and they haven't expressed the interest you have. The work I will do in physics and mathematics to do sound research should be counted as if I had taken those subjects. Obviously, access to and support from faculty as well as to labs and computers are a must."

Agamemnon asked her how she had become qualified to do what amounted to postgraduate work at age seventeen, and she replied, "How much time do you have?"

"For a promising student, as much as is needed."

"I was eased out of high school at thirteen. They told me I was a know-it-all. The irony was that except for a few teachers who knew what I didn't know, no one was sophisticated enough to know what I didn't know. All they saw was a social misfit who they had to protect from herself and others. I lucked out with two teachers in math and physics who weren't threatened by my being able to gulp down what they knew in a very few swallows and then question them about it. After that, they turned me loose to do research and learn on my own and occasionally gave me help to find source material."

"Why didn't you apply to college then?"

"My uncle and I decided that between my small size and thirteen-year-old social maturity, it would be better to postpone college."

"What have you done in the meantime?"

"Well, you must have read my admissions essay where I described what I did on Megantic last year. I taught math and French, went lobstering, coached basketball, and apprenticed with a man who creates 17th century Dutch masters."

Agamemnon couldn't resist asking, "Was that all?" He was beginning to like this young woman, even though he was having a hard time picturing her degree of brilliance. It was apparent she was up there and he had a sneaking suspicion that in a few weeks at Harvard, she might devour him. He had the thought that maybe she belonged at the Institute for Advanced Studies in Princeton, and then realized if she were there, he wouldn't have the pleasure of her exciting mind.

He asked her how she had managed to teach without a college degree and Nina told him that Renee, the principal on Megantic, was desperate for a substitute in math and French and recognized that she could handle the teaching without difficulty. Again she had the feeling he was asking questions he already knew the answers to. He asked her how it went and she told him about the results her students achieved on the state exams. This gave Agamemnon the idea that if Nina were made a teaching assistant, she would have more flexibility in what courses she took, she would have access to the stacks of the Widener Library, she would have better access to the faculty, and he would gain a superb teacher in his department.

Agamemnon suggested, "If I could get you a stipend as a research/ teaching assistant, would that make a difference in your choice of college?"

Sophisticated as Nina was, she was awed by what Agamemnon was suggesting. Thoughts came to her at the speed of light. She knew she didn't need the money because of what Karl had given her mother, but the opportunity to have what amounted to *carte blanche* at the University was tantalizing. She realized turning down the money might be off-putting. She was also thinking if he was offering the assistantship, he might do more. Why did he think she could teach? How did he know how much she knew in order to teach? What more did she want and need? Why was he offering her so much? Risking it all, she asked him, "How can you be so certain I'm as capable as you're assuming? You only know me on paper."

"I was wondering when you would get around to that. I know that you made the basketball team on Megantic a winning one, that you had your French students on the State Department foreign language proficiency test on level three, that your math students performed at unbelievably high levels, that you wowed the Maine State Education Commissioner and her staff with your incredible knowledge and your teaching ability, and that you have my friend Renee desolate about you leaving Megantic."

That answered the question of how Agamemnon knew so much about her. To give herself time to think, she asked him, "What else do you know about me?"

He told her that he and Renee had been friends in college and that he often visited Renee on Megantic. Renee had wanted him to meet Nina, but she wasn't on-Island then. He had introduced him to Red, telling him he was one of his promising students. "Renee told me that you and Red worked on an idea I would be interested in and I asked Red to tell me about it. He was reluctant both because he insisted it was your idea and because of his shyness. Renee drew him out by telling me that Red had done some of the preliminary math to identify what kinds of algorithms would work to trace the molecular history. Red's modesty told me a great deal and I concluded that the two of you worked closely on it. It was because of my interest in your project that Renee encouraged you to apply here. I'm glad he did."

They must have had a long talk about her. Now she knew why Renee encouraged her to go to Harvard. He must have known Agamemnon would seek her out and that they would exploit each other to their maximum mutual advantage. At Harvard, she would have the conditions to discover and create something that could be useful to mankind, and he would have the advantages of a sharp mind in his department, as well as the potential prestige of a major discovery coming from it. She debated with herself what more to ask of Agamemnon. She would need an office, and he already implied she would have unrestricted access to a lab and tools. She thought Red would be of considerable help in her work, but was that because she loved him or because of valid professional reasons? Agamemnon had just opened the door for her to ask for Red. Would asking for him to be her research partner be asking too much?

He said, "You're hesitating. Why?"

"I'm overwhelmed by what you're offering me. Renee said nothing about his conversation with you, and he didn't mention he had told you of my ideas about capturing sound from inanimate objects. He encouraged me to apply to Harvard, and now that I look back at it, I see he was subtly emphasizing I should go there. It surprises me he hasn't said anything, because he's always been straightforward with me. I suppose he didn't want to get my hopes up in case it didn't work out."

Agamemnon said, "I asked him not to say anything because I wanted to see what I could arrange before I talked with you. Is your hesitation about Red? I tried to get him as well. I talked with his parents, and they won't let him go, even though Renee said he could make it work on the academic side. He is under age and if they say no, that's it."

At first she thought Agamemnon wanted Red because he assumed that Red had originally come up with the idea of retrieving sounds. And then she realized that wasn't it, because Renee must have told him it was her idea. Having met Red, he wanted him because he knew Red could be of considerable help. But still, she was delaying committing herself. Why? Was it because it felt as if it had been arranged so neatly without consulting her? It hadn't occurred to her that it would be possible for Red to join her, and now that she couldn't have him it was awful. She wondered if it had been discussed with Red. Had he even been given a choice? If he had, why hadn't he told her? Probably Pearl hadn't even let it get as far as asking Red what he wanted. Here she was with the offer of plenty and yet confused and not able to decide what to do. And then there were the things on her application that Agamemnon hadn't mentioned. She had included that the Graduate School of Education wanted her to teach a course or a mini-course in how she had gotten her students in math and French to learn so effectively. She couldn't visualize how she could handle that along with what Agamemnon was planning for her. Being wanted in so many ways was the wealth of Croesus, but it wasn't all it was cracked up to be. She was facing a multiplicity of new experiences. A new school, two types of teaching, beginning serious research which she had never done, becoming a student again, new collegial relationships with faculty and students, and all to be done simultaneously.

She was hungered for by two departments, and yet it didn't feel as good as having been so admired and loved on Megantic. That it was her choice to leave the blessings and goodness of Megantic didn't help. But Harvard wasn't Megantic.

It was the first time she could remember being overwhelmed by what she was facing. Yes, she had been in many difficult situations before—being bullied because she was so small and considered a smart ass by her classmates, the awfulness of the time spent at Karl's so-called sanitarium, having to be incognito when Ogie was on the run—but in all of them, she was able to focus in a way to keep herself functioning. Now, without even being in the situation, she felt pulled apart by all its demands. She couldn't visualize what it would take to meet them. This was going to be different. It would require sophistication to teach highly abstract math to very sophisticated students. And while she had obviously done superbly well teaching high school on Megantic, she didn't know the first thing about what one teaches teachers. She had spent hours preparing for each of the two high school classes she taught, but it was material she already knew. Now she would be dealing with subject matter she had to learn and figure out how to teach. It was fine for her to figure out the theoretical possibilities of reading sound from solid objects, but she hadn't a clue about how to do the engineering for it, or for that matter, the highly complex math it would take.

She knew she had to make her coming incarnation work. She couldn't yet see how. All she could do was play the video in her head of the satisfactions she had experienced. She had generated excitement about learning in her students and helped girls who came to her for counseling feel better about themselves by making their boyfriends plan sex and use condoms. Nina had seen the change in the way the girls who did that carried themselves with dignity. She also saw how their boyfriends treated them with a thoughtfulness that had been lacking before. That Renee gave her the opportunity to teach at sixteen was incredible. Her rich friendship and affair with Red was life at its best. Leaving Red was the most painful, because he had lodged himself so deeply in her heart. She couldn't have believed she could have had so much profound joy.

Replaying her year gave her pleasure, but it also gave her the anguish of knowing she could not step in the same river again. The sands and rocks of a river are always changing and people are as well. She knew Meganticans would welcome her back, and Renee's open offer for her to teach was a comfort. But she had the wisdom to know that she too would change. And when she thought about what it would be like to be with Red again, she couldn't visualize how the highs of that relationship could repeat. She was certain it was a once in a lifetime love affair. She knew few people made the mechanics of sex true expressions of love and caring the way it had been for them. The word delirious must have been invented for what they had together.

When Red gave her the model of the Jenny T, she cried. He had carved it himself and replicated the colors of everything, including the sideboards, perfectly. It was a labor of love, because he knew what it meant to her. She had come to feel that Red and his grandfather were extraordinary, beautiful, sensitive, and bright people hiding under the mantle of dry Maine speech and mannerisms.

To cap off her heartbreak, when she arrived on the last day of school to teach her two classes, they had joined together in one classroom before she arrived. They proceeded to run the classes interactively among themselves in just the way she had worked so hard to get them to take responsibility for their own learning. They had become the owners of the material and of their own learning. They gave it to her as their gift, knowing she valued it more than a physical present.

She knew she needed to get her head in a different place. Dreading next year was insane. She had to turn it around and so she fantasized about how to excavate sounds and what uses a gadget that could do it could be put to. There had been attempts to retrieve sounds from pottery that were made when pots were thrown, which she wanted to know more about. But what she visualized was a very different approach, which if successful would broaden the field of acoustic archaeology immeasurably. While it was premature to picture the things that could be learned reading the audio molecular history of various surfaces, she couldn't resist doing it, because it fired her imagination. First she wanted to try it on the walls of the German caves whose paintings had been dated to about 40,000 years ago. If those people were sophisticated enough to do those renderings, they must have had complex speech. Would that speech have any relation to living languages? If not, how would it be possible to decipher it?

It then came to her that if sounds could move molecules, then could light do it? It didn't seem likely because she thought light would have less physical impact than sound would. But the effects of both were unknown, and as far as Nina knew, neither had been studied with a view to retrieving the history of sound or light on surfaces. She found it hard to believe that images could be retrieved from solid surfaces, but then it wasn't so long ago that the idea of sending pictures through the air would have been an unbelievable thing to do. As she thought of the unlikelihood of obtaining images from molecular readings on solid surfaces, she realized, wasn't that done chemically in darkrooms until recently? And then there was the possibility of reading magnetic effects on ancient cave walls. Perhaps images or sounds could be traced through them. It was delicious brainstorming all the possibilities and the richness that could transpire in the coming year. It might help assuage the losses she would feel.

END

gabrielhl@post.harvard.edu

40525548R00151

Made in the USA
Charleston, SC
08 April 2015